LIBRA

ZODIAC SERIES
BOOK 2

JOHN WEGENER

Libra

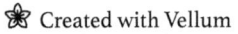 Created with Vellum

1

Duke Richelieu de Aquitaine glared at Duke Javier de Lorraine across the wide conference table. His expression screamed *How dare you suggest splitting up the Duchy of Champagne between us! It belongs to me. I have the rights to the whole duchy,* but his words were more tempered when he spoke. "I do not agree that it is a viable solution that you are offering — neither for us, nor for the citizens of Champagne. Confusion will reign with the division."

They sat in a conference room in the palace, which stood in the centre of Nouveau Paris, the capital of Franconia, the main planet of Delta Pavoni. Also at the table were Prince Léon Plantagenet of Franconia and Lord Chancellor Pierre, of the Duchy of Champagne.

"I don't consider it a problem," Javier said.

"No, no, no. That will not do," Prince Léon interjected. "The Constitution of Delta Pavonis states that we cannot subdivide an established duchy."

Javier looked at the prince. "Well, how are we meant to agree on who will control the duchy?" He heaved a sigh and added, "Are you sure Duke Olivier had no heir at all? Not even a bastard?"

"There is no heir," said the prince. "And don't presume they haven't searched. I agree it would all be much easier for everyone if there was."

"Why can't we just rule ourselves, like we originally proposed?" Lord Chancellor Pierre said, leaning forward, pleading.

Richelieu looked at him. *He can't be serious. What a preposterous idea!* He didn't understand why Léon had even asked the Lord Chancellor to the meeting. The negotiations were progressing poorly enough without the plebeians assuming they had any power. He sighed, wondering what Javier's actual intentions were. He felt sure he didn't really want the duchy. His own was large enough as it was. The only claim he had to it was through some long-lost family connection, one so far back that it didn't qualify as direct lineage.

"You can't rule yourselves as a democracy," Prince Léon said patiently to the Lord Chancellor, his tone condescending. "I've told you this before. The Constitution doesn't allow it."

"That settles it then. I'll take it all," Javier piped up, looking directly at Richelieu, a challenging glint in his eye.

Richelieu went black with rage. "I'll send my military in before I let you have it!"

Javier laughed. "Don't be ridiculous. We both know you can't afford a war. Your economy is in enough trouble without that."

Richelieu conceded that Javier was right. He really didn't have the finances to start a war with the likes of the Duchy of Lorraine.

"You're not having a war in Champagne," Pierre spurted out, his face crimson red.

"Calm down," Richelieu said, waving his hand at him. "No one's fighting in your territory. At least, not yet." He cast a wary eye at Javier. *This is going nowhere.* "Listen. Aquitaine is right next to Champagne. It would be easy to annex such a small duchy. Lorraine is on the opposite side of the planet. How on Franconia are you going to manage running it remotely?"

Javier studied the fingernails on his left hand, as if he had lost interest in the conversation, absently picking under the nail of his little finger. He lifted the hand to his mouth and blew at it to remove a particle and brushed it off his shirt. "I would manage."

"It's impractical."

"This wouldn't have anything to do with the wealth that you could strip from it, would it?"

Richelieu suddenly stood, fed up with Javier's prodding. "This is ridiculous. I will not stay here, if that's what we have to put up with."

"Sit down," Prince Léon said. Richelieu sat. It wouldn't do to insult the prince. Léon sighed. "We're not getting anywhere, as I thought might happen." He looked at both Javier and Richelieu. "You two go away and do some more thinking. Both of you come up with a proposal on how controlling the duchy would benefit the duchy and the planet. I'll look at them and decide."

"Hello, I'm here," Pierre said. They all looked at him. "Surely we have a say in it."

"No, you don't," Léon said bluntly.

Pierre's mouth dropped open as his face reddened again.

"Now, we have to prepare for the Senate Opening Dinner tonight. I take it you will both be there?"

"Yes," Richelieu said.

"I wouldn't miss it for the world," Javier said. "My wife enjoys these little dinners immensely. What about you, Richelieu? You bringing that grouchy old mother of yours?"

Richelieu refused to be provoked. "She's not coming tonight, no. I'm bringing someone else."

"She let you off the leash then?" Javier's interest was piqued. "Who's this mysterious date? Someone I know? Has Mother vetted her?"

"That's enough, Javier," Léon butted in. He would not allow his own family to be mocked in his presence.

Javier shrugged, unable to remove the smirk from his face.

"One day you'll go too far," Richelieu said, pointing his finger at Javier as he rose to leave.

"One must have a hobby." Javier stood up too.

Richelieu cast his eyes up to the heavens as though asking for restraint and walked out. He and Javier had known each other since boyhood but Javier had the knack of getting under his skin, and

Richelieu resented how easily he could get him worked up. It was almost a sport to Javier. He wished he had thicker skin sometimes, but it wasn't in his nature. His sensitivity won him no praise from his mother, although it seemed to go down well with his constituents.

Returning to the limousine flier, he sat back as the chauffeur flew him back to his Nouveau Paris residence. He closed his eyes to think. What sort of proposal could he put together to convince the prince that he had the right to take control of Champagne? Deciding not to worry about it for the rest of the day, he opened his eyes again and asked the steward to pour him a bourbon. He sipped on that for the rest of the journey.

2

"You stood up to that bully then?" Richelieu's mother, Camille of Aquitaine, asked as she barged uninvited into Richelieu's office in their Nouveau Paris residence. "Are you finally getting what's rightfully yours?"

The residence sat on the outskirts of the capital on a large estate. Other dukes had similar residences scattered around the city where they lived when the Senate of Franconia sat for business. Richelieu's office was located on the first floor of the residence, as far away from his mother's living space as possible, but she managed to negotiate the distance at her age with uncanny frequency all the same. The office sported wooden-panelled walls and a fresco ceiling, reminiscent of the decor of Renaissance France on Earth. His baroque desk of solid oak contrasted with the interface tablet he used to access his data hive and communication messages.

Richelieu sighed. He didn't need his mother badgering him as well, not today after the fruitless meeting. "No, Mother. We are still discussing it."

"What's wrong with you? You need to stand up to Javier. You're soft, just like your father. And where did that get him? Nowhere. You need to become a man. Maybe you could get a decent wife then."

Camille's late husband had adored her, but she thought him useless and resented the arranged marriage her parents (the then Prince and Princess of Franconia) had negotiated from the very first day. She could tell her husband had no backbone to him. The other dukes ran all over him, making her the embarrassment of the planet. She thought she had hope in rectifying the situation when Richelieu came along, and she could personally mentor and coach him, but she was now having doubts about him too. Maybe it ran in the bloodline.

"Mother!" Richelieu jumped from his seat and stared at her, enraged.

Camille stared back obstinately.

Unable to maintain the contest of wills, Richelieu looked away. "I'm getting ready for the dinner party." He walked out, leaving his mother to her own devices.

She smiled as he disappeared from view. Seeing the interface still active, she crept around the desk and looked at the messages her son had received. Several interested her and she read them closely, looking up occasionally to see if Richelieu was returning. She frowned at two messages that made unflattering comments about her, noting the senders. Not wanting to be caught snooping, she looked briefly around the office for any other useful information and left.

3

———————

Richelieu's butler knocked on the door of his dressing room as his valet helped him prepare for the Senate Dinner.

"Come," Richelieu called.

The butler opened the door and stood in the doorway. "Your dinner escort has arrived, sir. I have shown her to the library to wait for you."

"Very good. You haven't told Mother? I don't want her sticking her needles into her before we've even gotten to know each other." Catching the fleeting amusement between the butler and the valet, Richelieu instantly regretted his indiscretion.

"No, sir. I have made sure of her ignorance."

"Very good. I won't be long."

The butler closed the door again, leaving Richelieu to continue with his dressing. His valet straightened his uniform and he went to the full-length mirror to inspect himself. The reflection looking back at him wore the dress uniform of the Duchy of Aquitaine, with the planetary fleur-de-lis ensign on the right breast pocket and the thistle emblem of Aquitaine on the left; the gold cross of valor hung from a ribbon around his neck. He hoped he looked noble enough for his date. He had asked her to join him on the whim of the moment at the dinner party the Duke of Parisienne had thrown the week before, having materialized on the dinner party scene out of nowhere. She had impressed him because she looked both stunning and shy. He sighed. She probably would turn out like all the rest. Even if she liked him, Mother would scare her off before long. Squaring his shoulders, he removed the miserable thoughts from his mind and mentally prepared to meet her.

Descending downstairs to the library, he opened the door, freezing as his mother and his date turned to look at him. Terror filled him as he thought about the sort of mischief his mother could have achieved in a few minutes alone with her. A bead of perspiration appeared on his forehead, but his brow went up when his date, dressed in fine clothes and jewelry, smiled, first slightly and then with warmth. He looked back at her and her beauty threatened to overcome him, with the dress and jewelry she wore. "Mademoiselle Felicity, I see that you've become acquainted with my mother." He broke eye contact to glare at his mother before returning his full attention to Felicity.

"We've been having a brief chat," his mother said, smiling at her son as though butter wouldn't melt in her mouth. "You wouldn't leave without introducing Felicity, would you?" She added in a teasing tone.

"The thought had occurred to me."

"Lucky I saw her arrive then," Camille said with a laugh that could be mistaken for genuine amusement. "I'll leave you two to go to your dinner. Don't be late home now." With an affectionate glance at her son, Camille walked out.

Richelieu rolled his eyes as he walked toward Felicity. *When will I escape her? She's the reason I'm still unmarried. No one's ever good enough for me in her eyes, not unless she's hand-picked the woman herself. And anyone she suggests is so horrible, and so like herself, that I run the other way. She hasn't chosen Felicity, so I'm not sure whether to trust this apparent display of goodwill.* "I hope my mother hasn't been upsetting you. She can be a little blunt sometimes."

"Oh, Richelieu, she's charming. And I made sure we got off on the right foot."

He stopped and stared at her. *If she can stand up to Mother for more than one second, maybe she will last past one date.* Realizing he was staring, he bowed his head for a moment. "I am being rude. Welcome. Have you been comfortable while you have been waiting?"

"Yes, thank you for asking." Felicity walked up to him until they almost touched each other, making Richelieu a little uncomfortable. "I'm sure we will have a pleasant time tonight."

Unsure of what to do, Richelieu said, "We'd better be going then." Stepping back from the intimacy, he escorted her to the waiting limousine and they went to the dinner.

THE DINNER WENT as all such dinners did, with the dukes prodding each other for any snippet of information that they could take advantage of. They all stood in the large ballroom on the second floor of the palace, French doors open to a balcony overlooking the estate. Soft music played in the background as Richelieu stood talking to the other dukes with a cognac in his hand. He looked over to the ladies and saw Felicity conversing comfortably with the others, smiling and laughing as if she belonged. He felt happy. Things had gone well with her so far.

"Can I have a quiet word with you on the balcony, Richelieu?" Javier asked.

Richelieu looked at him suspiciously. "Sure." They both walked out to the balustrade of the balcony, away from the others. "What's on your mind?"

Javier smiled. "Some performance in there today." He looked at Richelieu as he took a sip of his cognac. "But that's not what I want to talk to you about."

"Good, because I wouldn't talk about it, anyway."

"You know that I've been putting together a bill to improve the rights of the Cetusians living on Franconia?"

"You can't go very far without someone talking about it. Whatever for is beyond me. Why would you want to improve their rights? They will only want more."

"It's not right. The way they're treated. Have you watched them? Most people treat their pets better."

Richelieu conceded that he had a point. Even though they weren't slaves, slavery was illegal, people treated them like that sometimes. The way some people barked their orders at them, including his mother, embarrassed even him on occasion. "So, what do you want from me?"

"I was wondering where you stood on the topic. I can see that maybe you're not as agreeable to the idea as I thought."

Richelieu rubbed his chin. "I didn't say I wouldn't support any change. It depends what's in the bill. I mean, one of the key arguments against improving their rights would be that it would increase their wages. No one will be happy with that."

"Especially you in your economic position."

"Now, that's unfair," Richelieu said, raising his voice slightly.

Javier winced. "Sorry. I didn't mean that. Can't help myself sometimes. The point is, I need your support on this. I know some other dukes look to you for direction, so if you give some sign of being open to some changes, you might sway them."

Straightening up with the compliment, Richelieu said, "Well, what are you proposing? How will it affect the economy?"

"This segregation thing is becoming unacceptable. I mean, it could even improve the economy if we allowed the Cetusians to mix with us more openly rather than having separate systems for them and us."

"That will cause a riot. People won't accept that."

"I admit we must ease people into the idea. The other thing. Have you ever seen where these people live? The slums? The condition of some of them is disgusting. You wouldn't put an animal in them."

"That's their own fault."

"Is it? You know it's virtually impossible for a Cetusian to buy property. They work unbelievable hours for a pittance."

Richelieu looked at Javier with more respect. He hadn't realized that Javier harboured such altruistic thoughts. He didn't think he had it in his nature. Richelieu took a sip of his cognac as he thought about what to say. Taking his attention away from Javier for a moment, he looked out into the moonlit garden. The sky was clear, and the stars sparkled in their sharp brilliance in the cool, clean air. "Give me an advance draft of the bill and I'll have a look at it. I'm sure there will be some aspects of it I can support." He looked at Javier. "It seems a little out of character, though."

Javier shrugged. "We're all full of surprises sometimes. Thanks. It means a lot to me."

"You're welcome. Let's go back inside before people get suspicious."

Javier laughed.

They both went back and Richelieu joined the others. He noticed Javier veer off to speak to a Cetusian who Richelieu knew worked for him. He watched as they started talking. The Cetusian got excited and waved his arms around. Javier looked around and quickly moved the agitated Cetusian out of sight. *Wonder what that was about?* A moment later Felicity approached him with a smile that instantly made him forget about the scene.

Felicity wrapped her arm in Richelieu's.

"Enjoying yourself?" Richelieu asked.

"Yes." She moved closer and whispered in his ear. "I'd like to spend some time alone with you, though."

Studying her, Richelieu pondered what she meant. Was she saying what he hoped she was saying? He had noticed the many looks of admiration some other males had cast her way at the dinner. He had also noticed that she did not return their gaze. She seemed to have eyes only for him.

"We shall see what tonight brings." He patted her hand, which had settled on his forearm. "It is getting late though. Maybe we should think about leaving." Saying his goodbyes, he walked out with Felicity at his side. Taking the elevator to the ground floor, they walked to the concierge, who arranged for Richelieu's limousine to come to the entrance, the two leaving as soon as it arrived.

Taking Felicity back to his residence, he saw her desire to stay, so he led her up the stairs to his bedroom.

RICHELIEU WOKE to persistent and urgent knocking on his bedroom door. He looked at Felicity, asleep, naked, and undisturbed beside him. He rubbed his eyes and looked at the chronometer. Five in the morning. What could be so urgent as to wake him so early? He got out of bed and put on his robe. Easing his way out the door, he stood in front of his valet, who looked shocked and worried. "What is it?"

"It's the Duke and Duchess de Lorraine, sir."

"What about them?"

"They're dead, sir."

"What!"

4

Yiska busied himself getting ready for the day ahead. He remembered the argument of the night before and frowned. He hadn't meant to get angry at the duke, but things just seemed to get out of hand when the duke said he might have to delay putting the equal rights bill before the Senate in the morning. No use staying upset over it, though. He'd patch things up with him when he saw Javier at the office.

A pounding on the door disturbed his thoughts, and he frowned again. Who could that be, and why were they wanting to break the door down? "Coming," he yelled. He walked to the door and unlocked it. The door burst open and strategic operations police officers rushed in, running throughout his premises to secure it.

Inspector Xavier Fay from the Nouveau Paris police walked in moments later and stood in front of him. "Yiska Powers?"

Yiska looked at him indignantly. "What is this about?"

"I have a search warrant for your premises."

"What on Franconia for?"

"Inspector," came a voice from another room. Xavier walked over, followed by Yiska. One of the other officers came out of the door holding a bloodied knife. Xavier turned to Yiska. "Yours?"

Yiska frowned. "No, it's not. What is this about?" Yiska suddenly felt his heart pounding in his chest as he realized the seriousness of his situation.

"Are you the only one that hasn't heard?"

"Heard what?"

"Someone murdered the Duke and Duchess de Lorraine last night."

"What?" Yiska's eyes widened.

Xavier watched him closely. "Throats cut with a knife. A knife very similar to that one, I suspect."

Panic set in and Yiska felt his temperature rise and perspiration coat his forehead. "You don't think I did it, do you?"

"People saw you fighting with him at the dinner last night."

"We had a short disagreement. Nothing to kill anyone over. We're working together. Why would I want to kill them?"

"A good question."

"Sir."

Xavier turned to the voice.

"A button, sir. Looks like the one from the duke's coat."

Xavier turned back to Yiska, disgusted. "You're under arrest." He looked at one of the other officers, who immediately came over.

Yiska protested to the man. "But I'm innocent, "I'm —" a fist to the jaw prevented any other words coming from his mouth. Hands wrenched his arms behind his back and he felt the restraints clamping onto his wrists.

"Don't be too rough with him," Xavier said, frowning.

"He's only a Cetusian."

"All the same. We only have circumstantial evidence at the moment. Take him back to the station and get a forensics team in here."

Yiska knew it was useless to put up any resistance. The police officer pushed him through the entrance door of his premises and to the waiting AGrav. He saw neighbors staring at him as they gathered to see what the commotion was about, some standing at their doors and a few peeking through the curtains covering their windows. Also being Cetusian, they made sure they stayed far away from the police. An hour later, he found himself in a cell, enclosed on three sides. The front buzzed with a blue-tinted force-field.

THE DUKE and Duchess de Lorraine murdered? That made no sense. He didn't want them dead. The duke was helping him in his equal rights campaign for the Cetusian population of Franconia. Yiska sat on a bench in the cell, his head tilted back and resting against the wall. His jaw hurt where the man had punched him. The skin felt tender when he touched it. He'd been lucky, though. Others had been roughed up much worse for more trivial matters than murder, although he couldn't tell what was ahead of him. They had taken everything but his clothes from him before they tossed him in the cell and had given him no indication of how long he would have to wait before someone came for him.

It seemed like many hours had passed before the main door to the cell block opened and two police officers walked in. They looked at him like they knew they held all the power and Yiska had none.

"Stand," one of them ordered.

Yiska stood up. The other officer turned the force-field off, and they both approached him, one with a stun pistol at the ready.

"Hands out."

Yiska obeyed, and the officer placed restraints on his wrists.

Without warning, the officer kicked him in the groin. Yiska buckled over in agony before being pushed to the floor. They both kicked him in the torso, winding him. One of them kicked him in the eye for good measure and Yiska felt the area instantly swell, closing it up.

"Get up."

Gasping for breath, Yiska tried standing, but only got halfway before another kick to the chest flipped him backwards.

"We'd better go," the one with the gun said. "They'll start wondering why we're taking so long." He looked at Yiska. "Get up."

Yiska dared not look at either of them for fear of upsetting them further and starting another bout of punishment. He slowly stood in a crouched position, not able to straighten fully from the pain. One of them pushed him and he shuffled forward. They directed him through the corridors and he found himself in an interrogation room five minutes later. Pushing him into a chair, they clamped the restraints to the table in front of him and walked out. He waited.

Inspector Xavier Fay walked in after what seemed like an immense amount of time. He stopped short when he saw Yiska. "Shit." He went back to the door and looked out. "Did you two do that?"

"He fell over," Yiska heard someone say.

Shaking his head, Xavier came back, closing the door behind him. He sat on the opposite side of the table and stared at Yiska. Yiska stared back at him, waiting for him to say something. "You're in serious trouble," Xavier finally said.

Yiska remained silent as he hadn't asked a question. He didn't want to antagonize the man; he seemed to have some decency about him.

"The blood on the knife matches that of the Duke and Duchess. Know how it got there?"

"No."

"When was the last time that you saw the duke or duchess?"

"At the Senate Opening Dinner last night. About 9pm."

"What did you do after that?"

"I went home."

"Straight home?"

"Yes."

"What time was that?"

Yiska frowned, trying to remember. "About 9:30."

"And you were alone?"

"Yes."

"How is it then that someone saw you at the scene of the crime at 1am?"

"What are you talking about? I was home asleep."

"We have two witnesses who saw you."

"They're lying."

"How did your DNA get there then?"

Yiska looked at the inspector, confused and unable to fathom what he was talking about. "I tell you — I wasn't there."

Xavier sighed and stood up. He paced the room, looking back at Yiska now and then. He came back to the table and leaned on it, both hands resting on the surface. "How did the murder weapon and a button from the duke's coat get into your apartment then, and why did we find your clothes with bloodstains on them?"

Moving his mouth, Yiska tried to speak, but no words came out. How was that possible? He had been home in bed asleep all night. How did his clothes get blood on them and how did the knife and button get in his apartment? Was he drugged? He felt afraid and didn't know what was happening to him. Nothing made sense. His breathing suddenly quickened and the unharmed eye bulged. "I don't know. Someone must have put them there."

Xavier stared at him. "Things will go better for you if you just tell the truth."

"I'm telling the truth."

"Pity I'm not GIA or I'd get a brain probe on you."

Yiska's eye bulged more. "But I'm telling the truth."

Standing straight, Xavier stared at him again. He left the room and came back five minutes later with a container of water, which he placed on the table in front of Yiska. Yiska bent over and sucked some liquid from the straw. Xavier watched. When Yiska straightened up again, Xavier said, "I've got a problem. I have two witnesses who have identified you at the scene of the crime at about 1am. I have your DNA at the scene of the crime and your blood-stained clothes and a knife with blood on it and you're telling me you were home asleep?"

"I was."

Xavier left, leaving Yiska in the room alone. He fell asleep after a while, being roughly woken up some time later. Confused with his surroundings, Yiska looked around as he became fully alert. Xavier stood in front of him. "Still sticking to your story?"

"It's the truth."

"Take him back to the cells," Xavier said to a police officer by the door. "And no rough stuff."

Yiska found himself back in his cell. The interrogations seemed to take days, trying to wear him down to get him to change his story, but he knew that he hadn't done it. He couldn't work out why there was so much evidence against him; he was innocent. After being manhandled back to the interrogation room yet again, he sat waiting for the same charade to happen.

Xavier walked into the room and sat. "Yiska Powers, I am formally charging you with the first-degree murder of Duke Javier and Duchess Emile de Lorraine. I suggest that you get an excellent lawyer, you will need one."

Yiska sat open-mouthed, not believing what he had heard. "But I'm innocent."

"We'll see what the judge thinks." Xavier rose and left the room. They escorted Yiska back to his cell moments later, his world falling apart around him as they beat him senseless before they left.

5

"Make sure you fertilize those camelias properly," Camille instructed the Cetusian gardener. She eyed him with contempt, knowing that he hated her, and enjoying the fact. *They get uppity if you give them any praise, and that's the last thing they need.*

The Aquitaine estate extended over a vast area of land sculptured into several functional areas. An outdoor amphitheater provided afternoon orations and such activities in the mild Franconian summers. A forested area provided pleasant strolls under the sheltering branches of the meticulously laid out trees. Many fountains, lakes and secluded benches also tapestried the estate. A promenade avenue beautifully bisected the layout from the chateau right through to the farthest boundary. Viewed from the air, the entire estate looked like a painting produced by one of the distinguished artists of years gone-by. Camille enjoyed the occasional scooter ride to view the work being carried out to maintain its beauty. Today she strolled through the fragrant flower gardens, enjoying the scents of the different species planted — camelias, roses and many other species.

She shuffled along the path of the grounds inspecting the lawns, which were smooth as bowling greens, and the multi-colored flower beds lined up on either side as she made her way back to the Aquitaine chateau, the chateau that had been home to her for more years than she cared to remember. She had such grand plans for the duchy when she married the duke, but his lack of assertiveness and ambition disappointed her. She would have divorced the simpleton if it wouldn't have lowered her status in society. Fortunately, he died early. She feared their son was turning out the same, though, despite her education and coaching. Maybe he needed a helping hand, a nudge. She would put more effort into the idea that he marry, although there was a risk that it might take him away from her influence, which was unacceptable.

The chateau, built in the baroque style of ancient Earth, glistened in the sunlight, the glow of the golden panels almost burning her face in the brightness. The breeze still floated the scent of the flowers over her as she prepared to enter the shadows of her opulent domain. The sound of breaking china rasped her ears, and she scowled as she rushed inside to identify the origin of the noise. Two Cetusian servants rushed to clean up the broken pieces of a delicate vase that had splattered on the polished marble floor in her entertainment salon. They cowered as they saw Camille enter the room.

Camille groaned. "Which one of you clumsy imbeciles did that?" she shouted as she rushed toward them.

The servants backed away in fear as she approached. "We're sorry," one of them said. "We were cleaning it and it slipped."

"What do you mean slipped? You're trained cleaners, how can it slip? I'll show you what happens when things slip. Now get out. You've broken my most precious vase."

Both servants rushed from the room. "You'd better be packing," she yelled after them. "If I see either of you again, I'll make sure you're punished tenfold for this."

The effort and emotion made Camille puff for breath as she glared at the doorway the servants had escaped through. She edged to a nearby seat to recover. *There is no excuse for such clumsiness.* Drawing her attention back to the shattered vase, she sighed in disappointment. It was one of her favorites and such a unique antique.

Why on Franconia would the Cetusians think they deserve better rights when they can't even clean a vase without breaking it? At least they're cheap. She stood and waddled over to the intercom and pressed the button.

"Yes, milady?"

"Get someone in here to clean up a broken vase and end employment for the two who broke it."

"Yes, milady." Having a computerized map of all the intercom locations, the answering servant always knew which room the communication came from.

Camille left and went to her study. She picked up her comm and called Felicity.

"Hello?"

"Felicity. It's Lady Camille. It's been a while since I've seen you. Is everything still progressing well with Richelieu? When are you coming over to enchant my precious son again. You seem to have made a big impression on him."

"Yes, he is enchanted with me. I hope that is to your liking. We have a rendezvous tomorrow evening."

"Good, he seems much happier with you around. I believe a blossoming relationship between you will suit both our purposes."

Felicity chuckled. "He's very charming when he wants to be, you know. I'm glad that you approve of me."

"As I said, you're making a world of difference with him. Make sure you see me tomorrow before you leave."

"Fine, I'll do that."

Camille sat back in her chair, suppressing a smile as she pondered the possibility of her son finding a suitable mate in Felicity. She then scowled. *She doesn't come from a pedigree heritage. That will not do for Richelieu.* However, Camille decided the relationship should continue for the time being. It made her son happy and that was important.

6

———————

The murders of Javier and his wife shook Richelieu to the core. Such a thing should not have happened. But he had to admit it placed him in a rather fortunate position, though. With the duke out of the way, he had the upper hand while the Duchy of Lorraine pulled itself together again. He called his political adviser to his office and busied himself with some routine matters as he waited.

A knock sounded on the door. "Come in." Richelieu finished what he was doing as his adviser, Archibald, came in, closing the door behind him. Archibald stood waiting.

Finishing his task, Richelieu said, "Have a seat."

"Thank you, sir." Archibald sat in the stuffed brown leather chair on the opposite side of the desk to Richelieu.

"The murder of the Lorraines is most tragic," Richelieu said, "but it provides me with a unique opportunity regarding the Champagne Duchy."

"Yes, it does."

"But first I was wondering how the Lorraine Duchy will change with the event that has occurred."

Archibald sat back, looking up to the ceiling for a moment while he thought. "The demise of the duke and duchess leaves the duchy in the hands of their nine-year-old son. He is the next in line." Archibald frowned. "In fact, he is the only heir to have claim to the duchy."

"You mean if, heaven forbid, something should happen to the boy, Lorraine would be in the same position as Champagne?"

"Yes, it would." Archibald looked at Richelieu with a conspiratorial smirk.

His expression disconcerted Richelieu. "Get those thoughts out of your head. I'll do nothing to harm the boy. Most dishonorable."

"I was just advising on the situation," Archibald said, returning to a sober expression. "It is my understanding that the current situation there is chaotic. They are uncertain who should be regent until the boy comes of age, and even how the process is to come about. It's never happened before."

Richelieu nodded.

Archibald frowned. "If I'm not mistaken, there is some connection between the Lorraines and your family somewhere back in the family tree. It might be possible for you to become Regent, depending on what the planetary Constitution says on the matter."

Richelieu's eyes lit up. *That's more like it. No underhanded executions. A legitimate means of controlling them.* "That would be worth investigating more fully. Please look into that."

"Wouldn't it be easier to just take them over?"

"No, not the Champagne Duchy and them, not both at once. Once I have Champagne, I can start thinking about Lorraine, but in the meantime, if there is a way I can control what the little duke can decide, it may amount to the same thing."

"Very well."

"When can we continue negotiations?"

"I would need to make contact and set up another session. It may take some time with all the confusion over who has authority."

"Yes, but we need to strike while things are chaotic. Otherwise they might start thinking of ways to thwart us, like Javier did."

"I will do my best."

Richelieu pondered what else he needed from Archibald and decided that was enough. "You can go."

Archibald stood and left.

Sitting at his desk, Richelieu turned in his chair slightly and looked out of the first-floor window of his capital residence. The gardens of the large estate cascaded into the distance as he pondered his thoughts. If he played his cards right, getting control of the Duchy of Champagne should now be less difficult than before. There were no longer any claimants to the duchy, at least until Lorraine got its act in order. He needed to move fast. He smiled. At last things were going his way. Standing, he ambled over to the window. The sun shone from the side and projected stunted shadows in the late morning light. The pencil pines that lined the central avenue of the estate stood erect and still in the windless air outside. Several Cetusian gardeners plodded through the greenery below, manicuring the gardens and lawns to maintain their appearance.

Breaking his concentration on the scene from his window, he walked into his strategy and communications room through the door adjoining his study. He switched on the meter-high holo-image of the planet, which featured a political map of the duchies. Lorraine lay at the top, surrounding the large North Pole of Franconia, and then plunging toward the equator. Champagne connected onto it with the slimmest of an isthmus, projecting to the east, hugging the northern equatorial region. His own Aquitaine covered the continent just to the east of that, straddling the equator with a narrow strait and several small islands between them. Burgundy comprised a group of large islands to the east of Aquitaine and west of Lorraine in the northern hemisphere. The capital duchy, Parisienne, or Ile-de-France, was located south of Champagne in the southern temperate zone. Lombardy and Picardie completed the duchies in the Southern Hemisphere, the seven duchies of Franconia.

Considering his options for taking control, he felt he had to achieve two key objectives to take over the duchy by force — gain control of the government and restrict any movement of personnel from Lorraine to Champagne across the isthmus. They could always fly infantry in, but that required air transport and stealth. He walked to the communications console and dialed Claude Baudin, his General of Armed Forces. The general's image came up moments later.

"Morning duke."

"Morning, Claude. I've been studying our plans for the forceful acquisition of Champagne. I still feel uneasy about how we will prevent Lorraine from helping across the isthmus. It seems a tough position to protect from land and air. They could even come in by sea."

Claude frowned, and his brow creased in concentration. "It would never be easy. Sometimes I wish we could revert to ancient times when they only had land and sea transportation. Completing the task would be so much easier."

"And so much harder for us bringing our own people across the strait."

"Yes, there is that. Anyway, we'll have two of our destroyers hovering just outside the atmosphere to make sure Lorraine doesn't come in from that direction. We will erect force-field barriers to stop any entry by land or sea."

"I see."

"I'm still nervous, Richelieu. Won't we upset the prince if we use our space-based military equipment? We're only meant to bring that out to protect the planet."

"It will be a delicate path to tread with the prince. I am hoping there will be no bloodshed and to beg forgiveness after the event."

Claude chuckled.

"It will be harder to pull us out once we take control," Richelieu explained. "Also, with the Lorraines both dead, the logic of having me take over the duchy is much more convincing. We can't really have a boy attempting to run his own duchy and simultaneously handle the difficulties of incorporating Champagne, even with a regent. Anyway, I'm hoping that the prince will allow me to assume control of the duchy without having to resort to military force."

"It would make life much easier. When will you next discuss the situation?"

"Next month, after the trial. Will you be ready, if I need you after that?"

"I'll be ready."

"Good, let's hope it doesn't come to that."

Richelieu ceased the call.

"About time you grew some balls."

Richelieu jumped and turned around. "How long have you been standing there, Mother?"

Lady Camille stood in the doorway to the room with a satisfied smile on her face. "Long enough." She had returned to the capital during the morning.

He glared at her. "You're not to come in here uninvited."

"Oh, don't be silly. You need someone advising you." She walked into the room as if she owned it. Seeing the holo-image, she waddled over to it and studied it herself. "Your plan may just work."

"Get out, Mother!" Richelieu's patience deteriorated.

"Don't you talk to your mother in that tone of voice. Now behave yourself. I'm just having a look around."

Blushing, Richelieu took some deep breaths. "Find anything amiss?" He asked in a cutting tone.

She looked at him. He could tell she almost said something else but changed her mind. "It's noon. We have a lunch engagement. Remember?"

Richelieu groaned. He had forgotten. He probably wanted to forget. She knew he hated the social engagements she forced him to attend. "Yes, Mother."

7

Satinka woke as the western sun streamed past the edges of her window blind, dimly illuminating the bedroom. She stretched and yawned as she sat up in bed and looked at the shamble of clothes on the floor. Being too tired when she got back to her simple apartment that morning, she had just let them fall where they fell before flopping into bed.

She got out and prepared to go see her mother before rushing back to work. She wanted to see how her mother was going, even though she dreaded the grilling she would get and the nagging about settling down like a dutiful Cetusian girl. Her one-bedroom apartment wasn't much to look at, but at least she had her own bathroom and kitchen, unlike the communal sharing of where she grew up. She shuddered as she recalled the ogling she had received whenever she went to the shower as an older teenager, fully developed and naïvely unaware of the desires of men, suddenly chuckling at the irony, given her current life as a stripper. Still, she would rather be where she was now than where she grew up. If she had stayed, she probably would be pushing out babies at regular intervals and be struggling to make enough money to feed herself and her growing brood — her mother's fate, and the fate of her brothers and sisters.

After a quick shower and something to eat, she rushed out of the door and to a bus stop to wait for an AGrav bus to the Cetusian Quarter of Nouveau Paris. The bus, crowded with Cetusian laborers traveling from work back to their homes, landed and Satinka got on, squeezing into the last space available, which meant she had to stand. There was no personal space for her and it wasn't long before she felt a hand squeeze her left breast. Fury exploded inside her and she slammed her elbow down on the intrusive forearm, a slight whelp of pain and then a chuckle coming to her ears from somewhere behind her as the hand retreated. She knew it wasn't just because she was attractive. Some creeps groped anyone if they could get away with it. A wall of blank stares met her when she turned to identify the culprit.

The bus emptied as it made its scheduled stops, and people disembarked. The stop she wanted finally came into view, and Satinka got off when the AGrav descended to the ground. She plodded down the dusty street, lined on both sides with the disheveled walls of buildings with dilapidated roofs. Just being there made her depressed. The smell of cinnamon, chili, curry and garlic, though, tantalized her, making her mouth water and bringing back memories of her mother's curries and the joy of watching her cook.

"Hello... Anyone home?" Satinka called, raising her voice as she cracked opened the door of her mother's humble shack and looked inside. She waited.

"Satinka. Come in," her mother said from the dimly lit interior. "Excuse me, I was just washing some clothes."

Satinka pushed the door all the way open, the hinges crying for mercy as she stepped into her past. The cramped room held every-thing her mother possessed. Another door on the opposite side allowed entry to an internal communal courtyard where the surrounding residents cooked, bathed, toileted and laundered, sepa-rate buildings in the middle allowing each function to happen. She saw the littered expanse through the adjacent window; the nostalgia made her sigh. "Hello, Mama." She said as she hugged her and gave her mother a kiss on the cheek.

"Come back to help your mama?"

"No," Satinka said, shaking her head with a 'not this argument again,' smile. "I just came to see you. Give you some money."

"What do I want with your money? You should come back and get a man to settle down with."

"Mama, I don't want to argue. Please. I just want to see you. See how you're going."

"What are you doing in that city that you have money to spare, anyway?"

Feeling her face redden, Satinka looked away. "You know I dance and sing in the clubs. It pays well sometimes." She had never told her mother that she was a striptease dancer and she wasn't going to now.

Her mother looked at her strangely. "And what do you have to *do* to get *paid well*?"

"Nothing... You put on an excellent performance; they sometimes give you a good tip." Satinka rolled her eyes. She hadn't told the total truth about her dancing, but she had told the truth about the tips and not having to perform any other services for it. "Want a cuppa?"

"Sure. Anything to change the topic."

"You brought it up." Satinka put the electric kettle on. "How are you doing?"

"What do you care?"

"Mama."

Her mother sighed and looked at Satinka and then looked down. "I'm OK."

"But?"

"I went to the doctor the other day."

Satinka's heart suddenly started pounding. She looked at her mother, alarmed. "What about?"

"Just been feeling tired lately."

"What did she say?"

"It's nothing."

"Ma-ma."

Looking at Satinka, worry in her eyes, her mother said, "She said I should have surgery."

"*What*? What for?"

"Something to do with my heart. But I can't afford surgery. We all have to walk across the brane sometime."

"Don't talk like that. You'll have the surgery. I'll find the money for it."

"Bah, it'll need more than tips from your dancing to pay for what I need."

Satinka reached out and held her mother's hand. "Mama, I'll find a way."

"Oh, Satinka, you were always the optimist. More than you brother and sisters."

The kettle boiled, so Satinka stood and made some tea for both of them, the rich Caerus tea that she brought with her sometimes when she could find it and afford it. How would she find the money for her mother's operation? She didn't want to sell her body any more than she already had at The Two Moons, but she had no ideas on how to improve her finances either. She would find a way. The aroma of the tea filled the room as she poured the boiling water over it, giving the impression of improving the light in the room at the same time. Bringing the cups over, she sat down again.

"What do the others say?"

"Who? Your brother and sisters? They say I need the operation, but they don't have any money to give. They're too busy trying to find enough just to fill their own families' mouths."

Satinka rubbed her mother's shoulder. "I'll think of something."

Her mother huffed but gave Satinka a loving smile.

Looking out into the austere courtyard, Satinka wondered whether her decision to leave this life was the right one. She saw more of the excitement and glitter of life further in the center of the city, but she couldn't look after her mother as she deserved. Still, she had a better chance of finding the money in the city than moving back here and finding a cleaning job or something else. She smiled inside as she tried imagining herself as a cleaner and couldn't.

It was time to leave and make the trip to her work. "I have to go now."

"Do you have to?" Her mother pleading for her to stay wrung Satinka's heart.

"Yes, I have to go to work."

"Please come again soon."

"I will." Satinka stood and took both cups to the small sideboard where a round bowl held other dirty dishes ready to clean. She hugged her mother and left, feeling a lot better on the trip back to the bus stop than when she came.

8

An hour later Satinka stopped in front of The Two Moons nightclub, its cavernous doorway beckoning to her to enter, inviting her back into her world. She appreciated the happy childhood her mother had given her, but that world wasn't able to give her what she wanted now, so she descended the steps into the world that she had chosen.

She had stumbled on the work by accident. One day while in the city looking for a job, she ran into an acquaintance who suggested she try her luck at the club. The manager had looked at her, listening to what she had to say about herself, and then asked her what she thought about stripping. Giving him an honest reply that she would be nervous at first but would get used to it, he looked her up and down again and told her the pay she would get before tips. It was much more than she received for the laundry work she had been doing, so, after confirming that stripping was all she would do, she accepted. Things had turned out over time and she was currently one of the most popular strippers the club had.

"You're late," the manager said.

"Went to see my mama."

"What's wrong?"

"Nothing."

He came over and grabbed Satinka's hand in his monstrous one, but cradled it, looking her in the eyes. "I can tell it's not nothing."

Shaking her hand loose and frowning with frustration and worry, Satinka walked away to control her emotions. She looked back. "She needs a heart operation but she can't afford it, and I can't afford to help her with what I earn here. I'm just trying to think of a way to get some more money to help her."

The manager looked at her, stern faced like a granite statue. He finally said, "I could help you with that, maybe."

"I don't want to sell myself or get into anything illegal," she blurted.

"I wasn't thinking of that. Listen. You have a fair idea of the intelligence of the other girls in here." He looked at her and she rolled her eyes. "Yeah, exactly what I think. You're different. You're very intelligent from what I've seen. You might have what I'm looking for in another venture I'm thinking of... a legal venture."

"Really?" Satinka couldn't tell if he really believed what he had just said about her intelligence or was leading her on.

"Really."

"And it would pay well?"

"Yeah. We might come to some arrangement for a loan too. You could pay it off with your work."

Satinka's eyes brightened. "What is it?"

"Let me think about it. I'll get back to you."

"Sure." She saw some customers starting to come in. "I'd better get ready."

9

"Shouldn't you be somewhere else?" Ahiga asked from the doorway to Alex's office.

The words broke Alex's concentration on the document he was reviewing and he looked up. "Huh?" He looked at his chronometer. "Shit! Chooli'll kill me if I'm late." He quickly grabbed his jacket and comm and stood, rounding the desk to rush out.

Ahiga chuckled. He made way for Alex as he sped past. "Say congratulations to her from Mai and me," he said to Alex's back as he ran down the corridor.

Many emotions went through Alex's head as he raced to his AGrav for the trip to the police academy hall complex where Chooli's graduation would take place. He remembered his own graduation and how naïve he was, until some experienced officers massaged him into shape as a proper detective. Chooli had struggled immensely to get to this day, mainly due to her own need for perfection, but also to make sure she would make Alex and, above all, her parents proud of her. He was proud of her, as he had continually told her, and pride filled him again as he raced to his vehicle. The last thing he wanted was to turn up late, as if her achievement didn't matter to him, because it did. It was more important to him than even he understood himself, which made him kick himself for getting distracted. Jumping into his AGrav, he raced out of the garage of the Tse Corporation office tower he worked in, entering the expressway to the Academy.

He smiled as he remembered their conversation that morning. "I'll come with you," he had said. "No. You go to work. I don't need you babysitting me. Just make sure you're there on time. You've got a seat next to Papa," Chooli had replied.

Nothing he said would budge her, as he knew it wouldn't, so he went along with her demand.

The travel along the expressway was smooth for fifteen minutes, but he suddenly came to a halt behind a traffic jam of AGravs. The cause of the delay remained hidden from his view, but judging by the number of vehicles, it had been in progress for some time. He sat in tense impatience as he watched the time slowly elapse and the start of the ceremony steadily come nearer. Seeing traffic flowing smoothly on a secondary airway, he turned from the expressway and joined that traffic flow, which provided steady, if slower travel to the academy.

After twenty minutes, the entrance to the academy public parking garage lay straight ahead and Alec went into it, parking in a space near an elevator. He looked at his chronometer and sighed with relief as he still had fifteen minutes before the ceremony started. Getting out of his vehicle, he put his suit jacket on, adjusted his clothing and rushed to get to the ceremony hall. Two minutes later he was standing in line while an usher at the entrance checked guests' invitation cards as they arrived. As he waited his turn, he noticed the odd look of disapproval from some of the Cetusians lined up. His turn finally came.

"Invite," the usher said in a bland tone. Alex gave him his card. The usher looked at him, his nose wrinkling slightly and eyes squinting in disapproval. "Near the front and to the left," he said as he handed the card back.

Alex became self-conscious of the disapproving attention he seemed to be receiving. *What's up with these people? Haven't they seen an Earth human before?* Despite being a resident of Caerus for some time now, he was still not used to such blind prejudice, but he put up with it remembering with some shame his own prejudice against Cetusians before he met Chooli.

He moved into the hall and walked down the middle aisle, looking for his seat. The hall was immense, with room for over six hundred seats. Only half that number occupied it now. Large columns loomed to the roof, defining the stage at the front. A banner with the coat of arms of the police force decorated the back of the staged area. The coat of arms comprised two crossed rifles and the two main moons of Caerus between the cross at the top, the background blue, rifles black and moons golden yellow. The words 'Integrity, Protection, Honor' encircled the emblem. People excitedly talked to each other as he walked down the aisle, but he noticed several stopping their conversation to stare at him as he passed.

Alex mentally shrugged off the unwelcome stares as he continued on, searching for Naalnish, Chooli's father. He spotted him not far ahead, one seat in from the aisle. Haseya, Chooli's mother, sat next to him. He walked to the row of seats. Naalnish saw him come and stood, as did Haseya.

"We were starting to worry," Naalnish said as he shook Alex's hand.

"So was I. There was a traffic jam on the expressway." Alex reached over and kissed Haseya on the cheek.

"Well, you're here now."

"Don't you want to sit by the aisle?" Alex asked both of them.

"No, no. I'm sure Chooli would want you to sit there," Naalnish said.

Alex raised his brow. "If you're sure?"

Naalnish nodded, and they all sat, Alex picking up the sheet of plasti-paper with the schedule of proceedings on it as he did so.

"How are things with you?" Naalnish asked in a hushed voice.

"Busy. Ahiga has me slaving away on a new mining agreement with some of his rivals. I think I'm earning every cent he's paying me at present."

Naalnish chuckled. "It's good that you're busy."

A person came to the stage and walked up to the microphone. "Can I have your attention, please? Welcome to this year's graduation of police academy graduates. The ceremony is about to begin, so could you all rise while the officiating officers, honored guests, and graduates enter the hall. Please remain standing while we sing the planetary anthem. You may then take your seats again."

Everyone stood and waited. An academy band started playing a marching tune soon afterwards, and the officials strutted up the aisle and onto the stage. They all faced the audience, waiting.

"Ten-shun!" reverberated from the back of the hall and the thump of a multitude of boots all stamping down at once followed. "Forward. March."

The rhythmic sound of marching followed as the graduates marched up the aisle two abreast. Alex saw Chooli march past on his side moments later. *Don't do it*, he thought as he saw Chooli's neck muscles straining to turn her head but resisting. He knew they forbade looking to the side. Sighing with relief when he saw her resist the temptation, he watched Chooli with pride as the graduates marched to their seats. The anthem music started from the band and everyone sang. The audience then sat, and the graduates were told to sit too.

The formalities and speeches out of the way, the awarding of the certificates of graduation started. It wasn't long before it was Chooli's turn. Alex heard her name announced and she walked to the side of the stage with the stiff formal military walk required, climbed the steps and continued her walk to the Commissioner of Police, who presented the certificates. She stopped in front of him, stamped her feet to attention and saluted the commissioner. He saluted back, gave her the certificate, and shook her hand. Alex saw that he said some words to her, and she smiled. They stood next to each other, and a holographer took an official holograph. They both saluted each other, and she proceeded back to her seat. The rest of the graduates filed through following the same procedure.

"That concludes the main presentation," the master of ceremonies advised the audience. "We are left with the presentation of the Outstanding Achievement award to the recipient for this year. I will request the Commissioner of Police to come forward to say a few words and announce the recipient of this year's award."

The commissioner came to the microphone. "Thank you and welcome to everyone here today. It is a proud day for all of us. It is always an honor for me to present the graduating students with their certificates, as I am sure it is a day to remember for them and for their families and friends. This year's class has been one of the most outstanding I have had the pleasure to meet. However, there was one graduate who..." the commissioner paused and looked vacantly into the distance, as if to find the right words, "... performed above and beyond the normal duties of a police officer, so there was no difficulty in selecting this year's recipient. Ladies and gentlemen, I present this year's award for outstanding achievement to Chooli Richards."

Alex looked over at Chooli with pride. He saw her sitting unmoved for a few seconds until the person next to her jabbed her in the side with his elbow. She came out of her trance and slowly stood, trying to remain formal and unemotional as she walked to the stage and climbed the steps. She took a deep breath and strutted to the commissioner. Standing stiff and straight, she saluted. The commissioner saluted back and attached the medal to the medal bar on her jacket. He shook her hand and said some words to her. Chooli shook her head, laughing and crying at the same time. Regaining her composure, she turned for the holograph with the commissioner, who then came to the microphone again. "Congratulations, Officer Chooli Richards."

The audience gave her a standing ovation. She stood facing the audience, licking and biting her lips, fighting back tears as she searched for her family. Her eyes locked on Alex and his on her.

Alex wanted to make a loud whistle, but thought better of it, giving her a quick wave instead. He turned to Naalnish and Haseya, still clapping. "You must be so proud of her."

A tear trickled down Naalnish's face as he faced Alex, the first sign of genuine emotion Alex had ever seen him display. "Yes, I am." Haseya also cried.

The clapping finally subsiding, Chooli turned back to the commissioner, saluted, and started returning to her seat. As she passed the sergeant, he stood and saluted her. He winked and sat again. She was taken aback as it was the first she had ever seen him relax his strict formality and discipline. Chooli continued on to her seat, although other graduates congratulating her and slapping her on the back hampered her progress. She finally made it and sat down.

The ceremony concluded, and the graduates marched out again, leaving the audience to file out as quickly as possible, talking and jostling for position.

Alex, Naalnish and Haseya walked out together. "That is some daughter you have there," Alex said to both of them.

Having recovered from his earlier emotions, Naalnish said pompously, "I hope she can now use her talent and not waste it."

"Oh, Naalnish," Haseya said. "Stop being so stuffy. You're as proud as anyone. I hope you tell her that when we see her."

Naalnish looked at Haseya, his formality melting, "I will."

They finally made it out of the auditorium and looked for Chooli. Alex spotted her having class holographs taken, and another one with the commissioner and other officials. The main holographs out of the way, Chooli waved Alex and her parents over.

"Would you like a holograph with your parents?" the holographer asked.

"Yes. Mama, Papa."

Naalnish and Haseya walked over and to either side of Chooli. Alex looked on as the holographer took the holograph, smiling at them.

"Alex. You too." Chooli said as she waved him over.

Reluctant at first, but relenting, Alex walked over and stood behind Chooli for the holograph.

"Just you and me," Chooli said as she turned to Alex.

Her parents nodded, so Alex stood next to Chooli, their arms around each other's waists and smiling as the person took the holograph.

They all walked away to the reception area afterwards and the next group assembled to have their holographs taken.

Naalnish placed his hand on Chooli's shoulder to stop her and get her attention. She turned towards him, her eyebrows shooting up. "You have made me very proud today, my daughter."

She burst into tears and hugged him. "Thank you, Papa. That means so much to me." They parted and she looked at him as she wiped her tears away. "That is what I have always wanted to do."

They continued to the reception and picked out items to eat and drink, stepping out of the way for others as they talked and ate.

A few minutes later, the commissioner walked over to them. Chooli started looking for a way to get rid of the things in her hands so she could salute, but the Commissioner smiled and waved her to stop. "You have an outstanding daughter there," he said to Naalnish and Haseya once they exchanged formalities.

"Thank you. I always wanted her to use her talent, so I hope that she can continue now that she is finally useful to you."

"Oh, Papa."

The commissioner laughed. "Oh... we'll make sure we use her fully — you needn't worry about that." He looked over to Alex. "And I presume that you are the famous Alex Warner."

Alex blushed. "At least you didn't say infamous. I don't think I am that famous."

"Your achievements have come to the department's attention. We've even analyzed some of your cases to see what we can learn from them. It would seem some of your talent has rubbed off on Chooli."

"We've had discussions about things from time to time. But you shouldn't presume that I've made much of a difference. I saw her intelligence the first time I met her. She is well suited to this profession."

Chooli blushed and hit Alex. "Stop embarrassing me."

"I hoped that you'd say that," the commissioner said with a

twinkle of mischief in his eye but failing to elaborate on what he meant. "Well, enjoy the rest of the celebrations." He walked off.

Alex looked after him as he left. "I wonder what that was about?" he asked, looking back at Chooli.

"Not sure," she replied thoughtfully.

Looking at Naalnish, Alex said, "Shall we celebrate?"

Naalnish nodded. "Yes, let's," he said, his aureola turning aqua with satisfaction.

Alex didn't know why the Cetusians had these aureolas. They had been genetically engineered a long time ago, giving them the ability to photosynthesize oxygen from carbon dioxide in the air to supplement low oxygen levels in the Caerus atmosphere. Th efficiency of the process diminished in higher oxygen content atmospheres. He could never find out how that engineering had occurred, its source lost in the dim mystery of the past. But it had resulted in Cetusians evolving a sort of halo or aureola. This distinction set them apart from other humans and had led to some humans regarding them as a sub-species. Many Cetusians resented this.

They started walking to the parking area, Alex with his arm around Chooli, feeling at peace with the world and full of joy for her success.

"Go back to your own planet, human scum."

They all looked around to see where the insult had come from. Alex saw two youths standing nearby.

"Yes, you. We don't need scum like you hanging around us and stop contaminating our women."

Alex tried saying something, but nothing came out. Chooli glowered in anger, her aureola a dark green, almost black, and she started walking toward the abusers, but Alex held her back. "It's OK. Let it go."

"No. I won't. They have no right to insult you. I'm a policewoman now. I may as well use my power."

"Please."

Chooli looked at Alex while deciding. Her shoulders slumped as her aureola returned to a normal pink color. "You sure?"

Alex nodded as they started walking again. He heard a couple of more comments, but the youths soon tired of it and left. *Why would they say that? What have I done to them to make them think like that?* The incident depressed Alex more than he admitted. He saw Chooli looking at him out of the corner of her eye and he looked back. She raised an eyebrow. He sighed, squeezed her a little harder for a moment and forgot about it, determined not to spoil her day.

10

---

lex sighed as he struggled out of his AGrav. The day had been long, and he was happy to return home for the evening. He smiled at the thought of Chooli and wondered if she had any news yet of where they would assign her now that she was a police officer.

Reaching the elevator, he went to the top floor where the penthouse he owned was located. He placed his palm on the scanner pad, which activated the face-recognition scanner and the door unlocked, disappearing into the cavity for him to enter. He walked in and the door closed behind him. "I'm home." Walking to the coffee table in the living area, he put his comm on it and kept walking to find Chooli. She stood looking out of the large full-wall-height window, gazing out at the city below. Alex wondered why she didn't turn but walked over to her and wrapped his arms around her. She leaned back and adjusted to his curvature so they joined neatly. Turning, she had a smile on her face. Alex saw joy, but also a hint of nervousness. They kissed. "What's wrong?"

"Nothing." She kept looking at him.

"Well?"

"Well, what?"

Alex stared with minor annoyance.

Chooli giggled. "Sorry. I got my assignment today."

Alex's eyes lit up. "And?"

"I'm starting with the GIA next week."

"What? The Galactic Intelligence Agency?"

"Do you know of any other GIA?" Chooli said, trying to lighten the mood. But Alex jerked away, his smile disappearing. He understood now why she had been nervous. She hadn't been sure how he would take it, and he wasn't taking it very well. He looked away, realizing he was being selfish. "Congratulations, I think."

Chooli came close again. "What's wrong? Aren't you pleased for me?"

He looked down. "Yes, I am... Maybe I'm jealous." Stepping to the window and looking out, he said, "I thought all that was behind me. Gave it up to be with you. And now you're going there. It's not a conspiracy to get me back?" He turned to look at her again.

"What? Don't you think I can get there on my own merit?" Chooli frowned, planting her fists on her hips.

"No... I mean yes. You are more than capable. You're better than some experienced officers that I worked with."

"Well?"

He looked into her eyes. They were like wells of delicious honey and he couldn't resist them. Smiling, he came close. "We should celebrate."

"What do you have in mind?" Her hand came up and her finger rubbed up and down on his shirt, a hint of fluorescence showing on her aureola.

"Not what you're thinking, not yet anyway. Let's go out to dinner."

Chooli pouted, but her smile returned quickly. "Where?"

"I don't know. Nothing fancy. What about back at the Intergalactic Hotel?"

"Want to relive old memories?"

"Why not? We haven't been there for a long time. Might meet some old friends."

"Okay. Let me get ready." She rushed into the bedroom.

Alex looked after her. He had to get changed, but he knew that he had plenty of time. Why did he feel so... jealous? Angry? He couldn't quite work out how he felt. His thought chafed at him. How would he feel with her going off investigating major crimes, being in danger sometimes, waiting for her to come home? Wondering if she would come home?

How things had changed for him. It made him appreciate what the partners of the people who worked with him in the GIA went through every day. He wouldn't be there to protect her. Looking back out of the window, his world seemed different from what it had been just five minutes ago, and yet nothing had really changed. Chooli would have been in just as much danger in the local police force as in the GIA, maybe more so. The appointment was a great acknowledgment of her ability, and he was proud of her, but he also wished she wasn't entering the world he had left to be with her. He wondered if Nascha was still there. He sighed and vowed not to dampen their celebration of her achievement.

Looking at the chronometer, he turned and went to get ready himself.

11

The days that followed his arrest were a blur to Yiska. He didn't have the money to hire his own lawyer, so they assigned a court-appointed lawyer to him. Yiska knew straightaway that this man thought he was guilty and wasn't going to put any genuine effort into preparing his defense.

The date of the trial finally came, and Yiska dressed in his best formal suit for his appearance. The guards and police had not attacked him for some time, so he had no physical bruises to show. He doubted things would have gone any better if he had. Being led into the defendant's seat, he waited for the trial to start.

The judge came in and everyone stood, sitting once the judge had. They selected a jury and the trial proper began. Yiska noted that not one Cetusian sat in the jury seats. It didn't surprise him, as he had read somewhere that Cetusians could not be on juries for murder trials.

The prosecution called one of the supposed witnesses to the stand. His appearance was so unprepossessing that Yiska couldn't believe that anyone would believe anything he said.

"So, Sebastian, what were you doing on the night in question?"

"I was walking past the Block II section of the Cetusian Quarter.

Then I saw something on the ground. When I got closer, I saw it was two bodies and someone was running away."

"I see. And did you get to see what this person looked like?"

"Yes, I did."

"Is that person sitting in the court today?"

"Yes, he is."

"Can you point him out to me?"

The witness pointed directly at Yiska. Yiska sat stunned. He had never seen the man before in his life.

"No further questions."

Yiska's lawyer stood and walked over to the witness. "How close were you to my client at the time that you allege that you saw him?"

"Less than ten meters away."

"I see. The weather records show an overcast sky on the night in question, and the nearest lighting is some distance from the scene. The person was walking away from you, it was dark, but you are sure that the person you saw was the defendant?"

"Yes, I'm sure."

The lawyer paused and looked the witness directly into eyes for dramatic effect. "No further questions, Your Honor."

Yiska looked at his lawyer in disbelief. Was that all the effort he would put into defending him? He shook his head. There was no hope unless he thought of something to save himself. The rest of the evidence and witness statements brought against Yiska went the same way. He finally took the stand and waited.

His lawyer stood in front of him, half facing the jury. "Where were you on the night of the murder?"

"I was at the Senate Opening Dinner for a time and then went home to bed."

"When did you last see the deceased?"

"I last saw Duke Javier at 9pm that night."

"And what time did you leave the dinner?"

"At 9:30pm."

"Did anyone see you leave?"

"I don't really know. I'm sure someone would have."

"Did anyone see you when you arrived at your residence?"

"No, I live alone."

"Did you murder the Duke and Duchess of Lorraine?"

"No, I did not."

"When did you first know of the Duke and Duchess's murder?"

"The morning afterwards when the police arrived at my door."

The lawyer went on with further questioning for another half hour before saying, "No further questions." He smiled at Yiska as if he felt the examination had gone well. Yiska couldn't see how he could think so, considering all the damning evidence presented so far.

The prosecuting lawyer stood up and came over. He stared at Yiska for five seconds, making him feel uncomfortable.

"You say that the first you heard of the murders was the morning after they occurred?"

"Yes."

"How is it then that they found your DNA at the scene of the crime?"

"I don't know."

"How is it the police found the knife used to kill the duke and duchess in your residence?"

"I don't know. It is not–"

"How is it they also discovered the button of the duke's coat at your residence?"

"I don't know."

"You seem to know very little."

"If you–"

"Did you or did you not have a heated argument with the duke at the Senate Opening Dinner in front of all the invited honored guests?"

"It wasn't–"

"Answer the question."

"Yes, we had an argument, but–"

"So?"

Yiska was getting increasingly frustrated with the style of questioning and knew that was exactly what the prosecutor wanted. The questioning went on for another hour, slowly wearing Yiska down. His lawyer gave no help or support, which frustrated him more. He knew what the verdict would be even now. He gave a sigh of relief when the prosecutor finished and walked back to his seat.

The summing up of the prosecution and defense started the following day, and the jury was released to consider its verdict shortly after the lunch recess. He went into the secure defendant room. It came as no surprise when the summons to return to the courtroom came through just an hour later. He returned to his seat in the courtroom, as did his lawyer and the prosecution. His lawyer gave him an encouraging smile, but Yiska saw no confidence behind the smile. The jury followed minutes later.

Yiska rose with the others when the judge came in. The judge sat, and the others did too.

The judge looked at the jury. "Chairperson of the Jury, have you come to a verdict?"

The chairperson stood. "Yes, we have, Your Honor."

Yiska started perspiring, and he felt a trickle slowly creep down his cheek as he looked nervously at the person.

"Would the defendant please rise?" the judge said.

Yiska rose and stood, his cheeks pale as he looked directly in front of him.

"And what is your verdict?"

"We unanimously find the defendant guilty of first-degree murder of the Duke and Duchess of Lorraine, Your Honor."

A murmur of satisfaction and relief rippled around the courtroom, as if everyone had known he was guilty all along and had been afraid he would get let off somehow.

Yiska staggered as the words of the verdict sank in. There was only one punishment for first-degree murder — execution. He licked his lips as anger boiled up inside of him. He was being made a scapegoat. But why? He would never know. It wouldn't be long before they carried the sentence out, of that he was sure. There must be something he could do. He knew his lawyer would be useless in finding a case for appealing the verdict. He might as well not have had a lawyer in the trial. He lowered his head in despair and yet the glimmer of an idea germinated in his head, something he had read about, a way he might get justice, He couldn't see how it would work, but he had nothing to lose. Yiska raised his head as he saw the judge turn to face him.

"Yiska Powers. We have found you guilty of the first-degree murder of Duke Javier de Lorraine. We have found you guilty of the first-degree murder of the Duchess Emile de Lorraine. By the powers invested in me, I sentence you to–"

"I appeal to the President of the Galactic Confederation," Yiska said in a firm voice.

The judge looked at him in surprise. An uproar erupted in the courtroom.

"Order, order." The judge pounded his holographic gavel on the bench.

The noise abated to silence again, and the judge looked back at Yiska.

"You what?"

Yiska stood up straight. "I appeal to the President of the Galactic Confederation to hear my case."

The judge looked at him in frustration. "This court is in recess for one hour," he finally said. He stood and walked out.

The hour passed, and everyone came back in, including the judge. "I have reviewed the precedents for your appeal and you are within your rights to have the case reviewed by the Confederation. So I remand you in custody, without bail, until the Confederation considers your case. Court adjourned."

12

T he Two Moons looked like a lopsided scale with girls wandering all over the club but few customers to serve. Satinka sighed as she sat on a stool, sipping on the lime-flavored cocktail in her hand, wondering why she stayed. Soft relaxing music wafted through the place, a welcome change from the usual blaring thump of bass and throbbing dance music more typical of the milieu.

They didn't get many nights like this, and this was the quietest she had experienced. She suspected the announcement of the guilty verdict for the murders of the Duke and Duchess of Lorraine had something to do with it. Emotions ran high in the Cetusian commu-nity, and several public disturbances had been escalated by the disgruntled groups that had congregated because of the murders. She had almost run into one such group on the way to work before diverting around the trouble.

The club manager walked toward her. Her unease ran high as he neared. He usually only came out of his hiding hole with unpleasant news, even though she got on well with him.

"Quiet night," he commented.

"Yeah." Satinka didn't want to offer any other comment before she knew what he wanted from her.

He eyed her, but had no body language for Satinka to guess what mood he was in. "Your mother still need that operation?"

The question surprised her. He had not followed up on his earlier hint that he could help her mother, so she had long given up hope of anything happening there. And she had no success herself in finding a solution.

"Yeah," she said, glum at being reminded of her failure.

"I might have a solution for you."

"You do?" Her spirits rose, but she remained suspicious until she heard what he had to say. She would not sell her body, no matter what.

The manager looked around. Frowning, he said, "Come with me." Satinka hopped off the stool and followed him back into his office. He closed the door behind them and invited her to have a seat, gesturing to a softly padded chair behind a coffee table. He sat in one next to it.

Her nerves were now stretched to breaking point as she anxiously waited to hear what he had in mind. It was only the third time she had been in his office, and the first time that he asked her to sit down. The other two times had been for a tongue lashing for some minor misdemeanor she had performed. She raised her eyebrows as she looked at him. "What's this all about?"

"We're looking to expand our business interests in Champagne. There seem to be opportunities developing there." She saw him eye her, presumably to gauge her reaction.

"What sort of opportunities?"

"Same as here. Clubs. But we want to have one with more class. Top-end clients with money to burn."

Something about her manager's idea piqued Satinka's interest, but she felt confused. "Why are you telling me this?"

"I want you to manage the project."

Satinka nearly fell off her seat, almost dropping the drink she still held. "What?"

The usually dour manager gave a broad-mouthed smile. "Thought you might get a shock."

She put the drink on the table as she started shaking with excitement. "But why me?"

"I told you before. I think you've got some brains and you're under-utilized in here." His smile increased. "I want to put you to work. See what you're made of."

Satinka gulped, eyes wide with fear. How would she do such a thing? What if she stuffed things up? What if she lost a lot of money? She temporarily suppressed the fear as a question came to her. "But how would this get me the money for my mother's operation?"

He chuckled. "Remuneration."

"Remuneration?"

"Yeah, remuneration. You don't think you'd have to do that and only get the measly pay you get here?"

A sly thought came to Satinka, "So even you think we don't get paid enough?"

"Hey, that's the going rate. Don't blame me for the oversupply of pretty girls."

She had to give him that one. She frowned. "All legitimate?"

"All legitimate."

Her heart started racing again as possibilities started sparking off in her mind. "What sort of remuneration are we talking about?"

"A retainer plus a share of the profits. If you do well, you'll get an interest in the place, give you some incentive."

Silence filled the room as Satinka pulled her jaw back off the floor. "An owning interest?"

"Yeah."

"But I don't know how to set up a place like this, let alone know how it's run."

"You don't give yourself enough credit. You've been here for a while. You know how things go down. I've let you take charge with some things when I've been busy. What you don't know, I can teach you."

It still seemed like a daunting task to her. How would she get something like that going? And top end. All the glitz and glamor that would involve. She looked at him. He sat looking back at her, his expression now blank, so she couldn't tell what he was thinking. She decided and smiled. "Deal."

He smiled in return. "Deal. First lesson. Don't let people know what you're thinking. I could read your face a parsec away and your aureola flashed like neon lights."

She smiled wider. "Lesson understood. So... when do I start?"

"You can start straightaway unless you want to wait for me to put together a package for you. I'm sure what I can offer you will be a good basis to negotiate over, though."

"You've always treated me fairly. I don't see why I shouldn't continue trusting you."

"Don't go trusting me too much, or anyone else. This is business and everyone is out to screw you." He coughed. "Pardon the language."

Satinka laughed. "I might have to get used to it."

"A toast?"

"Why not?"

He rose and went out the door for a few seconds, coming back in and sitting down again. One of the other women came in a minute later with a tray. It had a bottle of champagne and two glasses on it. She looked at Satinka questioningly when she saw her but sat the tray on the table.

"I'll tell you about it later," Satinka said to her.

She left.

The manager opened the bottle and poured them both a glass. He gave her one and held his up. "To a successful venture."

Satinka moved forward close enough to touch his glass and tapped it. "Yeah, to a successful venture and no more dancing."

He frowned. "That wasn't part of the deal."

She froze, alarmed she had put her new life in jeopardy before it had even started.

He laughed at her expression. "Just joking," he said. "You're welcome to keep in practice, though. Keep in shape."

Seeing that her prospects remained intact, she relaxed. "I'll think about it."

They both took a sip and Satinka started thinking. She looked at him. "Where would I work from?"

He smiled. "I like it. You can use one of the spare offices here for a start, but you'll need to set up an office over in Champagne, the capital Epernay probably."

They finished drinking the champagne and Satinka left the manager's office.

The eyes of all the women in the club converged on her as she closed the door of the manager's office. They knew something was up. She gave an enormous smile to reassure them that it was nothing bad and then walked over to them. They congregated around her and she told them about the change in her life. She couldn't wait to tell her mother.

13

Richelieu walked into Prince Léon's meeting room. Pierre, the Chancellor of Champagne, was already seated for the meeting. He rose as Richelieu entered. "Duke," he said as he bowed slightly.

"Chancellor," Richelieu replied. He could feel the tension in the room already, and all of it came from Pierre. He walked around to the other side of the table and sat facing Pierre for the discussions about to start.

Prince Léon sat at the head of the table and looked at both of them. He put his fisted hand to his mouth and gave a slight cough. "Things have changed slightly since last we met."

"They haven't changed at all, Your Highness," Pierre said, sitting up straight with a defiant look. "We still wish to have a democratic government in Champagne."

Richelieu sighed and looked at Pierre in exasperation and then at the prince. "We've been through all this. Let's get things over with and start drawing up the deeds for annexation of Champagne. All this is just wasting valuable time for no end."

"I agree it's wasting time," Pierre said, raising his voice. "You only need to acknowledge that Champagne can govern itself in peace and we'll all be on our way."

"Richelieu is right. We can't have you governing yourself—" the prince began.

Pierre slammed his fist on the table, his face red with determination as he interrupted the prince. "We *will* govern ourselves."

Prince Léon's voice grew angry. "I will not have you raise your voice at me."

Lowering his head, Pierre said, "I most humbly apologize, Your Highness, but we stand firm on this."

"You would prefer to be forced?" Richelieu asked.

Pierre looked at him with clenched teeth. "We will resist any force you wish to throw at us."

Richelieu admired the determination, but he wondered why Champagne was so determined to rule themselves.

"Listen," Pierre said, a pleading edge to his voice. "The late duke, God rest his soul, prepared us to govern ourselves from when he knew he wouldn't be producing an heir and the dynasty would end. In fact, he rarely had any input into our government toward the end."

"But the Constitution won't allow it," the prince answered.

"We believe it will," Pierre replied. "Our lawyers have been through it and believe there is room within the Constitution for a democratically ruled duchy to exist under the extenuating circumstances clause."

Prince Léon raised his eyebrows, "Really?"

Richelieu became nervous. They were serious if they were scouring the Constitution for justification to that extent. His opponent was wilier than he expected. "This is unacceptable, Your Highness. If Pierre and Champagne won't peacefully transfer power, then I must take it from them."

Pierre glared at him. "We will resist to the last."

"I doubt you have much of a military to do that."

"You don't know what strength we have, and what we lack in hardware we have in determination."

The prince looked on in horror.

"Come, come," Richelieu said, striking what he hoped was a concilliatory note. "Don't carelessly throw peoples' lives away. You know I have the manpower to overwhelm you."

"You want to try your luck?"

Richelieu studied Pierre intensely. He now knew Pierre was serious, deadly serious. He wouldn't give up without a fight. The discussions were coming to the worst result, both for Franconia and for him. Even though he had the power to pound Champagne into submission, he didn't want to do that. Apart from the waste of life, his finances weren't the best and the cost of rebuilding Champagne would add a further drain on his treasury — unless Champagne had more wealth tucked away somewhere than he realized. "If this is what you want."

Pierre stood. "If you won't allow us to rule ourselves, it is. This is war." He turned and stormed out of the room.

Richelieu and the prince looked at each other, disbelief etched on the prince's face. Richelieu felt nervous and uncomfortable. The meeting hadn't gone as he had planned or expected. "That didn't go well."

The prince shook his head, "No, it didn't."

"Is there anything to this constitutional acceptance of a democracy?"

"I don't know." The prince sighed. "I must get my lawyers to comb through it. It may need to go to the constitutional court for a ruling."

"That will take forever."

"Yes. And it will set a dangerous precedent if we allow it."

Richelieu stood.

"Where are you going?"

"To prepare for war."

"You're not going through with it?"

"I must. For the sake of my honor and for the good of Franconia."

"No, I won't allow it."

"What do you suggest? Let them get settled looking after themselves until you can decide what the Constitution says about it? No. This must stop, and it must stop now. We've been too soft on Pierre and the space-boy cabinet behind him. I must put them in their place and I will do it. Good day, Your Highness. I have a war to prepare for." Richelieu turned and left, his thoughts in turmoil as his footsteps echoed from the marble floor of the corridor he traversed, leaving the palace moments later to return to Aquitaine and a meeting with his war council. He felt pleased that he had prepared for such an eventuality, even though it was the last thing he wanted.

14

Returning to his estate in the early evening, Richelieu hurried to his study. He wanted to review the status of his military assets and the likely asset level of Champagne's military. Champagne was much smaller than Aquitaine, so it had a proportionally smaller military force.

Accessing his duchy hive, he drilled down to his secure area and opened the military file for Champagne first. It was much smaller. They had no space-based destroyers, and their ground strength was negligible in comparison. They had a large fleet of ships patrolling the coast, though, and a significant fighter fleet. A review of their army highlighted that they used a large proportion of Cetusians as soldiers. That surprised him at first, but he then remembered that Champagne had the largest population of Cetusians of any duchy on Franconia. It surprised him they trusted them to that extent, though. Maybe that's where the nonsense of a democratic duchy came from. He reviewed the strengths and weaknesses of the Champagne military and his own and decided the outcome of the war would come down to overcoming the ground forces and grounding the fighters quickly. He closed the files and sat back, letting the tension drain from him. He didn't want the war as much as the prince didn't, but he had no alternative.

The door opened. Richelieu didn't need to open his eyes to know who it was. "What do you want, Mother?"

"I wanted to find out what happened at the meeting. Have you gotten those renegades to accept us?"

"No, I haven't. They're still determined. I have no alternative but to go to war."

"Good."

Richelieu opened his eyes with a start. "What do you mean, good? How can you want a war draining our treasury?"

"Nobody else will put their foot down, will they? Not even Prince Léon. Maybe there is some of me in you after all. We can't have rogue duchies thinking they can do whatever they want, especially with all those Cetusian apes running around everywhere."

"The Cetusians are people like us, you know."

"That's what those idealists try to tell you but don't you believe it. You only need to look at them to see they're complete morons."

"Mother."

"Anyway, when are you going to get things started?"

"I need to talk to my military council first. What's it to you, anyway?"

Camille paced the floor in front of his desk, looking at her son occasionally. Richelieu could almost hear the cogs turning in her brain, and he didn't like it. That look meant she was scheming something. She stopped in front of his desk and placed her hands on it, leaning toward him. "I just don't want you to get cold feet, that's all." She had a cold, steely stare. She straightened and walked out, leaving Richelieu staring after her, wondering what on Franconia that was all about.

15

Chooli kissed Alex goodbye and left for her first day at the GIA. She felt excited about her new job and what it would entail and wondered what her first assignment would be. It definitely wouldn't be anything exotic or demanding, she figured, given she was just a graduate. She wondered if there were any initiation ceremonies for graduates. *I should have asked Alex.* She considered going back to ask him, but then let the thought drop from her mind. Surely, the agency was more mature than that.

When she arrived at the GIA offices in Arbor, the capital of Caerus, She heard a familiar voice.

"Hi, Chooli, or should I call you *Agent* Chooli? I heard you were coming today."

Chooli turned to the voice, her face and aureola flushed a little with a mix of embarrassment and pride at the mention of 'Agent.'

"Hi, Nascha. Good to see you too." She smiled. "I was shocked when they told me I was coming here."

"Not as surprised as Alex, I bet."

Chooli lowered her head as she remembered his reaction. "It surprised him. I think he felt a little jealous too."

"Oh, he'll get over it."

"He's over it. It just surprised him, that's all." Chooli looked sideways and then back to Nascha, leaning in to whisper. "There isn't any initiation, is there?"

Nascha grinned. "Not that I know of, but then maybe I wouldn't tell you if there was."

Chooli straightened and frowned, annoyed. "Hmm."

Laughing, Nascha patted her on the back. "Who are you meant to see?"

"Personnel."

"Oh. I was only joking about the initiation, but maybe you will get one."

Chooli raised an eyebrow.

"Follow me. I'll take you there." Nascha grinned and started walking. She passed reception, mentioning that Chooli was with her, and took her through to the secure area and through a door into the Personnel section of the office. After asking a few people, she found the person Chooli needed to see and introduced her. "We might have lunch together?"

"Yeah sure," Chooli said, feeling a little overwhelmed.

Nascha left, and the personnel officer put Chooli through her induction into the GIA. The morning elapsed before she knew it, and just before lunchtime they escorted her to her desk. Sitting down, Chooli looked at the desk she would call home when at work. It seemed unimpressive after all the study and other activities she had been through to get there, but it was her home at the GIA.

"Hungry?"

Disturbed from her thoughts, Chooli looked up at Nascha, "Yeah." She packed the things in her desk and stood, grabbing her bag. They started walking. "Where's your desk?"

"Over there," Nascha said, pointing.

"You get an office?" Chooli asked, her eyes wide.

"Us workers need our privacy," Nascha said, giving her a wink.

Chooli laughed. She didn't make herself conspicuous, but she couldn't help but notice the curious looks she got from some other agents as they walked through the office to the foyer, including some slightly lustful stares from two or three of the junior male agents. She chuckled to herself at the thought of their reaction when they found out she was partnered to Alex Warner.

Nascha led her to a cafe around the corner from the office and they sat down and ordered their meals, chit-chatting about what had been happening since they had last seen each other. Their meals came. Looking around to see who else sat around them, Nascha leaned toward Chooli. "Keep this to yourself, but I hear there's been a bit of trouble on Delta Pavonis. Some duke's murder."

"Really? Will the GIA get involved in that?"

"Maybe," Nascha said, shrugging. "It's being handled locally at the moment. What I wouldn't give to go there, though."

"You would? Why?"

"Haven't you heard about Delta Pavonis? It's the luxury system of the Confederation. Nothing is too exotic for those who have the money, and only those who have the money can afford to go there. It's the playground of the rich and famous."

"Oh. Yeah, I have heard about it. The name crops up in the celebrity news from time to time. Everything looks so glitzy."

Nascha looked a million parsecs away. "What are you thinking?" Chooli asked her.

Looking embarrassed, Nascha said, "Oh, nothing. I was just wondering what it would be like to have that much money."

Grinning, Chooli said, "It's not all it's cracked up to be, according to Ahiga."

"That's right, Alex works for him now."

"Yes."

"Didn't think he would settle for a corporate job like that."

Sobering, Chooli said, "He did it for me. It was the only way we could get Papa's blessing."

Nascha's eyes widened, "You asked for his blessing? That was courageous. I didn't think people did that anymore."

Chooli looked down and felt embarrassed. "I come from a fairly traditional family."

"Nothing wrong with that. Still, I didn't take Alex as one who could sit still for long. I wonder what it would take to get him back?"

"He likes it with Ahiga. He still gets his fair share of travel and excitement."

They continued eating in silence for a while.

"Any idea who you'll be working with?" Nascha asked.

Chooli shook her head. "It's been so busy getting all my security clearances and passes and everything else this morning, there hasn't been time to ask what I'll be doing."

"I hope it's someone who'll teach you something. There's a couple in the office who just waste the space they occupy."

Chooli giggled. She colored slightly afterwards, "I saw some guys looking at me when we walked out. They won't give me any trouble?"

"I've seen you in action. They won't give you any trouble. Besides, they'll drool when they find out you know Alex. He's quite a celebrity himself in GIA circles. Come on, we'd better get back."

They finished up and went back to the office, Nascha parting from Chooli to do her own business. Chooli returned to her desk and booted up the tablet on it. She surfed through the various GIA systems to familiarize herself while she waited for someone to tell her what she would be doing, getting up at one stage for a coffee. Boredom soon set in and she sat with her chin in her palm while she stared at the screen.

"Not disturbing you, am I?" a deep male voice said from behind her.

Chooli bolted upright in her chair and turned around. She went red, her aureola turning bright green, when she saw the name tag of the chief inspector for the office on the man's chest. "No, sir." She gulped. "I was just familiarizing myself."

The man chuckled. "I didn't mean to embarrass you. I know it's your first day, Chooli. I remember my first day and seem to recall it being boring."

It surprised her he knew her name. She sat waiting, wondering why he had come to her. He was much older than Alex, looking almost fifty with his hair graying, and he had an intimidating, muscular build, as if he worked out regularly. There was a friendliness in his manner, though.

"Can you come to my office, please?"

"Yes, sir." Chooli rose, ready to follow.

"You can get rid of the sir. Call me Shilah." He smiled.

"Yes, s-, Shilah."

He started walking and Chooli followed, entering his office soon afterwards. Shilah gestured for Chooli to sit in the chair beside the small square conference table that seated four. He sat next to her and studied her for a few seconds, making her feel self-conscious. "Been wondering what your first job might be?"

Chooli smiled. "Yes, I have been."

"How much do you know of the murders in Delta Pavonis?"

Wondering if he had eavesdropped on Nascha's conversation with her at lunchtime, she cautiously said, "I've heard about them."

Shilah looked at his notes, which he had picked up from his desk before sitting. "Someone murdered the Duke and Duchess of Lorraine on the primary planet there, Franconia, a few months ago. It was all being handled locally. They had the suspect and brought him to trial and found him guilty."

Wondering why he was telling her that information, she sat patiently and listened. "That seems straightforward."

"There's been a development. The defendant has appealed to the President of the Galactic Confederation."

"What does that mean?" Chooli asked, puzzled.

"It means that the GIA has to investigate the crime."

"That seems reasonable, but why are you telling me this?"

"Do you know much about the culture on Franconia, the population makeup?"

"No."

"Franconia is what you would call a luxury planet. The people there take immense pride in modeling themselves on the ancient people of France on Earth during their Renaissance period. That's why they have dukes and duchesses and model their political structure on the old French nobility. It has a principality and, just like in historical France, only males can succeed to the throne and the duchies. This makes for a patriarchal society. Anyway, the ruling humans on the planet have grown soft and refuse to do manual labor, so there is a large Cetusian population there. Apparently over the past few years, there's been increasing instability and grumblings about improving the rights of the Cetusians. I understand they treat the Cetusians poorly." Shilah frowned. "The accused is a Cetusian."

"Oh."

"Central GIA want a Cetusian involved in the investigation and have asked me for a candidate. I was wondering if you would be interested?"

Chooli sat dumbfounded, remaining speechless for a few seconds. "This is my first day, sir," she finally got out.

Shilah chuckled. "We're not sending you on your own. You'll be with a senior agent. A human."

"Who?"

"I don't know. They haven't told me. They said they'd get back to me in a few days when they know."

"But there must be other agents in the office much more suitable than me. What about Nascha?"

"She's too senior." He frowned. "Besides, they asked for you. I don't know why. They seem to know more about you than I do. I didn't even know that you had started today."

Chooli hoped that her nervousness and excitement didn't show too much. Why had they asked for her, though? That seemed strange and suspicious. She kept her hands folded on her lap to stop herself from fidgeting. "Yes, I would be interested."

Shilah smiled. "Thought you might be. I read your background file before I went to get you. You've already engaged in some exciting activities."

She looked at him sheepishly. "One or two."

"Well, I'll let Earth know. In the meantime, you might read up on everything you can about Delta Pavonis." He stood.

"I will, s- Shilah." Chooli, beaming with excitement at the prospect of adventure, rose and returned to her desk. She wondered who she would be supporting and couldn't wait to tell Alex. But then she frowned, wondering how he would take the news. The news of her joining the GIA had upset him. She realized he might be even less happy with her going off to another system for a while. Her resolve strengthened. He would just have to get used to it. She was a GIA agent now.

16

Alex's eyes followed Chooli as she left for her first day at the GIA. He felt happy for her but couldn't get a pang of envy out of his system. He realised he missed his time in the GIA.

Walking to the cabinet by the wall of the living room, he opened a drawer and pulled out his old badge, rubbing it with his fingers as he reminisced about old times. Sighing, he placed the badge back in the drawer and closed it. Those days were over and he had his job with Ahiga now, sorting out the multitude of security and other issues for his conglomerate of a business. At least it was as interesting as the work he had done in the GIA, and he enjoyed it. There were days, though, when he missed the danger of those times. He went into the bedroom and prepared for work, dismissing his previous thoughts.

His comm sounded back in the living room, so he walked out and picked it up, frowning when he saw who the caller was. Placing the call on visual, he said, "Commissioner Harris. Haven't heard from you in years."

"It has been a while. I had been intending on keeping more in touch. Things seem to keep getting in the way. How are you, Alex? You look fit."

Alex's suspicions grew as he sensed the commissioner buttering him up. "Yeah, I'm good. Been busy and keeping off the radar of the GIA, I hope."

Commissioner Harris chuckled. "I'm sure we have a file on you somewhere."

"I'm sure you do. To what do I owe the pleasure?"

The commissioner's mood became serious. "What have you heard about the murders in Delta Pavonis?"

Searching his mind, Alex said, "I think I saw something about it in the news. It was a while ago, though."

"Well, long story short, two months ago a duke and duchess on Franconia were murdered. Very important people. Top of the food chain. They convicted someone for it, a Cetusian, but he appealed to the Confederation."

Alex's eyebrows shot up. "Haven't had one of those for a while."

"No, we haven't."

"So why are you calling me about it?"

Harris shifted in his chair, his eyes trying hard not to look at Alex. "I was wondering if you'd take a break from what you're doing and help us on this."

Alex frowned. "Surely you have someone else you could use."

"There really isn't anyone I can trust like you. This is a delicate case at the highest level. Any slip-up could end up as a confederation issue."

Sighing, Alex looked him in the eye. "You know that I would if I were still in the agency, but I made a promise. That's why I quit. I really couldn't break that promise and leave Chooli here, even if I was happy to take on the case. Besides, I'm probably rusty by now."

"Come on, it's like riding a hover scooter. Once you've learned how to ride it, it comes back to you in no time."

Pacing the apartment with the comm in his hand, Alex ran his other hand through his hair. "I can't give you any answer before I discuss it with Chooli. She deserves to be involved in the decision. And I need to talk with Ahiga. It might be difficult for him to let me go for the time."

He saw Harris sigh. "I was worried you wouldn't give me an immediate answer. Okay. Talk about it with Chooli and call me when you decide. I'll start looking for an alternative in the meantime, but honestly, I can't think of anyone better qualified than you."

"You might have to settle on second best."

"You know me. I rarely do that."

"I know."

"Well, just think about it."

"I will. I'll call you back once I've had a talk with Chooli."

"It's been good talking to you again, anyway."

"Yeah."

He hung up, leaving Alex deep in thought. He couldn't understand why the agency thought they needed him. Surely the case wasn't that difficult to investigate. He needed to do some research. Reaching for his comm, he dialed Ahiga.

"Hi, Alex, what's up?"

"I won't be coming in today. Something's come up."

"Not anything serious?"

"No, I just need time to think something through. While you're there, how would you feel if I took some time off?"

"I'd miss you, but no one's indispensable."

"Thanks for the vote of confidence."

Ahiga smiled. "The business couldn't run without you. Does that make you feel all fuzzy inside?"

Laughing, Alex said, "I think I prefer the previous comment."

"What's this about?"

"I'd rather not say yet. I just need time to think about it and talk to Chooli, but it would involve being away from work for a while."

"How long?"

Alex shrugged.

"Well, whatever it is, I guess we'll cope."

"Okay, thanks. Probably see you tomorrow." Alex hung up.

He got his tablet out and sat at the table, searching for everything he could find on the murders Commissioner Harris had talked about. He had a fairly detailed knowledge of what was publicly available by the end of the day and why the commissioner had thought he would be good for the investigation. It seemed the situation on Franconia with the Cetusians and the rest of the population was delicate. Any spark of controversy might blow the Astatine reactor up into a full-scale uprising. It still didn't get him any closer to deciding on what to do. He just needed to talk to Chooli.

17

Alex was sitting out on the balcony sipping a beer when he heard the door to the penthouse open and close, and then the familiar footsteps of Chooli walking across the living space. He didn't turn around. Taking another sip, he wondered how to broach the subject of Commissioner Harris's call. She came out onto the balcony, sat in his lap and put her arms around his neck, leaning in to kiss him. "You're home early," she said.

"I didn't go to work today."

"Why not? Are you feeling sick?"

"No." Alex placed his beer on the table next to his seat and wrapped his arms around her waist as he thought about what to say. He went to speak but looked at her face again. She had the same happy but nervous look as she had when she told him about being in the GIA. "What is it?"

"What?"

"You have that, 'I've got something to tell you' look."

"No, I haven't."

Alex glared back at her until she relented. She unlinked her arms and touched his cheek. "I got an assignment."

"On your first day?"

"They don't want us to get bored."

"And?"

Chooli looked away. "They want me to help on a case."

"This is like drawing teeth. Please tell me before one of us dies."

"Well ... they want me to go to Delta Pavonis."

Alex felt her tense as she sat on his lap waiting for his response. *They want her to go to Delta Pavonis? The same day the commissioner calls to ask me to go? That couldn't be a coincidence.* He clenched his jaw and his mood turned dark.

"What is it?" Chooli asked as she rose from his lap. "I thought you'd be happy."

He rose as well and paced the balcony, slamming his hand against the wall of the building. "Those conniving bastards."

Chooli frowned. "What are you talking about?"

Alex shook his head and let out a loud laugh as he thought about how much they had thought about how he would react. He looked at Chooli, oblivious to the situation.

She crossed her arms and started looking angry. "Well?"

Turning his back to the wall and leaning back on it, he said, "I got a comm call from Earth this morning."

Chooli's brow creased, puzzled, "And?"

"From Commissioner Harris."

She jumped in surprise. "What did he want?"

"He wanted to know if I would do a special assignment for them ..." He paused for dramatic effect. "... on Delta Pavonis."

Chooli looked confused for a second and then burst out laughing. Her mood was infectious, and Alex started laughing too, although he couldn't see much that was funny. She came over, wiping tears from her eyes. "So you think they asked me to persuade you?"

"Don't get the wrong idea. I think your being asked is great and you would do well, but both of us asked on the same day?"

"Yeah, it is a bit of a coincidence." They fell silent as Chooli completed wiping her tears away. "So, what did you say?"

"About what? Oh, I said, I'd have to talk to you about it. He didn't give anything away that you were being asked."

"Maybe he didn't know. He wouldn't know who the office here would ask."

"We're talking about Commissioner Harris. He gets what he wants."

"He hasn't got you yet. Besides, he may have only thought about me after you brushed him off."

Alex fell into thought. "Maybe. Why didn't they ask Nascha or someone else?"

"That's what I asked. The inspector said that they wanted a junior Cetusian to assist. He didn't know who the senior person from Earth would be."

Alex walked back to his seat and picked up his beer, taking another sip. He looked at Chooli, "Want one?"

"Not beer. I might have a white wine, though."

"I'll go get it for you."

"Thanks."

Alex weaved his way around the furnishings to the wine fridge and pulled out a bottle of white wine, opened it and poured a glass, returning to Chooli. "What was your first day like, anyway?"

"Apart from that?"

"Apart from that."

She shrugged. "Typical first day, I guess. Had my induction. Had lunch with Nascha. She says hello, by the way. Played with the tablet and got my assignment. Started looking up information on Delta Pavonis after that."

Alex nodded. "Did they tell you what the case was?"

"A little. It's only my first day. I probably don't have the security clearances for all the details yet."

"You'll have your security clearance. It's a murder case."

"I know. That sounds a little mundane for the GIA to get involved in."

"I did a bit of digging after I got my call. Apparently, the situation on Franconia with the Cetusians is delicate. The murder of such high-profile people by a Cetusian hasn't helped. And now the Cetusian has appealed his conviction to the Confederation."

"That's unusual, isn't it?"

"Yes. I know of only one other appeal like this from my days in the GIA."

Chooli smiled. "That sounds more exciting. So, what are you going to do?"

"I'm having some dinner."

"I meant about accepting."

"I know what you meant. But I need to think and we need to talk."

THEY BOTH SAT in front of Alex's comm after dinner.

"Isn't it early in the morning on Earth?"

"Yes, it is. I've lost count of the number of times the commissioner's called me in the middle of the night. Maybe a bit of payback, since I can do it without getting disciplined for insubordination." He dialed Earth and waited.

The commissioner answered in a shorter time than Alex expected, and he had it on visual. "Alex?"

"Commissioner, I thought you might be in bed still."

"And ... you thought you'd get some payback?"

Alex grinned. "Something like that."

The commissioner frowned and then chuckled. "I can't do anything about it. I woke up and couldn't go back to sleep, so I got up and did some work."

"I've got Chooli with me."

"Hello, Commissioner."

"Hello, Chooli. Nice to meet you. I understand it's your first day at the Caerus office."

"Yes, it is."

"Did you have anything to do with her first case assignment by any chance?" Alex asked.

The commissioned let out a big laugh. "I knew you'd think so as soon as I saw who the junior agent was. No, I didn't. I've been too busy looking for an alternative for you, but maybe I need not worry anymore ...?"

"I can't very well let Chooli loose on the people of Franconia on her own."

"Hey!" Chooli protested, frowning at Alex.

"Is that a yes then?"

"Yes, it is, but you'd better have a big budget. I have a reputation to maintain now that I work for Ahiga."

The commissioned chuckled. "Don't worry, I won't make you slum it. You wouldn't stick to the budget if I wanted you to, anyway."

"You're right there."

"Well, good. I'll get the reinstatement organized immediately. You've still got your badge?"

"Yeah, it's safe in the drawer."

"You should be able to get anything else you need from the Caerus office. Sing out if you can't and I'll get it sent to you."

"Isn't there an office on Franconia?"

"No, there isn't. They oppose a GIA presence in their system. I think they don't want too many people sticking their noses into who comes and goes. I'll send you the details we know."

"Okay."

"Nice meeting you, Chooli. Keep him in order. I never could."

Chooli smiled. "I will."

"And Alex ..."

"Yes?"

"Thank you."

"You're welcome."

The commissioner ended the call.

18

Alex walked into the Caerus office with Chooli the next morning. The people working at their desks looked up as they walked in. Those who recognized who he was, dropped their jaws; those who didn't gave him a resentful look.

He looked around and saw Yas and Atsidi on the far side of the office. They both waved, and he waved back. He couldn't see Nascha anywhere. *Maybe she isn't in yet.* Following Chooli to her desk, he reminisced back to his first days. Staff were crowded into small offices back then, sharing it with two or three others. The open arrangement in this office was less claustrophobic. He found a seat and brought it over to her desk, sitting next to it, trying to keep out of the aisle as much as possible. The agent in the desk across the aisle smiled. He smiled back. The agent self-consciously went back to work.

He looked over to Chooli, who scrolled through her messages on her tablet. She looked to him. "Says here, I'm supposed to take you to meet the chief inspector when we get in."

"Better not keep him waiting then." Alex stood up again and put the seat away.

Chooli threaded her way to the chief inspector's office, Alex following her. It felt different following one's partner around the office. She knocked on the door of the chief's office.

"Come in."

Chooli walked in with Alex straight behind her. Alex looked over and saw how nervous she looked. He smiled reassuringly at her as they waited for the man in the seat to finish his current task. It wasn't long.

Chief Inspector Shilah looked up. "Oh, hello, Chooli."

"Hello, sir."

Shilah looked at Chooli.

"Shilah," she corrected herself.

He stood up and came around the desk. "And Chief Inspector Detective Alex Warner, I believe." He held his hand out.

Alex shook his hand. "Alex will do."

They heard a knock on the door, and all turned. Nascha walked in. "I don't believe it," she said with an enormous smile as she went to Alex and gave him a hug.

"Hi, Nascha."

"What are you doing here?"

"They've persuaded me to help in a case."

"Really?"

Shilah cleared his throat.

"Oh, sorry. Lunch?"

"Sure."

"See you then." Nascha disappeared.

"I read you two," he looked at Chooli, "or three, had an exciting case together two years ago."

"Yeah, she's an excellent agent."

"Anyway, take a seat. Coffee?"

Both Chooli and Alex declined but sat in the two seats positioned in front of Shilah's desk. He returned to his seat. "I never thought I would get to meet such a famous detective. Nearly fell off my seat when I saw the message from Commissioner Harris this morning."

"I don't know if I'm officially on the books yet," Alex said. "I haven't had time to have a look."

"Let's see." Shilah booted up his tablet and searched his hive data. "Yes, looks like it came through a few hours ago."

"Good."

"The commissioner's message said you are to have all leeway with expenses, whatever that means. You'll send them back to his office, anyway. What will you need from this office?"

"I'll need a tablet with full access to the hive, a maser pistol and zaser cannon."

Shilah's eyes opened wide. "That's some firepower, but we should be able to handle it."

Alex shrugged. "It keeps me out of trouble. Do you have a range nearby? I'd like to get some practice. I haven't fired a pistol for a while."

"Sure, I'll get Nascha to show you. Now, as far as the case is concerned, Commissioner Harris is sending through the background files." He flicked through the pages on his tablet. "You're to meet a Chief Inspector Xavier Fay in Nouveau Paris when you get to Franconia, but his details will be in the package you get. I'm envious of you two going off to Franconia. We can only dream of going to a place like that."

Alex smiled. "We're supposed to be working, not sightseeing."

"I know. Still."

Alex stood. "We'll get out of your hair. I'm sure you have a thousand things to do."

Shilah and Chooli stood, Shilah coming back around again to shake hands. "Anything you need, just give me a yell."

"Will do."

Alex and Chooli walked out. Chooli helped him with getting what he needed. He saw she wasn't sure either and had to ask many times where things were or who to see. He found an empty desk and spent the rest of the morning setting up his tablet how he liked it — when people didn't interrupt him by saying hello. He started feeling self-conscious, as if they thought he was a god or something.

They both went to the firing range in the afternoon, and Alex soon got his eye back with the maser. They had some kinetic weapons there, so he unloaded a few magazines of one of those. It almost felt like old times.

19

It took a week for Alex and Chooli to prepare for their trip to Delta Pavonis. Alex tested the commissioner's budget by booking a first-class cabin for the trip. He smiled as they boarded and saw Chooli's face absorb the luxury of space.

"I could get used to this," she said as she sat in the highly cushioned seat next to a window with a view outside.

Alex laughed. He enjoyed making her happy. "I just thought we should travel in style, since we are going to 'the' luxury planet in the Confederation."

"Won't the GIA complain?"

"They shouldn't have asked me to do the job."

Chooli frowned.

"Hey, I'm used to a bit of luxury working for Ahiga. Commissioner Harris would have known that before he hired me."

"So long as we don't get into trouble. I don't need any negative comments on my performance before I even start."

Alex laughed again. "You won't get into trouble. I'm the senior agent, remember?"

"Yeah, but maybe they think I can control you because of ... you know."

"Have you been successful with that so far?"

Chooli frowned again. "I thought I had." She smiled. "You just wait."

"I'm waiting."

A steward came into their cabin and asked, "Would you like some refreshments before we leave?"

They both ordered a champagne.

Alex bent over and kissed Chooli before placing his bag in a locker and seating himself. The champagne came, and they both settled in their seats, happy with their own thoughts for a while. The ship launched from Caerus, but neither of them felt it because of the gravity field covering the whole interior of the ship.

"Have you ever been to Franconia?" Chooli asked.

"No, this is the first time."

"What about any other leisure planet?"

Alex paused before answering. "I've been to one or two."

The reply piqued Chooli's curiosity, and she sat up, leaning toward him with a provocative smile. "And?"

"And what?"

"What did you do on them? Huh?"

Alex blushed slightly, which surprised him. "Nothing, I was working."

"Come on, you must have done some things when you weren't working."

"That was a long time ago," Alex said brusquely, getting a little uncomfortable by the intrusion into his past.

"I still want to know."

"Well, you'll just need to be happy not knowing."

Chooli flung her torso back in her seat in a huff, folding her arms across her chest, but made no further comment.

Alex looked over to her, feeling a little guilty and childish. Why shouldn't she know about his past? He might even tell her about his former partner who abused his trust, scarring him for so long — until he met Chooli. It's not as if he'd done anything wrong. Why did he feel guilty then, as if he had betrayed Chooli? He felt it strange for him to have such a reaction. She gave him the occasional glance, but stayed in her foul mood, although Alex wondered how much of it was pretence.

He sighed. "Okay then."

Chooli instantly came back to life and Alex proceeded to describe the leisure planets he had visited and the things he had done there, both work and recreational. She didn't react the way he had feared. He expected her to become jealous and disgusted in him, but she just took it all in as something new that was interesting to know. "... and that's about it. Your turn."

"I haven't been to any leisure planets."

"You must have some secrets from your past to tell me."

"And that's what they will stay."

"What?"

"Secrets."

"That's not fair."

Chooli just sat back in her seat with a smug smile on her face.

Alex shook his head and watched the holo-vision instead. He saw her looking at him again from the corner of his eye but pretended not to notice.

"I might tell you one day," she said.

"That's fine. We all have secrets we need to keep." He saw her wanting to ask him what he still kept secret but deciding against it, which made him smile slightly. They both sat back and watched the entertainment of their choice.

Nothing of particular interest happened on the five-day trip to Franconia, and they were eager to disembark when the time came. They walked from the spaceship onto the concourse of the spaceport in Nouveau Paris. Alex had seen nothing like it. Everywhere he looked, he saw opulence. There were vaulted ceilings throughout the concourse with frescoes showing fantastic scenes from history; whether Earth's or Franconia's, Alex couldn't tell. Gold shone everywhere, and the marbled floor echoed as he walked on it, geometric patterns decorating it. Alex looked over to Chooli, who gawped around in wonder, her eyes sparkling with excitement.

People rushed through the Arrivals hall in all directions as they jostled to the immigration area. Alex and Chooli followed the general direction of the crowd and the signage. They lined up together in one of the foreigner queues.

"Hey, you! Over there," someone shouted.

They didn't take any notice, not thinking the direction had anything to do with them.

An immigration officer strutted over to them and looked hard at Chooli. "Are you blind and deaf?"

Chooli looked at him confused for a moment until she found her composure again. "Is there a problem?"

"And insolent." He looked at Alex. "Is she your servant? Can't you control her? She's meant to go to the Cetusian line with the others."

Alex's blood pressure rose, as did his voice. "She is not my servant. She is a GIA agent, and I — we — would appreciate your treating her that way."

Others in the immediate vicinity started looking in their direction to see what the noise was about. They talked amongst themselves about the disturbance. The challenge and information about their identity took the immigration officer off-guard. A senior officer came over. "Is there a problem here?" he asked the other officer.

"I came over to advise the two here that the Cetusian needs to line up in the Cetusian line, sir."

"And?"

"They informed me they're GIA agents, sir."

The senior officer raised his brow. He looked at Alex and then at Chooli. A larger frown developed on his face when he looked at her. He looked back at Alex. "I apologize, sir. We are normally very strict with the rules here. It helps to maintain order."

"I'm not the one you should apologize to," Alex said.

"Sorry?"

"You should apologize to Chooli, not me."

The officer gulped. "This is very irregular." He looked at Chooli. It pained him to do so. "I apologize if this situation has caused you embarrassment. Perhaps, to prevent any further complications, it might be easier if both of you follow me to the diplomatic processing area." He looked back to Alex.

Alex looked at Chooli. "You OK?" She nodded. Looking back to the officer, he said, "That would be acceptable."

The senior officer led them to the cordoned-off area reserved for diplomatic clientele and they had no further trouble in the immigration process, although the officers seemed unsure how to treat Chooli.

"What was that all about?" Chooli asked Alex when they were out of earshot and walking to the luggage collection station.

"I don't really know. But I'm guessing it has something to do with sizeable Cetusian community here doing most of the menial tasks. We might be finding out why things are so tense here between Cetusians and the other franconians."

They collected their luggage and proceeded to the public area to find transport to the hotel. Crowds walked in every direction. Many humans strutted toward the exit in expensive dress, seemingly oblivious to the attention being given to them, with Cetusians struggling with the person's luggage behind them, getting the occasional reprimand for slowing the person down. Alex remembered his first day on Caerus and the porter he reprimanded when his case fell off the trolley; he now felt ashamed of his behavior. *How much I have changed since then?* He turned to Chooli, who looked at the scenes in front of her with distaste. "This may be more difficult that we thought," he said.

"Why do they let them treat them like that?"

"I don't know."

They saw many humans look at Chooli with disdain as they negotiated a route to the exit doors, both of them pulling their luggage behind them, unlike virtually everyone else with luggage, where the human left the luggage handling to a Cetusian to perform. Several Cetusians came up to Alex, asking if he wanted them to handle his luggage. Alex declined the offers and noticed they didn't ask Chooli the same question.

Finding the taxi queue, they walked over, placed their luggage in the next one in line and got in. "The Nouveau Hôtel Lutetia please," Alex said to the voice input of the taxi. Moments later, it lifted off and sped on its way.

Alex looked over at Chooli, who looked upset. "You OK?" he asked, as he placed his hand on hers.

"It's one thing being told about the discrimination, experiencing it first-hand is a shock. Will they treat me like that everywhere?"

"Hopefully not. We'll just have to set them straight if it happens." He smiled and Chooli smiled back. "Let's look at the scenery."

They both looked out the taxi windows at the surrounding area. The landscape looked very industrial as they left the spaceport, but gradually segued into suburbia as they traveled toward the city center. They passed over several areas that looked like slums and were out of place with the rest of the city. The grandeur of the city started unfolding as they approached the main precincts. Gold-colored buildings with impressive architectural designs towered up into the air, but the most notable sights were the relatively small but still vast one- and two-story buildings in the baroque style of Earth from long ago, which sat in huge estates of gardens, lakes and other features.

"Look at those buildings," Chooli said, pointing to one of them. "I wonder who lives in those."

"People with more money than us, I would think."

They arrived at their destination. Alex paid the fare with his credit chip and they disembarked. A Cetusian porter instantly came over to help with the luggage, although he looked twice at Chooli before deciding to unload the items, anyway. He placed them on a trolley and followed Alex and Chooli into the hotel.

"Diablo," Chooli said with a smile of fascination as they entered the foyer. They walked on a deep burgundy polished marble floor. Gold-gilded chaise lounges stood throughout the space, with matching side tables and pedestal lamps. Gold-gilded designs covered the ceiling, also from the baroque period on Earth.

"I didn't think it would be like this when I booked the place," Alex said, smiling as he took in the view.

Humans of all ages strutted through the area, some headed for the entrance, others to the reception desk and still others toward arched doorways to dining rooms, bars and salons on the ground floor, their wealth reflected by the amount of jewelry they wore. There wasn't another Cetusian in sight except for the porters and some maids. Alex and Chooli headed for the reception desk. Two customers waited in front of them. The one directly in front looked around and shuffled to the side away from Chooli when she saw her next to Alex. Chooli looked up to the ceiling and sighed.

"How may I help you, sir?" the receptionist asked Alex after the couple ahead of them had moved on.

"A room booked for Alex Warner and Chooli Richards."

"Let me see. Ah, yes, Mr. Warner. That is for two weeks?"

"Yes."

The person busied herself with the check-in process. "Passport chips?"

Alex and Chooli handed over their chips, which she scanned and handed back to them. After another minute, she said, "Okay sir, I have placed you in one of our Chateau suites on the third floor. It has a spacious room for your servant and —."

"What do you mean, servant?" Alex interrupted, his anger rising with his voice.

The receptionist looked at him in shock. She opened her mouth several times, but no sound came out, her cheeks glowing bright red. Finally, she looked at Chooli and back at Alex, "I'm... sorry, sir. I assumed —."

"Well, you assumed wrong."

Having seen the exchange from her office, the manager came out and over to the receptionist. "Is there a problem here?"

"Yes, there is a problem. Everyone assumes that Chooli is my servant, just because she's Cetusian. I will not tolerate it. She is a person like everyone else, and a fully paying person at that."

Chooli became uncomfortable with the attention and placed her hand on Alex's arm, squeezing it slightly. He looked at her but couldn't calm down yet.

The manager looked at the receptionist and then back at Alex. "I am sorry, sir. It is unusual for a Cetusian to come here as a guest, although not unheard of. You must accept our apologies for the assumption of our receptionist." She gestured with her hand for the receptionist to move aside and looked at the booking. She rapidly typed on the keypad. "As compensation, I have upgraded your room to one of the penthouse suites for you and Chooli to use during your stay. I have also included a full drinks voucher on your chip for the duration. Again, please accept our apologies for the misunderstanding." She looked at the receptionist and back to Alex and then Chooli. "It is an honor to have agents of the GIA staying here." The receptionist's eyes widened at the mention of the GIA, as did those of several other people in the immediate area.

Placated, Alex calmed down and looked at Chooli, who still had her hand on his arm. "I accept your apology. Do you, Chooli?"

She nodded, "Yes, thank you." She smiled as she looked at the manager.

The manager noticeably relaxed with the easing of the tense situation. "Well, I hope that you enjoy your stay with us. Business or pleasure, if it isn't too rude to ask?"

"Business, unfortunately," Chooli said.

The manager smiled. "Well, I hope that you can see some of our many tourist attractions and activities while you are here." She handed over the room chips and gave the receptionist a frown before returning to her office.

Alex saw quite a lineup of people when he turned. He gave an apologetic smile to the person behind him and moved away from the reception desk, Chooli following him. The porter with the luggage instantly appeared next to them, a smile on his face. Alex assumed that he had heard the heated exchange and approved of Alex's stand.

"Room?" the porter asked Alex.

Alex looked confused. The manager hadn't said which penthouse suite they had. "Do you know?" he asked Chooli.

Chooli looked at her chip, which had no identification of the room. "No, I don't."

The porter held out his hand to Chooli, "If you give it to me, I'll scan the chip and it will bring up your room on the screen." Chooli gave him her chip, and he got the room number. "Good," he said, handing the chip back. "Please follow me." He led the way to the elevators and up to their room.

The inside of the room impressed Alex, and Chooli's eyes opened wide. The porter deposited their luggage, pointed out the key features, and left.

"Diablo," Chooli said, using her favourite word for anything she found amazing, as she walked her way through the room.

Alex let out a sigh and went over to a desk, leaning his rear against it. He put his hands to his face and rubbed his eyes before looking around again. Chooli smiled at him and walked over. "Thank you."

"Well, it shouldn't have come to that. I can't understand these people. How are we meant to work with them with an attitude like that?" She leaned against him and kissed him, stirring his desire. Alex's comm sounded, and he groaned. "Yes?"

"It's Chief Inspector Xavier Fay here. Is that Alex Warner?"

"Yes, it is."

"Please accept my apology. I meant to meet you and Chooli at the spaceport, but someone mixed up the time of your arrival."

"That's fine."

"Do you want me to come over now and meet you?"

Seeing it was late afternoon already in Nouveau Paris, Alex said, "No. Maybe we'll begin first thing in the morning."

"That sounds good to me. Shall I pick you up at eight?"

"Yeah, that would be fine. See you then." He disconnected and looked back to Chooli. "Where were we?"

"By the gist of that conversation, we have the rest of today to ourselves?"

"Yeah and we were just about to do something."

Chooli gave a seductive laugh. "Let's go have a look around."

"But ...," Alex said as he pouted in disappointment.

She laughed again. "Plenty of time for that later."

Alex shook his head and started unpacking some things. They headed out half an hour later.

20

Alex and Chooli entered the foyer of the hotel at eight the next morning after having had breakfast in the hotel restaurant, where Chooli had received some surprising looks from time to time.

Alex looked around for any sign of a person who might be there to pick them up but couldn't see anyone. He commed the number that had called him the previous day and a man's voice answered.

"Hello."

"Inspector Fay?"

"Yeah."

"Alex, turn around," Chooli interrupted, pointing to someone. "That might be him."

The person she indicated turned and Alex waved to him. They hung up and Xavier was with them a few moments later.

"Welcome," Xavier said as he shook Alex's hand. He looked at Chooli for a moment. "And you must be Agent Chooli." He hesitated briefly but then shook her hand too.

"Thank you," Chooli said.

"I've read up on you," Xavier said to Alex. "Both of you." He turned to Chooli. "You have quite a reputation." He turned again to Alex. "I hope that won't impede what you are here to do."

Alex frowned. "What do you mean?"

"This is delicate. I need to tell that not everyone is so sympathic to why you're here."

"I think the people here have given Chooli a taste of what your people think of Cetusians."

Xavier looked alarmed and turned to Chooli. "I hope it wasn't anything serious."

"Only a misunderstanding about my relationship to Alex. I'll get over it."

"And what is your standing on the subject?" Alex asked.

Xavier paused before answering. "I have to admit that I have my prejudices, but there's no doubt we treat Cetusians poorly and their rights on this planet need improvement. Attitudes are hard to change, though."

"Well, I'll let you know if I'm pissed off," Chooli said.

Xavier looked at her in shock, but then laughed. "You do that."

"Well, shall we interview this detainee of yours?" Alex said.

"Let's." Xavier led the way out of the hotel and to his AGrav and to the police headquarters in Nouveau Paris. He parked, and they went up the elevator to his office. They walked through an area where people were busily working. Some looking up as they strode through the office to the far side. Several of them said hello to Xavier, but a miasma of disdain seemed to drift through the air toward Chooli.

"You need to freshen up?" Xavier asked both of them.

"I might quickly, if you don't mind," Chooli said.

"Through there and to the right." Xavier pointed.

Chooli went off and Alex followed Xavier into his office. They made small talk while waiting for Chooli to return. A little later, a commotion erupted from where Chooli had gone a little later, and they both went to investigate.

"What's going on?" Xavier asked when he saw Chooli holding a detective in an armlock.

"He wanted to hit me because I wouldn't make him some coffee," she explained

"You idiot, Harold — she's an agent. You're lucky she doesn't have you arrested."

Chooli let go of the man and tidied herself up.

Harold went bright red. "How was I to know, sir?"

"Does she look like one of our maids?"

"Not really, I suppose."

Xavier sighed. "Make yourself useful somewhere else." He turned to Chooli. "Please forgive him. As I said, attitudes are hard to change."

Chooli nodded but gave Harold one last hostile look before following Xavier and Alex back to Xavier's office.

"So, I believe that we have transmitted all the information of the case over to you," Xavier said.

"Yes, it has been, thank you. Chooli and I have worked our way through it on our trip here. We have a few questions, but we'd like to interview the detainee first."

Xavier looked at the chronometer. "I've arranged for his transfer from the prison. Let me just check where he is." He made a few calls. "Good, he's waiting for us downstairs in one of the interview rooms. Let's go." He stood up and led the two to the elevator and down to the lower level. The warden on duty escorted them along a corridor and into an observation room adjoining the room that Yiska sat in.

Both Chooli and Alex looked shocked when they saw Yiska. "What have you been doing to him?" Chooli asked.

Xavier looked embarrassed but also angry. "Who did this?" he asked the warden.

"He fell over."

Alex butted in. "If I hear of him falling over again, I'll make sure you're held accountable, understand?"

The warden gulped. "Yes, sir."

The warden left, and they watched Yiska through the window for a while. He looked in terrible shape, even apart from the beating he had obviously recently received. Alex thought he looked like he had given up hope of ever seeing the open air again. Alex and Chooli went next door.

Yiska looked up when they came in. He looked at them both with wary eyes as he watched them sit on the opposite side of the table to him.

Alex looked at his notes. "Hello, Yiska Powers. I'm Chief Inspector Detective Alex Warner from the GIA and this is Agent Chooli Richards, also from the GIA."

A glimmer of light came into Yiska's eyes when he heard that they were from the GIA, but the light disappeared as soon as it had come.

"Do you mind if we ask you some questions?"

Yiska said something to Chooli in native Cetusian, which Alex couldn't understand, and Chooli said something back, also in native Cetusian. He said something else.

"What is he saying?" Alex asked Chooli.

"He said he will only talk to me. He doesn't trust humans."

Alex eyed Yiska. "That's fine with me," he said. "But can you please speak in Galactic standard? It's for your own benefit that I understand face to face, instead of through a translation."

Yiska said something else to Chooli, and she said something else back. He finally nodded. "Okay."

Chooli looked to Alex for direction.

"You read the same notes I did. Use your training," Alex encouraged her. "I'll fill in the gaps."

She nodded and smiled. Turning back to Yiska. "Can you tell us what happened that night?"

"You already have the file."

"Please, we would like to hear it from you again."

He looked at Chooli and then at Alex. Looking back to Chooli he said, "I went to the Senate Opening Dinner to talk to the Duke de Lorraine about a matter. I stayed around for a while longer and then left."

"It says that you had an argument with the duke. What was that about?"

"Nothing really. I'd been working closely with the duke to develop an equal rights bill for Cetusian citizens to put before the current sitting of the Senate. He said that he wanted to delay it until he settled the business with the Duchy of Champagne. I went off at him, saying that he had delayed it long enough and he was just trying to back out of it. We exchanged a few other heated words, but we then settled down. I apologized for my outburst and he said he would reconsider bringing it to the current sitting. That was all. We parted amicably."

"And you didn't threaten to kill him?"

"Goodness no! Why would I do that? He was trying to help Cetusians. Now the bill will probably never go to the Senate."

"What did he mean by the business with the Duchy of Champagne?" Alex asked.

Yiska looked at Alex and stared for a moment. He appeared to decide and looked back to Chooli. "The Duke of Champagne died recently and left no heir to the duchy. It is my understanding that one of the other duchies is to assume control of it."

"So, he had substantial involvement in discussions on that?" Chooli asked.

"Maybe. I don't really know."

Chooli looked at Alex. He gestured for her to continue. "What happened then?"

"I left."

"What time was that?"

"Around 10:30."

"And you went home?"

"Not immediately." Yiska looked guilty.

"That's what you said."

"I know."

"So ... where did you go?"

"I went to a gentleman's club first."

"A gentleman's club?" Chooli looked at Alex, confused.

"A striptease joint," Alex enlightened her with a slight smirk.

"Why didn't you say this before?" Chooli said, looking back to Yiska.

"I didn't think it was relevant."

"Not relevant? It could be your alibi."

Yiska moved uncomfortably in his seat. "I didn't want that information out in the press. It would have been detrimental to the cause."

Chooli sat back, shaking her head. "Men. When did you leave the 'gentleman's club'?"

"About 11:30."

"And where did you go?"

"Home."

"Straight home?"

"Yes."

"Is there anyone who can verify you were at the club?"

Yiska shrugged. "There should be someone who saw me. I am fairly regular."

"You didn't have any personalized service then?" Alex chipped in.

Yiska looked to him. "No."

Chooli raised an eyebrow at Alex. He shrugged. "Could have helped verify he was there. Got a name for the club?"

"The Two Moons."

Alex smirked and Chooli again looked confused. "I'll tell you later," he said to her, and then back to Yiska, "It's a Cetusian club then?"

"Yes."

Alex nodded for Chooli to continue. Although Yiska had clearly warmed to having Alex involved, Alex thought the experience of leading the interview would be good for Chooli.

She looked at her notes. "So you went home. What happened then?"

"I went to bed, woke up and prepared to go to work. The next thing I knew, the police were tearing my place apart."

"Where they found the murder weapon."

"So they say. I didn't put it there."

"How did it get there then?"

"I don't know. I've been asking myself that, but I can't understand how it got there. I have a security system on my apartment. It would have gone off if someone had sneaked in and planted it there, but it didn't."

"The report says they found your DNA at the murder scene too."

"I don't know how that got there either. I've never been to that place. Why would I go there?"

Chooli paused. She looked at Alex.

Alex looked at Yiska, thinking about what other useful information he could provide at that point. They needed more information about the murders first. He had to see where it happened and chase up some other points Yiska had provided that weren't in the original investigation or seemed questionable. They needed to visit this gentleman's club. He felt sure Chooli would enjoy that — not. "Is there anything else you can tell us at the moment that you think is relevant?"

Yiska shrugged. "Would it matter?"

Chooli bristled slightly at the apparent insolent reply, but Alex understood. He had seen it before in people who felt defeated. "Listen. If you are innocent, we are trying to help you here. Your only chance of defeating this charge is to tell us everything you know. If you are innocent, we are on your side. If you lie to us, we will come down on you so hard, you will wish you had never asked for us to get involved."

Yiska sat defiantly for a moment but after looking at Chooli, who sat passively confirming what Alex had said, his shoulders slumped. "That is all I can think of."

"I'm sure we'll want to talk to you again. In the meantime, if you think of anything no matter how small, get someone to contact us."

Yiska nodded.

"Let's go."

Alex and Chooli left the room. Alex had a furrow of concentration on his face as he left. Something didn't add up. Yiska seemed sincere and telling the truth, but there was a lot of circumstantial evidence against him. No one had seen him commit the crime, and yet his DNA was at the crime scene. Someone could have planted it there, just like the knife, but why?

Xavier came out of the observation room. "You finished with him?"

"For now, and I meant what I said about him falling over again. Let's go back upstairs." He turned to Chooli. "You did good in there."

Chooli straightened herself. "Thanks." She went to say something else, but Alex gestured for her to stay quiet.

Xavier showed them to a conference room they could use as an office while they were in the building. Alex closed the door when they entered. He set up his tablet and took a black box from his bag. It had one switch on it and a dial. He toggled the switch to the on position, rotating the dial until a green light came on and placed the box on the table. "We can talk now."

Chooli looked at the box. "What's that?"

"A signal jammer. No one can see or hear what we do or say with that on."

"There are windows."

Alex sighed. "Apart from looking through the window."

"You really think someone might eavesdrop?"

Alex looked at her as he composed what he wanted to say in his mind. "We don't really know. This is a very high-profile case, and I'm sure our progress and what we find out will interest people. Something's not right. Do you really think that guy could have done what he's accused of by talking to him? He seems just as bewildered as we are."

"He could be acting."

"Bloody talented actor. No, my gut says something doesn't add up here."

Chooli looked out through the window of the room. "And you think it involves the police?"

"I don't know. We can't rule them out if something is going on in the shadows."

"And that's why all this jamming and secrecy."

"Yes, at least until we know who we can trust."

21

Camille looked out over the chateau lawns, where people were gathered in resplendent pavilions. She smiled with satisfaction. The high tea was coming along splendidly — and all the prominent ladies of Franconia were there for her to glean information from. She so enjoyed putting on these events. Her face soured slightly as she cast her eyes on her Cetusian servants, but even their ineptitude would not spoil the occasion for her. She descended the steps and moved to the closest group of women, four duchesses and Felicity.

"Ah, Dame Camille," one said. "What a splendid gathering you have organized. Up to your usual standards, I see."

The others in the group smiled. Camille couldn't tell whether in agreement or in mockery. "Why, thank you, Sophia. It is so nice of you to say so. I am pleased that you came. It has been such a long time since we caught up with each other."

"Yes, it has. We are all busy. And you more so than most at the moment. Making sure your son manages the war well."

Camille gritted her teeth but maintained her smile. "He can manage his own affairs. And how is life in Picardie? Did Allard come? I haven't seen him yet."

Sophia's eyes narrowed. "Yes, he's here somewhere. Things are going very well at present, thank you."

"Oh, I'm happy to hear that. I heard the drought is causing a severe drain on your economy. I hope it isn't causing you to tighten your belt."

"They have exaggerated the effects of the dry season out of all proportion. We are managing with no cutbacks at present. Talking about tightening belts, I presume you will have to, given the war draining your coffers."

Picardie must be suffering, Camille thought. *I thought I had seen that dress before, and now I remember it from the commemorative holograph. She wore it to the Senate Opening Dinner.* She smiled. "I doubt that. Felicity, have you met everyone?" Camille face Felicity, who had gravitated to the circle of duchesses, and smiled.

"Yes I have. It's been such a pleasure to meet the people that Richelieu mingles with. You are all very friendly and charming." Felicity gave a fake smile as she raised her glass of champagne for a sip.

"And what is your pedigree?" Sophia asked.

Felicity glanced at Camille and back at Sophia. "My pedigree is intermixed with off-world business interests amongst influential families in the Confederation."

"You must be pressing all the right buttons if you meet with Camille's approval," one of the other duchesses said, chuckling.

A servant maid came over with a tray full of sandwiches with a variety of fillings, offering them to the ladies. She stumbled as she stretched to offer a lady further away, spilling some sandwiches onto the ground. The maid went bright red. "I am so sorry, my ladies. I will clean it up immediately." She went to leave but stood transfixed by Camille's face.

"What clumsiness," Camille said between gritted teeth, remembering where she was. She calmed down and sighed, her smile returning. "It's very difficult to train Cetusians these days."

"Yes, dutiful servants are hard to find in some duchies," another woman said, to the sniggering of the rest in the group.

Camille glared at her. "Yes, I hear you have trouble. Anyway, I must mingle." She made eye contact, challenging the woman to reciprocate the barb in front of her peers. The servant came rushing back and cleaned up the spilled sandwiches, eying Camille occasionally to check she wouldn't attack her for her clumsiness. She rushed off again when she finished. Seeing the challenge declined, Camille walked off, hearing whispers and sniggers behind her. She relished the sparring matches they all engaged in. It provided so much useful information.

Ambling through the crowd of people, Camille reviewed her servants' work. They seemed to cope with their assigned tasks well. She saw a general scattering of servants throughout the gathering, offering both food and drinks. The function's smooth running put a smile on her face.

"You idiot!" came an angry male shout from somewhere ahead.

Rushing toward the shout, Camille anxiously scanned the crowd for the source of the commotion. Her eyes locked onto an apologizing Cetusian, the man he faced rubbing at his shirt where a large wine stain was spreading. She hurried over, embarrassed by the mishap. "Don't just stand there apologizing, go get a cloth to clean up your mess," she said to the servant. She faced her angry guest. "I am so sorry, Duke Fabien. I shall reprimand the servant severely."

"I should think so. Such clumsiness is unacceptable, Dame Camille. But I know how hard it is to find good labor these days. If it's not ineptitude, it's insolence with all this talk of equal rights. Forgive me for talking evil of the dead, but it's fortunate the demise of the Duke and Duchess de Lorraine seems to have put a stop to all that nonsense."

"Hear, hear!" Duke Bouchard de Lombardy said, "Our labor costs are high enough without that nonsense putting ideas in their heads."

"Quite right," Fabien said. The servant came running back with a cloth. Fabien grabbed it out of his hands and gestured for him to leave before he thought about punishing him himself.

"You are so understanding," Camille murmured, slightly lowering her head in obeisance. "I hope this hasn't dampened your stay."

"Not at all. I'll not wear it again, anyway. Too damn embarrassing having people look at the spot when you meet them."

Camille turned and joined a group of women behind the men. She took part in their discussion until the men's conversation pricked her ears. She prided herself on her ability to engage in one conversation while simultaneously listening to another.

"Have you heard the latest development in the murders?" Fabien was asking.

"No. What has happened?" someone else said.

"The accused has used a little-used law to try wriggling out of execution."

"Really?"

"Yes. I would have thought you had heard. It was in all the holo-casts."

"Yes, yes," Bouchard butted in. "The culprit appealed to the Confederation for a re-investigation. We have to oblige, so they say."

"Yes. As I said, it's some obscure law," Fabien continued. "They have sent two agents from the GIA to investigate."

"Two? What a waste of money. Everyone knows the scoundrel is guilty," another man said.

"Well, they convicted him on circumstantial evidence," someone else said.

"Circumstantial? They found the knife in his abode. How much more evidence do you need to convict a Cetusian?"

"True, but the man was working with Javier putting together that equal rights bill."

"Just goes to show how temperamental they are. Javier probably disagreed with him, so he slit his throat."

"Anyway," Fabien said, "they have arrived and one is a Cetusian."

"You're kidding?"

Fabien nodded. "A pretty little thing she is too, I'm told." The others laughed.

"And what about the other agent?" Bouchard asked.

"The other one is a man. Human. Experienced, they say. I heard he put up a right old stir when they arrived at the hotel. He wasn't too happy about the receptionist mistaking the other agent for his servant."

"You don't say," someone said.

"Well, at least the man should sort this all out in no time," Bouchard said.

"Let's hope so. These agents can be sticklers for evidence, though. We'd be better off without them if you ask me," Fabien replied.

That is interesting, Camille thought as she tuned out of the conversation and tuned into the one in front of her.

22

Richelieu wandered over to the group of men next to Camille and joined their conversation.

"How are the war preparations going?" Fabien asked.

"They're all coming together," Richelieu replied as he picked up a glass of champagne from a passing tray. "A pity the duchy isn't as agreeable as this drink." The others laughed at his comparison.

"What do you think of these agents coming here from the GIA?"

Richelieu shrugged. "They have a job to do. I really don't have an opinion one way or the other at present. So long as they sort it out, so things can move on."

"Yes, yes. Anyway, you've put on a pleasant event here today, as usual."

"You should thank my mother for that. She's the social manager. I'd avoid them if I had my way. They take too much time away from more important things."

"Like wars?"

Richelieu smiled. "Like wars."

"Talking about distractions," Bouchard butted in. "I hear a certain lady has been making inroads into your time lately."

"Yes. What is her name again?" Fabien asked. "I know you told me, but I'm terrible at remembering names."

Richelieu blushed. "We're exploring one another at present – nothing serious yet. It's Felicity. She's here somewhere. Mother saw fit to invite her."

"The eternal bachelor finally getting hooked then?" Bouchard jested.

Richelieu laughed. "Have you been talking to Mother?"

The others laughed.

"Would make her happy," Fabien said. "Wouldn't it?"

Bouchard changed the subject back onto the possibility of war. "So, what do you think about Champagne, Richelieu? How serious are they?" He asked. "I don't recall them having a large military."

Richelieu sighed. "Unfortunately, they're very serious. That's one of my headaches, estimating how long it will be before they see reason and start negotiating."

"Well, I hope there isn't too much bloodshed. It might damage the economy of the entire planet, if there is. People might stop coming here and spending their money."

"I don't know," Fabien said, flippantly, "they might pay extra to experience a war zone."

Richelieu frowned. "Yes, I hope I can resolve it quickly. I would prefer to prevent deaths on both sides." He finished his drink and placed it on the tray of a passing servant. "Well, I must be off. Enjoy the rest of the afternoon."

23

The next day started warm with the sun shining and a slight breeze blowing. Alex and Chooli prepared to visit the place where the murders allegedly happened. Xavier came with them and they brought the holographic recording of the victims with them so Alex and Chooli could see the virtual victims in situ.

Xavier's AGrav took them to the location, and they all disembarked. They stood in a dead-end alley on the tee junction of two major streets in the primary Cetusian district. Old three-story buildings with no windows stood on either side of the alley, and a synthetic concrete slab blocked the end to fence it off. It was dark even at the time of day they arrived, which was late morning.

Alex walked the length of the alley, looking for anything unusual. With so much time having elapsed since the murders, he didn't expect to find anything, but it didn't hurt to look. He looked up and scanned the buildings. "No security cameras?" he asked Xavier.

"There is one at the entrance," Xavier pointed to a camera mounted ten meters in the air. "But it was out of order when the murders took place."

"That'd be right," Alex said sardonically. He looked at the ground and went about two-thirds of the way in. "This is where they found the bodies?"

Chooli looked at the spot and looked at Alex, surprised. "How do you know?"

"There is a faint blood stain here."

"Yes, that's it," Xavier said. "I'll get the holograph equipment set up." He went back to the vehicle and got the equipment. Chooli helped him set it up. Checking its correct assembly, Xavier turned the holograph projector on and an image of the dead duke and duchess appeared where Alex had deduced the victims had laid.

Alex went back to the entrance of the alley. It was quite a distance from the bodies, so it would not have been easy to discover them by accident. "Who found the bodies?" he asked Xavier.

"That's a little tricky. People saw two men stripping the bodies of valuables."

"Who?" Alex asked. "Who saw the men?"

"It was an anonymous tip-off. We arrested and convicted the men of that crime and some others."

Chooli looked at him, disgusted at the thought of people robbing dead bodies. "Where are they now?" She asked.

"Serving time in the penal colony on one of our moons."

"We might want to talk to them," Alex said.

"You might have to go there for that. The penitentiary does not allow them off the moon until they've served their time."

Alex nodded his head and then walked back to the site of the bodies, shaking his head while walking around them as though something was troubling him. The duke lay front down with his head turned to the side, mouth and eyes open and a gaping slash in his throat from ear to ear. His wife lay front down too, half on top of her husband, her head on one of his shoulders. She had a matching slash in her throat. Alex crouched, studied the scene for some time, and frowned. Looking up at Chooli, he asked, "What are your obser-vations?"

Chooli jumped slightly, surprised that he was asking her. She crouched for a closer look, leaning over to study the duke's shoulder where the duchess lay. Her brow wrinkled. She stood and took a step back. "Something's not right," she said to Alex.

"What isn't right?" Alex asked, intrigued to see if she would come to the same conclusion that he had.

"I don't think they killed these people here."

"Why not?"

"There isn't enough blood. Look at the man's shoulder. If the woman bled out here, there would be blood saturating the clothing. There is very little blood stain. And the general amount of blood — it's far less than what one would expect from two people having their throats cut at this spot."

Alex smiled. "Anything else?"

Chooli looked again for some time. "No, I don't think so."

"I can't be certain until I talk to a forensic medical examiner, but I believe they cut the throats postmortem."

Xavier frowned. "You mean the knife didn't kill them?"

"I don't believe so."

"But that was the only injury on both of them."

"Hmm." Alex stooped over the bodies for a closer examination, scanning every area of skin he could without having the clothing digitally removed by the projector, which he didn't want to do. His focus finally centered on the necks of both of them, just above the knife cuts. "That's odd."

"What is?" both Chooli and Xavier said in unison.

"Look, this puncture mark. It's on both their necks in the same spot. I don't recall reading that in the autopsy report. Actually, I would have thought the medical examiner could distinguish between a premortem cut and a postmortem cut." He stood and rubbed his chin, thinking. "I've only ever come across a puncture wound like that once before. From what I was told, it's a terrible way to die."

The others looked at him expectantly.

He explained, "An assassin nano-bot. It burrows into the flesh and finds a bloodstream, the primary artery in the neck usually. It then manufactures a lethal poison within seconds from the person's own blood. Death is within a minute or two. It doesn't show any of the poisoning symptoms or manifestations, which is why it's so hard to tell and why it's so useful to an assassin." He smiled grimly. "This was a professional hit. No way could Yiska have done this."

Xavier stood stunned, facing Alex. He looked down. "This is rather embarrassing."

Alex felt for Xavier. "You can only work with what you've got. Still, I'd like to talk to the medical examiner to see how he came up with the findings in the report."

"So where were they killed?" Xavier asked no one in particular.

"Good question. We must retrace their steps and see what we find. We're finished here. Let's go give the examiner a visit."

Xavier and Chooli packed up the holographic equipment and they traveled to the coroner's office, where all the forensic autopsies of murder victims were conducted. Fortunately, the chief medical examiner could see them immediately. Xavier, Alex and Chooli filed into the examiner's office.

The examiner closed the door and invited them to sit. "So, Xavier, what can I do for you?" he asked after the introductions were over.

"We're reexamining the Loraine murders, Hugo," Xavier replied. "Maybe I'll let Alex explain." He looked to Alex to continue the conversation.

"We've just come from the alleged murder scene and viewed the holographic file," Alex said. "There seem to be some inconsistencies between the autopsy report and my observations. Now, I know I'm not a medical examiner, but I've seen many murder scenes including those involving the victim having their throat cut, and it would seem to me that the cuts are postmortem."

Hugo looked at Alex, indignant at the questioning of his department's expertize. He looked at Chooli and frowned further. "I think we can tell the difference between a premortem and postmortem cut."

"Why didn't you pick this up then? Even I can tell its postmortem from the holographic image. You should have been able to pick it out straight away on the real bodies."

Hugo sighed. "Let me get the report out and have a look." He unlocked his tablet and searched for the files, a deeper frown appearing after a time. He kept typing away on the keypad, the finger strokes becoming more pronounced and forceful as his frustration increased. Giving up, he looked back at them. "They've disappeared." He had a look of incredulity on his face. "I've never had that happen before."

"How can they just disappear?" Xavier asked. "Maybe someone accidentally filed them elsewhere."

Hugo shook his head. "I just did a search, and they're not coming up. Someone's removed them."

"How can that be?" Alex asked. "What about your backups?"

"I've looked there too and someone's wiped them too."

"Do you mind if I get one of our GIA analysts to look at your hive?"

"What good will that do?"

"If they didn't remove them professionally, they may be recoverable. Although, I suspect it was a professional job and they are not."

Hugo hesitated.

"I can get a warrant, if that will help?"

Hugo let out a breath and sighed. "No, that won't be necessary. I'll authorize access."

Xavier scratched his head. "Where does that leave us, Alex?"

"Can we see the bodies then?" Alex asked.

"We have released them for burial."

Alex's eyes widened in surprise. "Is it usual to release the bodies before you execute a conviction?"

"Normally not, but in this case, it seemed to be open and shut. I saw no reason not to release them to the estate."

"And who requested the bodies?"

"I can't tell you that either." Hugo gave a sad smile.

Alex gritted his teeth. "I take it that normally they would have been shipped back to the Lorraine Duchy estate?"

"Yes, each noble house has a family mausoleum for burial," Xavier explained.

"We must get a warrant to disinter the bodies."

Xavier and Hugo looked at Alex in shock.

"What? Is that going to be a problem?"

"More than likely. It's difficult enough to disinter a normal body but disinterring a member of the nobility is unheard of. People would consider it sacrilege," Xavier said.

Getting frustrated, Alex forcefully said, "Do we want to find out what killed them or not?"

Xavier sighed. "I'll get one of my people onto it." He stood up and went out of the room, coming back a minute later.

Alex looked at Hugo. "Have you come across assassin nano-bots before?"

Raising his brow in surprise, Hugo said, "No, I haven't, why?"

"I believe that's what killed the duke and duchess."

"Then it would have had to have been a professional hit."

"Yes, it would have." Alex sat in thought for a moment. "I don't think we can do much more here then. Thank you for your time, doctor." He rose from his chair. Chooli and Xavier followed his lead.

Xavier's phone rang, and he answered it in private mode. He listened and looked at Alex with a frown before hanging up. Alex looked at Xavier expectantly. "They cremated the bodies."

Alex groaned and looked up to the heavens. "Typical. Why do I get these cases?" He sighed and looked back to Xavier. "Let's get back to the office then."

They left the medical examiner's office and Xavier took them back, depositing Alex and Chooli in their makeshift office when they returned. Alex collapsed in a chair and leaned back as far as the pivoting chair would go, putting his hands behind his head and closing his eyes to think. After half a minute he said, "Haven't you got something better to do than look at me?" He heard a slight giggle and opened his eyes again.

"No, I haven't. I'm waiting for you to tell me to do something," Chooli said. "Anyway, what's wrong with looking at you? I can think of worse things to look at." She looked at him even more alluringly.

"No fraternizing at the office," Alex said, his grin contradicting the instruction. He leaned forward to let the chair return to its upright position. "I suppose technically, this is only your second day on the job." He thought. "Can you organize one of our cyber experts on Earth to look at the medical examiner's hive? I'll see if we can get a ship to take us to our two dodgy witnesses tomorrow. We need to go by this gentleman's club on the way back to the hotel and verify the time Yiska was there." Chooli nodded and went to work.

Alex stood and went out to find Xavier. He came back ten minutes later. "All fixed. We have a transport ship to take us to the penal colony at nine tomorrow morning. The Chief Warden will meet us when we arrive."

"And I've organised for an analyst to look at the hive tomorrow."

"Good." Alex let out a tired breath. "Not much more to do here today. Let's pack up and head off to this gentleman's club."

Xavier organized for a department AGrav to be seconded to Alex. Alex and Chooli hopped in and instructed the interface where to go. They both sat back for the flight.

"What was with all the sniggering yesterday about the name anyway?" Chooli asked.

"You don't know? Really?" Alex grinned. "The two moons?" His eyes dropped from her face to her breasts.

"Oh." Chooli reddened slightly with the revelation. "You men have a one-track mind."

"I don't see you complaining most of the time."

"That's different."

Alex grinned again and sat back for the trip to the club.

THEY ARRIVED FORTY MINUTES LATER, in the early evening. Getting out, they went to the entrance and descended the stairs into the dimly lit club. Plush velvet covered the lounges scattered around a stage area. Other chairs and stools were also scattered around the floor, mainly positioned facing the stage. Some surrounded small tables. Alex saw that the stage included a pole-dancing pole. He watched Chooli look around, and presumed it was the first time she had been in such an establishment.

"Can I help you?" The question came from a tall, muscle-bound Cetusian man, clearly a bouncer. He looked like he spent a lot of time in the gym, and Alex suspected he might take the odd steroid as well to build up the muscles further.

"I hope so," Alex said. "I'm Inspector Warner and this is Agent Richards from the GIA." He and Chooli showed their credentials. "We have a few questions for you."

The man looked at them both suspiciously. "That depends."

Alex chuckled. "This isn't a raid or anything like that. We just want to find out when one of your customers was here to confirm his alibi. You maintain the required archives of your surveillance system?"

"We keep a strict confidentiality policy."

"I can make a few calls and have this place inspected for compliance. It might take some time and shut down the place for the night."

The man's eyes widened. "I don't think it will come to that. What do you want to know?"

"We want to verify that a Yiska Powers was here on ..." Alex looked for his notes.

"... January 25th this year," Chooli said, helping Alex.

The man's eyes widened again. "The man who killed the Duke and Duchess de Lorraine?"

"Allegedly killed."

"I thought that was all over. Yeah, we can find that out. He was a regular, actually. Had a special girl he always wanted to see: Satinka. She's here tonight. You want to talk to her?"

"Please," Alex asked.

The man went away and came back a minute later with one of the most beautiful women Alex had ever seen — human or Cetusian. She was Cetusian. She walked with a rhythmic, mesmerizing gait and smiled seductively at Alex as she approached him and Chooli. She had very little on, which added to the allure. He saw Chooli's aureola flash dark blue with jealousy before she got her emotions under control again.

Satinka stopped in front of Alex, "And what can I do for you?" She looked at Chooli. "Or is it both of you?"

"They're from the GIA," the muscleman said.

Her smile broadened. "It doesn't bother me what they do for a day job."

The spell breaking, Alex said, "We're after some information. I understand that you know Yiska Powers."

Her smile disappeared. "Yes, I do ... or I did. He's in prison, isn't he?"

"We're investigating the murders people allege he committed. We understand that you were with him on the night of the murders."

"I may have been. That was a long time ago. If he was in here, I probably spent some quality time with him." Satinka's eyes sparkled at Alex when she said, 'quality time.'

"Well, how can we find out?" Alex asked her and the man.

"Follow me," the man said. Which they all did, including Satinka. Alex noticed that she stayed close to him, too close for Chooli's comfort. He turned toward Chooli and smiled. He knew he shouldn't play with her emotions, and he wasn't going to. It just felt good knowing that she was protective of him and their relationship.

They went into a little office where they all barely fitted, Satinka nestling close to Alex with Chooli trying to get some separation between the two. The man manipulated the information on the security tablet for the establishment. He finally got the night in question and let the holo-image play for the entrance to the club. Yiska walked in at 9:53pm. The man switched cameras and followed Yiska. He met Satinka, and they went off to a room.

"Where is that room?" Alex asked. He started feeling uncomfortable as Satinka rubbed up against him. He looked at her. She just continued smiling.

"Just out there. I'll show you in a minute," the man said.

The holo continued, and they both came out at 11:09pm, Yiska leaving shortly after. The man turned the holo recording off. "Follow me," he said, and they all followed him to the room Yiska had used. It had four walls with no windows — no escape except through the door they had come in by. He looked at Alex.

"That seems to be conclusive," Alex said.

"Anything else?"

"No. Thanks for your time. We let you get on with running your ... business."

They all walked to the stairs. Alex and Chooli turned to climb them.

"Don't forget to come back for some quality time," Satinka said to Alex as his gaze passed across her.

He smiled. "Maybe some other time."

Chooli scowled.

They climbed the stairs and left in the AGrav. Chooli pummeled Alex with her fists when they had some privacy, much to Alex's pain and delight.

"Stop it, will you?"

"You shouldn't have led her on."

"Led her on?"

"I saw your eyes."

Alex laughed. "I sense some jealousy."

Chooli finally relented her attack and sat fuming.

Seeing her hurt, Alex stroked her cheek with his forefinger. "Chooli?" She looked at him. "You have nothing to worry about. I love you. I wouldn't do anything to hurt you or betray you. Okay?" He saw her aureola slowly change from anger to calm and then to a tinge of happiness.

She finally smiled cheekily, "You'd better not." With that said, she jumped across to sit on his lap and kissed him.

24

A lex and Chooli waited at the spaceport, ready to board the transport to the penal colony. They arrived at nine in the morning as arranged. A man walked over to them several minutes later. "You two coming with me?"

"If you're going to the penal colony, the answer is yes," Alex replied.

"Follow me then."

The man started walking to the hatch of the transport, not looking behind him to see if Alex and Chooli followed. Frowning, Alex wondered if he cared much about anything. Once inside, Alex saw mostly cargo in behind five seats for passengers. He and Chooli sat in two of them. The hatch closed moments later, and they rose into the air soon after.

Alex looked out of the porthole, wondering where the investigation would lead. There seemed conclusive evidence that the charge against Yiska was false, but why accuse him in the first place? Was it because he was Cetusian and expendable? Did it have something to do with the rights bill he was working on with the duke? Or was there something more sinister involved? There was very little respect for the Cetusian population, from what he had seen so far. He found that the treatment the Cetusians received annoyed him, almost angered him. *How had such prejudice grown?* The Cetusians were as human as he was.

A sudden jolt rocked the transport and Chooli yelped, shooting out a hand to hold Alex's arm. "Sorry about that," came over the ship's comm, the voice dry and unconcerned. "There's an asteroid belt along the way and some smaller wayward ones get in the way sometimes. Nothing to worry about."

"That's easy for him to say," Chooli said, looking scared.

"I presume that's not the first time he's hit one. He didn't seem worried."

"I'd prefer him not hitting any, if it's all the same with him."

Alex lifted his arm and put it around her shoulders. They encountered no more collisions along the way, arriving at the moon three hours after liftoff. The transport landed, and the pilot came out from the cockpit, opening the hatch and walking out with no word about the arrival or what they were to do. Looking at Chooli with a perplexed face, Alex rose, as did Chooli, and they both followed him. Another man waited for them as they walked down the steps to the surface below.

"Detective Warner?" The man said. He frowned when he saw Chooli. "And Agent Richards?"

"That's right," Alex replied. "And you are?"

"Chief Warden, Martin Noyer. Call me Martin. Welcome to Lune-de-Diable penal colony. There has never been a successful escape from here."

Alex sensed pride in the announcement. "Thanks for agreeing to have us interview the two people of interest. Do you mean there have been unsuccessful ones?"

Martin chuckled. "Yes, there have been a couple. Unfortunately, they didn't adequately prepare themselves against the vacuum and coldness of space. Please come this way. We have the two in separate interrogation rooms, as requested." He started walking. Looking behind, he said, "You don't have a lot of time. The transport is likely to leave without you, if you delay him for long."

"We'll keep that in mind," Alex said as he looked at Chooli.

They continued walking through the corridors of the domed colony entrance until they arrived at an elevator. They got in and descended an indeterminable distance, from Alex's perspective. The doors opened, and they entered an extensive underground area, lit with glaring lights. Following Martin, they walked until he came to an office block, which they entered and Martin showed them to a room. It was an observation room where they could looked into two other rooms. There was a prisoner in each with a guard standing in the corner. The prisoners each sat at a table, restrained to a rail with a magnetic cuff. They sat slumped in their bright orange prison overalls, looking bored.

"There they are. They're all yours for as long as you want. Just tell the guard at the desk outside when you're finished and I'll come and take you back to the surface."

"Thanks," Alex said.

Martin walked out, leaving them to their tasks.

"Which one first?" Chooli asked.

"Does it matter?"

"Not really, but that one looks like he'll talk," Chooli said, pointing to the one on the left.

"They'll both talk by the time I'm finished with them, but let's go by your suggestion." They left the room and entered the left interrogation room.

The prisoner looked up, wary. He leered when he saw Chooli. *Hasn't seen a woman in a while*, Alex thought. *Not that Chooli doesn't have desirable features.* He saw her give the man a steely look. The man quickly looked away.

Opening his tablet, Alex brought up the file on the man. He read it again, making him wait. He looked up. "Says here that you saw the murderer of the Duke and Duchess de Lorraine leave the scene of the crime."

The prisoner looked at Chooli and back to Alex with an uncertain gaze. He finally sat back, a smug look on his face. "That's what the report says."

"In the dark?"

"Yep."

"From ten meters away?"

"Yep."

"Bullshit."

The smugness left the man's face as he seemed to realize he was there for more than some questions.

"Were you really there?"

"Yes, I was."

"Doing what?"

He became worried, stammered, "Th-this and that."

"This and that what?"

"L-looking for th-things."

"What things?"

"Th-things we could sell."

"What, on the bodies?"

"Y-yes. They weren't having any n-need for them."

Alex sat back and looked at Chooli. *She was correct in choosing this one. He was a pussycat.*

She looked at the man without disguising her disgust. "You didn't really see the man you accused, did you?"

The man looked at Alex and then Chooli. He licked his lips, the nervousness apparent. He finally lowered his head. "No."

"Why did you say that you did then?"

"They said they'd reduce my sentence. He was only a Cetusian, anyway." The man's head jerked from Alex to Chooli immediately after he said the words, his face turning bright red. "I-I mean, th-that's what th-they said."

The disgust on Chooli's face deepened. "So the other witness was your partner?"

"Y-yes."

Alex rubbed his chin in thought. "Who's 'they'?"

"W-what?"

"They. You said *they* would reduce your sentence."

"I-I don't know. I presume they were the police."

"Did they look like police?"

"They didn't look like anyone, but who else would interrogate us?"

Alex paused, thinking. *Another fall-guy. I wonder if they were really the police?* He looked at Chooli, "You got any more questions?"

"Did you get a reduced sentence?" Chooli asked.

The man looked glum. "Not really. Especially when they put you in a place like this."

Gets you put out of the way, Alex thought. Whoever was behind this has gone to some considerable lengths to get Yiska put away. But why? Surely his work with the rights bill wasn't causing that much of an outrage. Why him? Or was he just someone convenient they could use as being believable enough to a prejudiced society looking for blood? He looked at Chooli again. She shrugged. "That will be all." Alex stood and left the room with Chooli close behind him.

They interrogated the other prisoner but got no more information from him than the first one. Completing their interviews, Alex called for Martin, who arrived ten minutes later. He escorted them to the surface, and they left the moon in the transport soon afterwards. The pilot had been waiting impatiently for them. To fill in the time, Alex went over with Chooli what they knew so far. "So what do we know?"

Chooli thought for a moment. "Someone murdered the duke and duchess, but at a different location to where they found the bodies, presumably by assassin nano-bots, and they had their throats cut after they died and somewhere else."

"They cut their throats where they found the bodies. The amount could be consistent with having them cut postmortem."

Chooli nodded. "Someone planted Yiska's DNA at the site and placed the knife in his home, assuming he is innocent."

"Oh, he's innocent all right."

"Yiska has an alibi for the time of the murder."

"And we have two bogus witnesses to the crime."

They talked for some time, discussing what they knew. At the end of the discussion, Alex sat back. "We'll just have to go back to when they were alive and put together a timeline from there. See if we can get a clue as to where the murder took place and who did it."

"That would be the Senate Opening Dinner."

"Yes. Fancy a visit to the prince's palace?"

Chooli's eyes sparkled. "Never been in a palace before."

THEY ARRIVED BACK on Franconia and Alex received a message from Xavier for them to see him, so they got in the AGrav and went to police headquarters, going immediately to Xavier's office.

He looked grim. "Follow me," he said. He took them to the elevator and to an upper level. *This is ominous*, Alex thought. *Up usually means someone higher up the food chain.* The elevator stopped, and the doors opened. A vast office area stood in front of them with just a personal assistant and an enclosed office. Another area held a conference room. The assistant looked up when they arrived. The man looked at Chooli in disgust, quickly shifting his gaze to Alex and Xavier. He picked up a comm and whispered into it. Looking at Xavier, he said, "He will see you now."

Xavier led the others into the enormous office. There was no doubt who was in charge when one entered, with a vast desk facing them and a man in an equally immense chair behind it. The man stared at them as they filed in. Alex could see that Xavier was nervous and worried. Alex wasn't sure if he should be too. The man behind the desk had obvious power, but only on Franconia. Maybe that was enough for Alex to share the worry. He would find out.

"Inspector Fay," the man said. The man stood and his slight stature surprised Alex. Such a man with a lot of power, not a preferred combination in Alex's opinion. He looked in his sixties and had black rings around his eyes, showing signs of sleep deprivation. He was stocky, but not obese. He walked around the desk to the three.

"Commissioner Gros, sir, may I introduce Chief Inspector Detective Alex Warner and Age–"

"I know who they are." Commissioner Gros stood first in front of

Chooli and looked her up and down with a disapproving look. He moved on to Alex and looked him up and down too. Alex felt like he was in an inspection of the guard. The obvious use of power to intimidate intrigued him, though. What did this man want? He had a calculating look in his eye when Alex looked at him. "I've had some reports come to me inferring that you believe this Yiska Powers is not guilty of the crime of murder."

Alex looked at Chooli, whose anger he saw festering, and then at Xavier. He answered noncommittally. "We have reached no conclusions yet. I'm not sure where your information has come from." Alex saw Xavier cringe slightly out of the corner of his eye. The man in front of him was Xavier's boss and could get rid of him in an instant, but the man would not intimidate Alex, although he was interested in where the man's information had come from. He was ruffling feathers in some quarters. Beforehand, Alex wasn't sure if he should stand to attention or not, but now he stood in a relaxed stance and looked impervious to the attempt at intimidation.

"I see. And when will you reach a conclusion?"

"When we have finished our investigation."

The commissioner stared at Alex. "You have finished it now and have concluded that Yiska Powers is guilty as charged."

Alex bristled. "I can't do that, sir. That is against procedure and not in line with justice being done and seen to be done."

A beetroot redness spread across the commissioner's face. "You have finished your investigation," he shouted, a bit of spittle flying into Alex's face.

Alex gave the man an equally steely stare. He lifted his hand and wiped the offensive fluid from his face. "Why do you want the investigation stopped?"

The commissioner took a step back, obviously not used to having his orders questioned. "I will have your badge," he whispered.

"Fortunately, I don't report to you, commissioner. You are welcome to file an official complaint to my commissioner, if you like, but, until then, I will continue with the investigation. Now is that all?" Alex had had enough of the jerk in front of him. He

had better things to do than be intimidated into sending an innocent man to his death, and he was sure Yiska was innocent. He
just had to find proof that he was. He saw Xavier almost having a
fit of his own next to him, and Chooli struggled to contain a
smile.

"Get out, get out! You'll be sorry you didn't take my advice."

"Is that a threat, sir?"

"Get out. Xavier, remove them from my presence."

Xavier gulped. "Yes, sir."

Happy to comply with the commissioner's demand, Alex turned
and followed Xavier out with Chooli behind him. The personal
assistant looked at them in shock as they passed and waited for the
elevator to arrive. When the doors of the elevator closed behind
them, Alex asked, "What was that all about?" He looked at Xavier.

"You've just made a powerful enemy," he said.

Alex shrugged. "But why would he want the investigation
stopped? Who's leaning on him?"

Confusion crossed Xavier's face, worry replaced it. "I don't know.
He mixes with some very important people. It could be any of several
people."

"Come on, Xavier. The murder of a duke and duchess and it looks
to me it was a professional hit. There can't be too many people with
that much power and means to pull that off."

Xavier recoiled as if Alex had shot him.

"I'm sorry. I didn't mean to have a go at you. I just get worked up
when something like that happens, and it usually happens because
someone wants to hide something."

Placated, Xavier replied, "It could be several people. Some rich
and influential businesspeople could do it, or another duke. Even the
prince, if you wanted to include everyone."

"You don't want to include the prince, why is that?"

"He would have nothing to gain. It makes his position more
onerous."

The doors opened.

"What do you mean?"

Xavier looked around the office. Several people were still working at the late hour. "Let's go have a drink."

Alex looked at Chooli, who shrugged. "Okay then. Lead the way."

"There's a bar just around the corner." Xavier led the others out of the building and into the bar. He found a table in a corner, dimly lit and positioned where he could see who came and went. They ordered drinks. The waiter looked twice when he saw Chooli but said nothing. Xavier took a sip from his drink when they came and fiddled with his glass as he thought. "One duchy of Franconia, Champagne, has no duke. Without an heir, the noble line is extinguished. Our Constitution says that a duke must run each duchy, and the prince was, and still is, trying to get either the Duke de Lorraine or the Duke de Aquitaine to take it over. They are closest geographically and in lineal connection to the defunct Champagne line. Now, with the death of the Duke and Duchess de Lorraine, that lineage is also in danger of ending. They had a nine-year-old boy, so he would be the new duke when he comes of age." He took another sip of his drink.

"Who runs the duchy in the meantime?" Chooli asked.

"A regent together with a council of elders."

"And who is the regent?"

"That's the point. No one can agree who it should be. Prince Léon is pulling his hair out, trying to get people to agree on someone."

"So, what you are saying is," Alex said, "with the Duke of Lorraine out of the way, the Duke of Aquitaine is in a prime position to take over Champagne without a fight for it."

Xavier nodded his head. "Except Champagne wants to rule itself. They want a democratic government, something their duke had been working toward."

"Someone didn't bump him off too?"

Shaking his head, Xavier said, "No. He was an old man. He died naturally."

"Would Champagne benefit with the Lorraines dead?"

"Only in that they would have one party to fight off, instead of two," Xavier said after some thought.

"Why didn't you tell us about this before?"

"I didn't think it was relevant until that little showdown with the commissioner."

Alex raised his brow. "Little?"

Xavier chuckled.

"Well, you've given us something else to ponder," Alex said as he finished his drink.

"Listen, tomorrow's Sunday, our usual day off. What do you want to do?"

Alex looked at Chooli, "What do you want to do?"

She sighed. "I could use a rest, but it's up to you."

"Sounds like we'll take a day to recharge. We need to work through what you just told us, anyway."

"Go see some sights. It's fairly easy to get to most of them from here," Xavier said.

"Might just do that. Might be the only time we can afford to come here."

They all finished their drinks and went their separate ways.

25

Alex groped for Chooli as he woke the next morning, only to find air where she should have been. He opened an eye, making sure he hadn't missed her. The bed was empty. He rubbed the sleep from his eyes and sat up, looking for where she had gone. It was such an enormous apartment, compartmentalized into rooms. He saw immediately that she wasn't in the bedroom. She wasn't in the bathroom either as the door was fully open and the room vacant. He frowned as he rose out of the bed and put a gown on. Chooli's back appeared as he entered the living room. She sat on the balcony in a lounge chair, basking in the sun with very little on. The sight of her nakedness aroused him as he approached her.

"About time you got up," she said, not bothering to look around.

Alex flinched. *How does she do that?* "What are you doing?"

She turned toward him. "Basking." Looking lower, she asked, "What's on your mind?" as she saw a bulge in the gown.

"Nothing," Alex said, blushing. He moved over to her and leaned over to kiss her. "Unless you have ideas."

Chooli smirked. "One track-mind."

Alex stood up again, slightly insulted by her remark. *He didn't always have that on his mind ... only when around her, especially when she had no clothes on.* He sighed. "Why are you up, anyway?"

"We should do something relaxing today. Something to recharge us."

"Like what?"

"I don't know. There must be something. You're the chief detective — find something interesting we can do or look at."

"Chief detectives get their juniors to do the legwork."

Chooli stuck her tongue out. "Your junior is on strike today."

Alex moved in to tickle her, but she saw him coming and jumped up. They jumped from side to side, Chooli looking for a means of escape, bursting past Alex and into the living room. He expected her movement and caught her around the waist. She yelped, feigning an attempt to get away, but she wrapped her arms around his neck and kissed him instead, as he walked her to the bedroom.

"I'LL GO ASK DOWNSTAIRS," Alex said half an hour later, Chooli snuggled up next to him.

"Hmm?"

"I'll go see what we can do, or have you changed your mind?"

"No, what about breakfast?"

"We can go downstairs or have it up here today."

"Can we have it up here? I don't like the way the people look at me all the time."

"Sure. You order room service, while I check out the tourist attractions."

"You'd better put some clothes on first."

Alex rolled his eyes. "Thanks for reminding me." He showered and got dressed, going downstairs while Chooli organized breakfast. She sat eating through hers when he returned, looking like she had been thinking as she sipped on a coffee.

"Didn't want it to get cold," she said as she looked at him.

Alex nodded as he sat down to start on his food. "Need to keep up your energy," he mumbled under his breath.

"I heard that," Chooli said with a smile.

Grabbing a glass of orange juice, Alex asked, "What were you thinking about?"

"Nothing really. I was just thinking about what Xavier told us last night about the dukes and everything. This might be more complex than we thought."

"What makes you say that?" Alex asked. He had come to the same conclusion but was interested in what her reasoning was.

"Well, the Duke of Aquitaine had an obvious motive, and, as Xavier pointed out, the Champagne people may have also had one. But then one of the other dukes may also have wanted the Lorraines out of the way. Maybe they want to get rid of the boy and take it over like Champagne. Or maybe someone wanted to get rid of them for other reasons. We know the duke was looking at more rights for Cetusians on the planet. What if someone with a lot at stake got rid of him to stop anything going through the Senate?"

Alex smiled. He liked her thinking but being reminded of all the possibilities was giving him a headache. "All thoughts I've been mulling over, but let's follow the evidence and see where that leads us. In the meantime, let's enjoy our day off."

"What have you found?"

"There's a place called 'The Slide'. The concierge says it's a must-see attraction on the planet, but only the bravest ever use it."

"Why's that?"

"He wouldn't say. He only smiled. Anyway, I made a reservation for a guide to take us there in an hour's time."

"An hour?"

"What's wrong with that?"

"I have to get ready." Chooli jumped from her chair and started for the bedroom.

Alex rolled his eyes. "Women."

"I heard that."

AN HOUR later they were sitting in the vehicle the tour guide had organized and were speeding across the surface of the planet. The site they traveled to was near the North Pole of the planet, and in the Duchy of Lorraine. The landscape below fascinated Alex. He could see why it was a popular tourist destination. Everything looked pristine in the naturally landscaped areas. But there were also large recreational parks that the tour guide pointed out, explaining all the activities people could enjoy in them, including joy rides of various sorts and going from the mundane through to the outright dangerous or erotic, depending on one's tastes.

Three hours later, two tall peaks appeared on the horizon straight in front of them, looming higher as they got nearer.

"That is where we are heading to," the guide said.

"What are they called?" Chooli asked.

"The Fangs," the guide replied. Despite being human, she didn't seem bothered by Chooli being Cetusian. She was one of the few unprejudiced humans they had met on this planet.

"Why are they called that?"

"They look like two snake fangs. They rise on two sides of a waterfall, which is what we want to see."

Chooli looked at the snow and ice below and across the landscape all the way to the two mountains. "In this climate?"

The guide laughed. "It thaws out in the summer months, but the attraction is in the winter. You will see when we get there."

Alex could see a large plateau either side of the two mountains as they approached and a massive escarpment to the valley below.

They slowed and landed half an hour later in a parking area at the base of the waterfall. The guide gave them both heavily insulated coats and hats to protect them from the cold outside. Getting out of the AGrav, Alex and Chooli looked around and up in awe. A mass of frozen water extended up to the saddle between the two mountains.

"Amazing, don't you think?" the guide said.

"Diablo," Chooli said, her mouth staying open as she kept looking up.

"We can go to the top and you can slide down it."

Chooli looked at her, horrified. "No way am I doing that."

The guide chuckled. "Probably an excellent choice. It's one of the most popular extreme sports for the ultra-rich brats that come here. It has a significant mortality rate, but that doesn't seem to dissuade anyone."

"Well it dissuades me," Alex said with a laugh. "How high is it?"

"About 2000 meters."

"What?" both Alex and Chooli said at the same time.

"It's almost a vertical drop most of the way down," Alex continued.

Still smiling, the guide said, "That's what makes it interesting for them. They use bobsleds. It's almost certain death if they fall off or the bobsled rolls."

"I like a bit of excitement, but no way am I doing that," Chooli said.

"I would have to agree," Alex said.

They looked around for a while longer. The guide took them to the top to show them the view from there. She showed them several other things of interest on the way back to the capital and their hotel. They both thanked her for the interesting day.

A handwritten message sat on the coffee table in the living area of their suite when they got to their room. Alex picked it up and read it, surprised by the message.

"What is it?" Chooli asked.

He looked at her. "The prince has invited us to see him tomorrow at eleven."

26

Alex arranged for Xavier to pick Chooli and him up for the visit to the prince's palace. Chooli, who had rushed out after receiving the invitation to buy a new outfit, spent ages getting ready for the event, despite Alex telling her she should just treat it like any other day in the life of an agent. She was finally ready just before Xavier arrived.

"Maybe I should try getting a princely title," Alex said as he looked at her.

"You're always my prince."

Alex had nothing to say to that, so he waited for Xavier, who commed them five minutes later to say he was waiting in the hotel foyer. They went straight down.

Xavier looked at Chooli as they approached, taking in not only the new feminine outfit she wore, but the string of stunning emeralds around her neck. Seeing his look, her hand went to her neck and she said, "They're a gift from my grandma. I always carry them with me, but it's not often I get a chance to wear them."

"Wish all my officers dressed like that," he said, adding, "I mean, all the women."

Chooli blushed. "It's not every day that you get to meet a prince."

"True. I'm sure he'll appreciate it too. I've heard he enjoys elegance and beauty."

Alex looked at Xavier and then Chooli and back to Xavier. "Are you making a pass at her?"

Xavier laughed. "I'm a bit too old for her. Besides, I've got a perfectly good wife and family at home. Still, if I was twenty years younger, you might have some competition."

"Hello, I'm standing right here," Chooli said, feigning indignation but enjoying the attention.

"We'd better be off," Xavier said. They all left the hotel and got into Xavier's AGrav for the trip to the palace.

The Royal Palace of the Prince of Franconia was in the foothills just outside the capital and was half an hour's distance from the hotel. They sat back in the vehicle considering what might lie ahead.

"Any idea what the prince wants to see us about?" Alex asked Xavier.

"No idea. Royal invitations are rare. I'm fairly sure he's not angry with you. He would have gotten his royal guard to fetch you if that were the case."

"Oh my God, look at it," Chooli said in astonishment as the palace came into view. It stood in the grandeur of the baroque period, based on the design of the original Versailles Palace in France, coated in gold and shining in the morning sun, as if advertising that the occupant was the Sun King himself.

They arrived at the entrance to the estate moments later. Xavier had a word with the sentry. He got the invitation from Alex and gave it to the man, who scanned it and waited for clearance for them to enter, which came a few seconds later. The guard directed them to the entrance of the palace. When the AGrav stopped, they got out and all of them gaped at the magnificence of the entry vestibule. A guard stood at attention on either side of the doorway and a page waited for them. Alex noted that the page was Cetusian.

"Welcome," the page said, his eyes widening slightly as they rested on Chooli. "Come this way."

They followed the page through the vestibule and up a set of stairs, walking through a long corridor until they stood at a set of doors with another two guards either side of them. "Wait here," the page said. He entered and closed the door behind him, opening both doors thirty seconds later and gesturing for them to enter.

They walked into a large antechamber with a gilded desk and chairs directly in front of them. Large paintings with gilded frames of ancestors lined the walls. They all stood frozen in amazement at the spectacle. "Please," the page said, gesturing for Alex and Chooli to enter the set of doors to the side of the antechamber. He showed Xavier to a seat where he could wait for them.

Alex and Chooli moved forward, their footsteps echoing on the polished marble floor. The prince sat busy at his desk as they entered and another page showed them to seats at a small table by a set of French doors, which were open to allow the pleasant air to circulate through the room. They sat and waited.

The prince put down his stylus a minute later. He stood and walked over to them. "Sorry to take you away from your work," he said as he stood by the table.

They both stood, not knowing what to say. Alex finally said, "Not at all ... Your Highness ... The truth is, I wanted to come here, anyway."

"Forget about the highness rubbish. That's archaic. Call me Prince if you must, or just Léon," He looked at Chooli. "You look elegant, Agent Chooli."

Chooli blushed bright redder aureola green with a hint of gold. "Thank you."

"That is an exquisite necklace. Where did you get it, if I may ask?"

"It was my grandma's. She gave it to me before she died. Said it would look better on me than her."

"Well, if it looked anywhere near as elegant on her as it does on you, she must have been quite a woman."

"Thank you."

The prince looked around and then said, "Let's sit and chat." He gestured to a nearby servant for food and drinks.

"Your invitation surprised us when we got back to the hotel yesterday."

The prince laughed. "I'm sure that your detective Xavier noted the rarity of such an invitation."

Alex's brow rose in surprise.

"Yes, I know he's just outside."

"We weren't sure how to get here, so we asked Xavier to bring us. Hope that was all right."

"Certainly. This is a private audience, but I will make sure to say hello to him before you leave."

The servant came back with maids who carried trays of tea, coffee and various cakes and biscuits, together with cups, saucers, plates and utensils. They served the prince, Alex and Chooli, paying particular attention to Chooli as they were all Cetusian like her.

Alex saw the exchange between the maids and commented when they left. "The maids seemed intrigued by Chooli's presence."

Prince Léon chuckled. "I know there's a lot of tension within the realm between the human and Cetusian inhabitants. Totally unnecessary. We are all people. I wish the suppression of the Cetusians would cease. I'm trying to get the Senate to do something about it, but they seem to be taking an eternity to change their opinion on the topic. But I digress. There are few Cetusians who have an audience with the prince. I'll ask one later, but I suspect that they consider it an honor to them all."

"Can't you pass a law?" Chooli asked.

"Unfortunately, no. The Constitution doesn't allow the prince to make laws. It must be the Senate."

"Why are you prince, instead of king or maybe president?"

"Good question. Our system is modelled on French aristocracy — that's why we have dukes and duchesses among other things. When the present political structure came into effect, they wanted a head of state that fitted with that. King seemed too archaic and president too modern. So they settled on prince."

They sat in silence for a moment while they sipped some tea.

"And how is your investigation going?"

"Progressing well," Alex replied. "As with many investigations, I'm coming up against a few puzzling questions."

"Any you can tell me?"

Alex smiled. "I would have thought I would have to tell you anything that you commanded."

Léon laughed. "The prince is not above the law here, although some people of lower status sometimes think they are."

Alex thought before he said, "I don't think the duke and duchess were killed where the police found them."

"Really? What brings you to that conclusion?"

"Mainly lack of blood."

"I see. Where were they killed then?"

"I don't know."

"And that's why you were intending to come here."

Alex was surprised that the prince remembered his earlier comment. "Yes. This is the place where they were both last seen alive. I want to trace their movements from here to where the police found them, if I can."

"So you will need recordings of anything from here for the night of the Senate Opening Dinner then?"

"Yes."

"I will have my security team fully cooperate with you on that."

"Thank you."

"I want the incident fully investigated. We have a right to justice here. So, I take it you have doubts of the guilt of the accused?"

Alex looked at Chooli before answering. He wasn't sure what he should say.

"We suspect that the man may have been set up to be a scapegoat, but we are still keeping an open mind," Chooli said for him.

"I see." The prince sat back, thinking. He suddenly became stern and serious and looked directly at Chooli. "I suspect there are many reasons someone would have wanted them out of the way."

Chooli sat in shock as his eyes drilled into her.

"Has anyone threatened you?" the prince asked.

Alex and Chooli looked at each other. "Not yet," Alex said. "Why do you ask?"

"There is a sinister element to our society. If what you suspect is true, there is more afoot than a straightforward murder. Those responsible have many means of silencing those getting too close to the truth. Be wary of what you poke. It may reach out and try to bite you."

Alex felt shaken by the prince's warning and he saw Chooli was too. "We will keep our guard up."

The prince's mood changed as quickly as it had before. He became cordial again. "Have you seen any of our attractions?"

"We went to see The Slide yesterday," Chooli said.

"Ah yes. A very popular attraction. Did you try it?"

"Not on your life."

The prince laughed. "It is dangerous. I doubt I would do the ride either." He looked across to one of his servants and sighed. "Unfortunately, this is all I have time for. It has been a delight to talk to you both."

Alex and Chooli smiled. "The pleasure is ours, Your ... Léon." Alex said.

The prince held out his hand and shook Alex's. "If this is not too presumptuous," the prince said to Chooli before leaning forward in front of her and kissing her on the cheek. Alex saw several servants raise their brows in surprise. The prince stepped back and grabbed both Chooli's hands, "My, you look magnificent." Chooli went red again. He turned to Alex, "You are a lucky man."

His comment completely took Alex by surprise. "How did you know? We try to stay professional at work."

Laughing again, the prince said, "I can see it in your eyes. Genuine love. We cannot hide it."

It was Alex's turn to blush. "I see you are very observant."

Letting Chooli's hands go, the prince said. "I truly must get back to work but stay in the antechamber while I give the instructions for my security personnel to help you. I had better say hello to the inspector, though." He walked out with them and went over to Xavier, who instantly stood and half bowed in reverence for his prince. "Please, Inspector, at ease."

Xavier stood straight again and gulped, looking at Alex and Chooli. Alex thought Xavier couldn't decide whether to stand trembling or burst with pride at meeting the prince.

"I wish to thank you personally for escorting our two visitors here today."

"My pleasure, Your Highness."

"They have further business here with my security team. Please accompany them and keep them out of trouble," the prince said with a wicked smile and a wink at Chooli. She giggled.

The prince turned and left them.

"You seem to have hit it off well with him," Xavier said to Chooli.

27

Alex, Chooli and Xavier sat in the antechamber of the prince's office for another five minutes. One of the staff came in then and asked them to follow him. They went downstairs and to the basement level of the palace, eventually arriving at a large security office with a wall of screens on one wall of the room. Ten security officers sat in front of the screens, each of them assigned a bank to observe. Their guide went up to the supervisor and talked to him. They both came back to Alex and the others.

"I hear you're after some footage," the supervisor said.

"Yes," Alex replied. "We'd like to see the security footage of the Senate Opening Dinner. We are interested in following the movements of the Duke and Duchess of Lorraine."

The supervisor nodded. "Follow me. We'll let the others continue their work in peace." He led the way to a side office, also with several screens on one wall and a terminal. Sitting at the terminal, he typed in some data and the screens came to life. Typing some more brought holo-vision for the time of the dinner on the screens. Twelve views displayed at the same time. He took the time further back in history to the start of the dinner. "There you go. There's the couple arriving."

"Is that their vehicle?" Chooli asked.

The supervisor turned around and seemed to contemplate whether to deign to answer a Cetusian before changing his mind and answering respectfully, "I don't know. I presume that it is. The dukes usually have several limousines at their city residences."

Chooli nodded. "Where do the vehicles go while the dinner is on?"

"There's a secure parking lot." The supervisor turned around, typed on the terminal and a view of the parking area displayed as one view on the screen.

"And what do the drivers do?"

"There's a common waiting room they stay in next to the parking lot."

"Thank you."

The scenes on the displays played out, and they watched the duke and duchess mix with the others. At one stage, the duke met another, and they went outside.

"Who is he talking to?" Alex asked.

"That is Richelieu, Duke of Aquitaine."

"I take it you don't have audio?"

The supervisor chuckled. "No, we give them some privacy. A lip reader might work out what they say." He typed again and a view of the two on the balcony came up. They both went back inside ten minutes later, at which point they saw the Duke of Lorraine walk over to Yiska. The heated discussion was obvious and Yiska walked off in a huff, the duke returning to the dinner. They all went into the dining room after that and sat down.

"Speed it up a little," Alex requested.

After typing a command, the supervisor made the holo go faster. People ran around unnaturally as the clock on the displays raced though the time. The dinner ended and people started leaving.

"Real time," Alex said.

The supervisor slowed the holo down again and they watched as people prepared to depart. The time was just after 10:30pm. They saw the driver for the Lorraines get into his vehicle and drive off from the parking area, and the duke and duchess leave the hall area. When they arrived at the entry, where they had arrived that night, someone directed them to another side area. They seemed confused, and the duke had a brief discussion with the person who seemed to explain something apologetically. The duke and duchess finally walked off.

"Who is that person?" Alex asked.

The supervisor stopped the recording and zoomed in on the face. "That's strange," he said, creases marking his forehead. "I haven't seen him before."

Alex looked at Xavier with an inquiring expression.

Xavier sighed. "This is the first time I've seen this. I'll see if we can identify the person." He made a note.

Starting the recording again, the supervisor waited for another question or request. He typed instructions in the terminal and other views came onto the display, following the duke and duchess as they walked down a corridor. They walked through a door. When the supervisor brought the view of the other side onto the display, static confronted them, making the supervisor jump in his seat. He stopped the playback and retyped his instruction with no better result. "I'm terribly sorry," he said. "The camera appears to have gone down. That should not have happened. I'll check the maintenance log to find out what the problem was." He restarted the playback, speeding the replay up. Twenty minutes went by and the recording from the faulty camera came good again. There were no signs of the duke or duchess. The supervisor stopped the playback.

"What is that room?" Alex asked.

"It's a side entrance to the palace," the supervisor said. He typed in a command and a view of the outside came on one view. "This is outside the doorway." He rewound the recording, and that screen went static at the same time as the one inside.

Alex rubbed his chin. "We have a missing twenty minutes where anything could have happened."

"It would seem so," Xavier agreed.

"Can we re-watch the twenty minutes in real time?" Chooli asked.

"Why would you want to do that?" Xavier asked.

"Not sure. There might be something we can pick up."

Alex shrugged, "Sure."

The supervisor rewound the recording, and they started watching.

"Stop," Chooli said after watching five minutes of static. "Rewind a bit and slow it down."

The supervisor did as she asked, and the recording restarted at one-tenth speed. A flicker came across the screen and then disappeared.

"Stop," Chooli repeated. "Just rewind a bit and play frame by frame."

He rewound the recording and started again; the supervisor setting the replay frame by frame at a one-second delay between them. It started with static. Half a minute into the replay, a frame came up with half an image. The next frame had a full image, and the next returned to static. The supervisor stopped and reversed the replay frame by frame until the full image came up. It showed the duke and duchess lying on the ground and two people standing over them as though in conversation with each other. One of them was facing away from the camera, but the other was facing toward the camera. It was impossible to tell if the first one was male or female, but the other was definitely a man; his face wore a chilling smile and one of his hands held what appeared to be the knife used to cut the victims' throats.

"Well, I'll be," Xavier said, exhaling a breathe. "Did you see that before?" He looked at Chooli.

"I just thought I saw a flicker," Chooli said, slightly embarrassed.

"It would seem we have the site of the murder," Alex said. "Can we have a look there?"

"Certainly," the supervisor said.

Alex looked at Xavier. "We need to identify that man."

"Already noted."

Alex turned back to the supervisor. "We will need two copies of those recordings."

"All of them?"

"All of them."

"I'll have them made and sent to you."

"Let's go see this room."

The supervisor rose and escorted the others through to the side entrance of the palace they had just viewed. "This is it."

Alex had a meticulous look over the entire room and outside the exit door but found nothing of interest. "We'll get a forensics team here and see if we can find anything, although I doubt that we will after all this time. It seems the murderers did an expert job cleaning up after themselves."

28

Having exhausted everything they could do at the palace, Alex, Chooli and Xavier got back into their AGrav and left, arriving back at police headquarters half an hour later. Xavier led Alex and Chooli into the traffic-monitoring center.

Alex frowned. "What are we doing here?"

"I thought we could track the vehicle the duke was in as it exited the palace grounds. See where it goes."

"Oh. Good idea." *Why didn't I think of that?*

Xavier talked to the officer on duty, who went to work searching back through the records they had of traffic cams and satellite feeds for the night of the murder. Alex and Chooli stood behind the man, watching on with interest. A satellite image of the palace came on the screen in front of them and the man zoomed in to the palace gates as the feed played out in real time at the time the murders had taken place. A vehicle emerged a few minutes later. Freezing the image, the man looked around. "Is that the vehicle in question?"

"Can you zoom in anymore?" Xavier asked.

The man tried magnifying the image but became frustrated by the pixilation when he zoomed in much further. He typed away at his terminal and brought up a different feed for the same time. It showed the vehicle from a fresh angle and could magnify the image further.

Xavier looked closely at the vehicle. "Yes, that's it. The Lorraine insignia is on the door."

"Good, we can track it now." The man tagged the vehicle and zoomed out. He let the feed play again.

After ten minutes, the vehicle made a right-hand turn and headed in a different direction. "That's not the direction to the Lorraine city residence," Xavier said.

Alex could feel excitement mount up in him. "Let's see where it goes then. Is it toward where you found the bodies?"

"No. That is in the other direction too."

The vehicle traced its way across the city for another twenty minutes and then disappeared.

"What happened?" Alex asked, startled by the sudden loss of the tag.

The man rewound the feed until the vehicle came back again, stopped play and zoomed in. Warehouses came into view. He started the feed again, and they watched the vehicle turn and enter a warehouse. The tag disappeared when it went inside.

"We need to go look at that warehouse," Alex said.

"Let's see if it comes out again," Xavier said. "Can you increase the speed two times the normal speed?" The man increased the playback speed. Another vehicle came out of the warehouse ten minutes later. They watched the vehicle as it traveled across the city. "It's going to the spot where we found the bodies."

"Can you identify that vehicle?" Alex asked.

"I'll try," the man said. "It might not be possible since it's night time."

"Do your best — and see if the other vehicle comes out. Let's go have a look at that warehouse." Alex started toward the door. Xavier and Chooli followed, and they all headed to the garage and their AGrav.

Xavier slowed the vehicle as they approached the warehouse, housed in a large industrial area. The one of interest was on the edge and in an older and more dilapidated part of it. Some slum shanties stood nearby. Driving up to the front of the warehouse, Xavier stopped, and they all disembarked. The frontage stood right on the roadway where vehicles descended to enter it from the traffic lanes above. There were no windows to look into. The door held firmly when Alex tried opening it, locked with a keypad combination lock on the wall next to it. He reached into his pocket to retrieve the small box he usually carried with him for just such emergencies. It wasn't there.

"Any ideas on how to get in?" Alex asked, trying not to look sheepish.

"We should really get a warrant," Xavier said.

"That would take too long and, besides, we have cause to see what's inside."

"I could try picking the lock," Chooli offered.

The others both arched their eyebrows. "That's a side of you I didn't know about," Alex said.

"I learned it so you can't keep any secrets."

Alex wasn't sure whether she was joking. "Go ahead. Can't hurt to try."

Chooli retrieved a gadget from her bag and went to the lock mechanism. She worked away at it for several minutes before they all heard the clunk of the door unlocking. She tried the handle, and the door slid to the side with minor effort. They all entered. The warehouse extended back two-hundred meters and was seventy-five meters wide and twenty meters tall. The Duke of Lorraine's vehicle sat to one side.

"Your guy doesn't have to worry about finding this one," Alex said to Xavier.

Xavier huffed and walked to the vehicle, his footsteps echoing through the almost empty building. Careful not to leave fingerprints or DNA to contaminate the area, he opened the door of the AGrav. A stench instantly surrounded them all. Chooli gagged and Alex and Xavier covered their noses.

Alex looked inside. "The driver, I presume." A body lay on the floor of the vehicle in an advanced stage of decomposition. It looked male and had a chauffeur's uniform on. "Didn't anyone report him missing?"

"We could never find him. We listed him under missing persons," Xavier said.

"I don't understand. How did all this get missed the first time?"

Pulling back and straightening, Xavier replied defensively, "We were under immense pressure and it looked like an open and shut case. There didn't seem to be any loose ends. Besides, we were told to stop any further investigation once we had our case against Yiska watertight."

"By whom?"

"Who do you think? Commissioner Gros of course."

Alex shook his head. He couldn't believe they would just leave it like that. In the brief time he had known him, he had felt respect for Xavier, but he felt a sense of disappointment in him now. He changed his concentration to what was inside the vehicle. Blood covered the seats and a clutch purse lay on the floor with the Lorraine coat of arms on it. Alex presumed it belonged to the duchess.

Chooli started wandering around the warehouse, looking for other clues. "Hello," she said.

Alex pulled his head from the vehicle and looked at her. "Who are you saying hello to?"

Chooli pointed. The top of the heads of two children were just visible looking into the warehouse through the door. She started walking toward them, but their heads disappeared. "You don't have to be frightened," Chooli called after them, trying to sound soothing to make them feel comfortable with her. The heads returned. More of them were visible than before, and it was obvious they were Cetusian children. "Come in. We won't hurt you." She reached the door and stood just inside the building. Both children slowly walked a little toward her, keeping a watchful eye on Alex and Xavier. They were boys about eight and ten years old and had scruffy clothing covered in dirt, as were their faces. Alex, becoming interested in the children, started walking over to them too. They started retreating. Chooli looked around at Alex and then back to the children. "Don't mind him. He won't hurt you. I'll tell him off if he does."

Both boys' eyes opened wide. "Aren't you afraid of him?" the older one said.

Chooli smiled. "He's my boss, but I'm a police officer too."

"You're a police officer? But you're Cetusian."

"They have a lot of Cetusian police officers where I come from."

"Really? Where do you come from?"

"A planet called Caerus in the Tau Ceti system. Do you know of it?"

The boys looked at each other and back at her, shaking their heads.

Alex stood next to Chooli and looked at both of them. "What are you doing around here? Do you live in the houses we saw at the edge of this estate?"

The boys held their heads down and nodded.

"You can look at him," Chooli said.

They both shook their heads. "Not allowed," the older one said.

"Well, you can look at me then, can't you?"

They slowly raised their heads and looked at her. She smiled and looked at Alex. He smiled in return. "Do you explore around here a lot?" she asked as she bent over slightly to lower her head to their level.

"Sometimes," the older one said. He seemed to be the spokesman for the two of them.

"What about during the night?"

"We're not allowed out at night."

"But do you sneak out sometimes?"

"Sometimes." Both the boys had sheepish grins.

"It's all right. I won't tell anyone. Do you see anyone coming into this warehouse?"

"Not for a long time," the older boy said, feeling more comfortable. "There were some people here a long time ago." The boy looked at the vehicle. "It was dark, but they drove that vehicle in here," he said, pointing a grubby finger at the AGrav.

Xavier had walked over to them in the meantime and stood listening to the conversation.

"Did you get a look at any of the people?" Chooli asked.

The boys shook their heads. "It was too dark."

"How many were there?"

The boys looked at each other. The younger one put up two fingers. The older one nodded. "Two, we think."

"Did you see anything else?"

"They drove off in a different AGrav about half an hour later."

"You have been very helpful. Thank you."

Both boys puffed their chests out and smiled.

Chooli stood straight again. She looked at Xavier and frowned. "What do you teach these children?"

Xavier sighed. "It's part of our society, I'm afraid."

Alex looked back at the vehicle. "See anything else useful?"

"No," Xavier replied. "I'll get a forensics team down here straight-away. They might find something. But if this is a professional hit, my guess is they wiped everything clean."

"You're probably right. Let's get back. I've got some thinking to do," Alex said.

The boys left, and they took a last look around before closing the door and going back to the office.

29

Richelieu followed the page through the corridors of the prince's palace to his study, a route he had walked many times before. Prince Léon's call sounded urgent, which surprised him. Urgent business with the prince was rare. The page left Richelieu in the study antechamber and left, leaving Richelieu waiting patiently for the prince's attention. He didn't have to wait long. The prince walked through the door from the study. Richelieu noticed black-rimmed eyes, as if he needed sleep badly.

"Please come in, Richelieu."

"At your pleasure, Prince," Richelieu replied, gesturing for the prince to lead him in.

The prince pointed to the table and chairs next to the window. "Drink?"

"I would appreciate a nice cognac."

Léon nodded to the butler standing nearby and sat. Richelieu obliged and sat too.

"I appreciate your coming to the capital at such short notice to see me," Léon began.

Richelieu gave a small smile. "One does not refuse the prince."

"I suppose not. Still, I wanted to see you and felt time was of the essence."

The butler came and placed two snifters of cognac on the table in front of them. They both raised their glasses. "Cheers ... Now I wanted to talk to you again about this problem with Champagne ..." Léon raised his hand when Richelieu started protesting. "I know your feelings on the subject, but please, hear me out." He looked at Richelieu with steely eyes, and Richelieu waited patiently for him to continue. "We both know that, constitutionally, Champagne is standing on shaky ground with their claim that a democratic governing body is acceptable. I find it unpalatable myself and accept that morally you have the best claim to the duchy. But do we really need a war? Consider the economic impact a war will have on the planet."

"Your Highness, I want a war as little as you do, but what choice do I have? You saw the obstinate stance Pierre took. He won't budge."

"Don't you think you drove him into a corner? You gave him no room for negotiation."

Richelieu frowned, feeling frustrated. "What do you suggest? I will not tolerate a duchy without a duke running it, and I am entitled to that position. There really is nothing to discuss from where I sit."

Léon looked forlorn. Richelieu could appreciate the awkward position the prince was in, but he wouldn't give up the duchy without a sound reason.

"Could you come to some kind of arrangement where you are duke by name and let them run their own affairs maybe, give them basic autonomy and only provide general guidance in their affairs?" Léon suggested.

"You saw Pierre. They want complete autonomy. They don't want people looking over their shoulders, making sure they're doing the right thing. Even if I were open to the idea, they just wouldn't accept it. I think you are clutching at straws. I know this will dent the economy and the reputation of our great planet, but we must take a stand on this. Otherwise, we'll have others going down that path.

Lorraine, maybe, given the age of the young duke there. You know this is the right thing to do."

Léon gritted his jaw and stood. He strode over to the window and looked out to the gardens below. Richelieu watched him carefully, waiting for him to reveal his mood. Léon turned his head. "You disappoint me, Richelieu. I always felt you to be a reasonable man, but this uncompromising insistence on war makes me wonder if there are other reasons you want this war to happen. Reasons hidden from my eyes?"

Richelieu felt righteous indignation. He stood and declared, "I do not deserve this accusation. I'm a reasonable man. I tried to negotiate a resolution acceptable to us both, but they will not budge. What will you have me do? Roll over and let them laugh at me?"

Léon sighed. "Of course not. I'm just trying to get you to reconsider. I knew it was hopeless, but I had to try, anyway. The other duchies are grumbling to me, no end."

"Let them grumble. They would do exactly the same if they were in my shoes. If they want to complain why don't they complain to me?"

Walking back to the table, Léon took another sip of cognac. "Well, good of you to come."

Richelieu also sipped, allowing the liquid to calm his temper. "I appreciate your efforts, Prince, in trying to find an amicable solution. There just isn't one until Pierre and his cronies come to their senses."

"There is a sizeable population of Cetusians in Champagne. Some say they are the reason for this drive for democracy."

"I doubt that. They are a timid people. I find them very tame."

Léon finished the rest of his drink, and Richelieu did the same.

"Again, I appreciate your coming all this way. Hope you have a pleasant flight back. Unfortunately, I have other things to do or I would ask you to stay for dinner."

"My pleasure. I too have things to attend to."

A page escorted Richelieu from the room and he flew back to Aquitaine deep in thought. Richelieu wondered if the prince had a point about the Cetusians. They made up a considerable proportion of the Champagne population. They would make a lot of expendable soldiers, if nothing else.

30

Arriving back at the estate, Richelieu went straight to the dining room for dinner ... and, unfortunately, his waiting mother. The dining table stood ready for the meal with places set for Camille and himself at opposite ends of the table.

Camille sat in a lounge chair by the open French doors, a glass of sherry in her hand. A warm evening breeze wafted into the room bringing the scent of roses with it. She almost looked content from where Richelieu entered.

Camille looked up when Richelieu walked in, eyes intent on her son as he took the few weary steps over to her and placed the obligatory peck on her cheek. "What did the prince want?" she asked as she sipped her sherry.

"He wanted to talk me out of this war."

"That's not possible, is it?" Camille asked a bit too hastily, Richelieu thought. He stared at her for a moment, wondering what had brought about the rapid response.

"No, this war will happen regardless. He made an excellent point, though. He mentioned the large number of Cetusians in Champagne."

Camille frowned. "Why would he mention that? They're insignificant. They don't have a brain cell between the lot of them."

"Mother. They are the same as us, and you know that. Stop debasing them all the time."

"I'm not. I'm just pointing out the truth. They make excellent servants despite my bickering over them, but I doubt you need worry too much about them fighting our troops. We would make quick work of them. Wouldn't we?"

"Yes, Champagne doesn't have much of a military, from what my sources tell me. That's what's so disturbing. They know I out-gun them, but they want to go down this path anyway."

Richelieu saw his mother look at him as she thought over the new piece of information. "Always look for what's up their sleeves, Richelieu. You don't want any surprises with this."

"What do you mean?"

"Are they hiding something you don't know about? Have they been secretly training a reserve?"

"Not from what our spies tell us. What are you driving at?"

"My brother must have mentioned that for a reason. How could they use a large population of Cetusians to their advantage? Just think about it. Now, let's have dinner."

"Yes, Mother."

31

C amille sat at the breakfast table, content with eating toasted bread and honey and sipping her strong, black coffee. She smiled as she thought about her conversation with Richelieu the night before. The drive in her son pleased her. It was nothing like the procrastinating demeanor of his father. She wondered again what she had seen in such a man, other than a means to stay at the top of the social hierarchy of society. Maybe that was all there was. That and producing a son worthy of her at last. She could parade her influence even further when he took over Champagne. How she would enjoy the envy of the other duchesses and their kin. She would rise to her rightful status in Franconia, one she deserved as sister to the prince. It wasn't right that male heirs alone could fill the pinnacle of political positions, she thought bitterly. As the prince's elder sister, she would have been the reigning Princess of Franconia.

Her comm rang, bringing her out of her reverie. She frowned. Unusual for Sophia, the Duchess of Picardie, to call. "My darling Sophia, to what do I owe the pleasure?"

"Camille, hope I'm not disturbing you. I just heard the most amazing piece of gossip and I had to tell you. I'm sure you'll be interested in it."

"Well, what is it then?"

"You know some detectives from the GIA are investigating the Lorraine murders again?"

"Yes, yes, I know all about that," she replied impatiently.

"But did you know that they don't think the Cetusian did it?"

Camille frowned again. "No, I didn't. Why would they think that? Wasn't the evidence against him watertight?"

"Just telling you what I heard."

"Oh, they must be saying that to justify their existence. They have to make out they're doing something better than our own police can do, otherwise people would start wondering why we have them here."

"They seem to be asking a lot of questions. They even talked to Prince Léon, I heard. He doesn't give just anyone an audience."

The news disturbed Camille. They shouldn't be poking around where they're not wanted. "They must think they own the place. You know how obnoxious some of these off-worlders can be."

"Yes, I know. Well, I must be off. I have things to do. I'm sure you have too."

The comm went dead. Camille glared at it. Silly busybody, hanging up like she did, as if she's more important than anyone else. Still, she had told Camille some useful information. She frowned, wondering why Sophia had especially wanted to tell her that. Why her, as if it affected her in some way? They weren't particularly close. Camille drew great pleasure in making fun of her and embarrassing her sometimes. What was she up to? What did she want in return for sharing it? It all seemed a bit of a puzzle to Camille. She shrugged her shoulders and finished her toast and coffee, humming to herself as she rolled the conversation over in her head.

A maid came over, asking her if she needed something else. She scowled and told her to come back when she was finished. She suddenly remembered the conversation with Richelieu and the ever-increasing population of Cetusians in Champagne. Maybe they were the troublemakers. Their potential influence on the outcome of the war worried her, not that Richelieu was in any doubt of winning it, but they might prolong it, escalating the expense far beyond what it needed to be. Surely, Richelieu could think of something to minimize the costs. She wouldn't want him telling her to curtail her expenses. He was a smart son. He would think of something.

32

Alex lay in bed thinking about what he now knew of the mysterious murders of the Duke and Duchess of Lorraine. Chooli snuggled up next to him, sharing her body warmth as she slept. He had woken early and couldn't get back to sleep but didn't want to remove himself from Chooli's side. The night still lingered outside, with just the orange glow of one of the four moons orbiting Franconia providing any light to see by.

The murders had taken place at Prince Léon's palace, and they had the facial image of one killer. Alex felt sure that the face wouldn't turn up in any database on the hive. The murders had been a professional hit, and the assassins would have covered their identities. He wasn't sure what direction the investigation should go if they couldn't get any lead on the identity of the killers. The duke had had one other major discussion at the dinner. He had talked at length with the Duke of Aquitaine. They were also at odds with the absorption of the Duchy of Champagne. Alex felt he should talk with Richelieu to get a complete picture of events prior to the murders. The takeover of a complete duchy would be a huge motive for removing any other contenders, although Lorraine still had the boy and it sounded like the Duchy of Champagne would put up a fight to prevent itself from being taken over by anyone. Or were they fighting already? In the gloom of the early morning, Alex couldn't remember exactly what Xavier had said. He saw the first signs of dawn as he continued to lie in bed thinking. He would visit the Duke of Aquitaine.

Feeling better for having made a decision, he tried to get some sleep. Chooli moved and snuggled closer. Barely had he shut his eyes when a slight noise came from the living area of the hotel apartment drove all sleep away. He shook Chooli awake and instantly jumped from the bed, grabbing the maser pistol he kept within reach at night. After a moment of confusion, Chooli was straight behind him, shocked but alert. She ran to the dresser by the far wall and pulled her pistol from her bag. "What is it?" she whispered.

Alex lifted his forefinger to his lips as he stepped slowly to the bedroom door, making sure he wasn't directly in front of it. He motioned Chooli in the dim light to go to the other side of the bed. Moments later, the door disappeared, the shrapnel residue exploding into the room and the noise deafening Alex and Chooli. Two assailants rushed into the room and shot at the bed before realizing it was empty. Alex shot one and Chooli the other before either of them could turn to look for their intended targets. Both were dead before they hit the floor.

Rolling into the other room, Alex squatted and scanned it for any others, but the room was empty. He stood and took a deep breath as the adrenaline slowly drained from his system. Thinking how ridiculous he would look in his nakedness, he nonetheless put the light on. The entry door to the apartment was closed, but the balcony door stood open. The two must have come in through it. He walked over and closed it again before going back to the bedroom. Chooli still stood where she had been, pistol held in front of her and eyes wide, looking at the dead people on the floor.

"You OK?" Alex asked.

"That's the first time I've ever killed someone," she said as she started shaking.

Having seen this reaction before in young recruits, Alex quickly moved over to her. He removed the gun from her hands and put his arms around her. "It's OK." Alex stroked her hair as he held her close. "It's OK," he whispered again, as he looked over at the destroyed bed and then the two dead bodies. *Who the hell are they?*

Chooli slowly recovered and pulled away. She looked up at him. "We'd better put some clothes on."

Alex laughed. "Yeah, we'd better."

They got dressed and Alex called reception to tell them of the invasion. He then called Xavier, who said he'd get police over to him straightaway. Police arrived half an hour later, followed by Xavier fifteen minutes after that. Dawn had come and gone, and the rays of the sun shone into the living room where Alex and Chooli sat.

Xavier looked at both of them with a grim face. "That was a close call."

"Yeah, it was. Lucky I was awake and heard them open the balcony door."

"First one?" Xavier asked Chooli, who sat staring at the bedroom door before looking up at him.

She nodded.

"Make sure you don't lose that feeling. I've seen too many taking a liking to the killing and get overly trigger-happy."

Alex initially thought Xavier was giving her unusual advice, but he realized how true it was. His first killing was buried somewhere in the distant past in his mind, and the extinguishing of a life seemed to have numbed his senses through practice over the years. He wanted to believe that he held every life precious, despite what the person had done. He looked at Xavier. "Someone wants us to stop poking our noses where they don't belong."

"Yeah, that's pretty clear."

"Any idea who they are?"

Xavier shook his head. "Their faces match nothing in our databases. I'll get forensics to do a DNA search."

"They were professionals too." Alex looked at Chooli and clenched his jaw. "I'll find these bastards." He looked back to Xavier, "And whoever is pulling the strings. I'll get their descriptions back to the GIA on Earth. See if they turn up in any confederation databases."

"We'd better find you two another place to stay."

"You can't lock us away in a safe house. We've got a job to do."

"No, but I can make sure you get a good night's sleep without worrying about unwanted visitors."

Alex nodded. "Well, we can't sleep in that bed." He pointed in the direction of the bed in the other room. The maser-powered weapons the assailants used had destroyed it. "Anyway, I want to visit Richelieu."

Xavier looked at Alex as if he were mad. "You can't just knock on the duke's door and ask to see him."

"Why not? I'm sick of treading softly. If people want some action, I'm ready to give them some. Let's go ruffle a few feathers."

Xavier groaned. "I'll arrange a long-range AGrav then." He walked out of the room.

Alex and Chooli packed their bags and moved to another room while Xavier organized the AGrav and somewhere else for them to stay. Xavier came back two hours later with a suitable means of transport. They all got in and Xavier set course for Richelieu's estate in Aquitaine.

33

They reached the front entrance of the estate at midday.

"I sent a message through that we're coming. Not sure how well they'll receive it," Xavier said.

"I don't really care how they receive it," Alex said as they emerged from the AGrav. Alex walked to the sentry building with the others and entered. Several men sat there in military uniform. "Chief Inspector Detective Alex Warner from the GIA, I want to talk to your boss."

"I'll get the supervisor," one man said.

"No, not him, the big boss, Richelieu."

The men looked at each other.

"He knows we're coming."

The man who had spoken got up and went to another office in the building, and another man came back with him a few moments later. He looked at Alex, sneered at Chooli, and looked back to Alex. "I hear you want to make an appointment to talk to the duke."

Alex shook his head. "No, I don't want to make an appointment. I want to see him ... Now." He stared back at the man.

"He's rather busy."

"I don't care. We will charge him with obstructing a Confederation investigation if he refuses to see me."

Several men gasped when Alex made his threat, and the man in front of him gave up any pretense of authority or of holding the upper hand in the encounter with Alex. "Wait here." The man went back into the office he came from. They could hear him talking to someone, but it was too soft and muffled to hear what he said. He came back out five minutes later. "You may proceed to the estate chateau. Someone will meet you at the entrance to escort you to the duke."

"Thank you for your cooperation," Alex said with a fake smile. He turned around and saw Chooli trying desperately to contain a grin while Xavier looked deathly white. They all exited the building and got back into the AGrav. The force-field at the entrance lowered, and they flew into the chateau entry area. A man in military uniform met them and led them to a room.

"What's with the uniforms?" Chooli asked.

"They're fighting Champagne for control of the ducky," Xavier said.

"So, the war's started already?"

Xavier nodded.

They waited in a study. It had bay windows that looked out onto the lawns and gardens of the estate. Cetusian gardeners busily worked the plots, bent over in their toil. A portrait of a woman hung from one wall. She stood in a proud and regal stance. A royal dress and regalia bedecked her, and a tiara sat on her head. She looked twenty or maybe thirty to Alex as he stood in front of the painting. He turned to Xavier. "Who's she?"

Xavier shrugged. "Don't know."

They waited fifteen minutes before a man strutted into the room, dressed in military uniform, and of obvious high rank, judging by the number of stars planted on his shoulders. He looked at the people in front of him, eying Alex and Xavier up and down and stopping with a look of fascination when he saw Chooli. He came out of the spell. "What is it you want? I'm in the middle of a war, you know."

Alex stepped toward him. "You are Duke Richelieu of Aquitaine?"

"Who are you?"

"I'm Chief Inspector Detective Alex Warner and this is Agent Chooli from the GIA," Alex said as he gestured to Chooli. He pointed to Xavier. "This is Chief Inspector Xavier Fay from your central police department. We're investigating the murders of the Duke and Duchess of Lorraine."

"So you're the one making a nuisance of himself."

"Just doing my job, Duke."

"Well, I don't know what all the fuss is about. It's obvious the man's guilty."

"That's just the point. It's not obvious to us. In fact, it looks just the opposite."

Richelieu looked surprised. "I was told it was an open and shut case."

"Fresh information has surfaced. That is why we are here. We understand that you had a discussion with the duke at the Senate Opening Dinner at the beginning of the year."

"Yes I did," Richelieu said warily. "But there is nothing suspicious in that. We often talk about things, as do all the dukes, especially on such occasions."

"And what did you talk about?"

Richelieu frowned in concentration. "He was preparing to put forward a bill in the Senate that would provide equal rights to the Cetusians." He looked at Chooli. "He wanted to know what support I would give it. I had told him in the past that I might be amenable to granting improved rights to Cetusians."

"And were you going to support him?"

"I said I wanted to think about it further. I wanted to see the last draft of the bill he would be proposing."

"That was all?"

"Yes."

"Nothing about threats to gain control of Champagne?"

Richelieu stiffened. "What do you take me for? First, we would exchange any such threats at the negotiation table, not the Senate

Opening Dinner. Second, there is an honor amongst dukes. We would never threaten another duke's life."

Alex eyed him closely, but it seemed he was telling the truth.

The door opened, and an elderly woman walked in. She bore a remarkable resemblance to the woman in the painting. "What's all this commotion about?" She looked at Chooli, who stood looking back at her. The woman reddened with anger. "Lower your head," she demanded. "How dare you look directly at me?"

Chooli's jaw clenched, and she flared in anger, but she stood her ground and continued looking, making sure the woman felt her direct eye contact. The woman started strutting over to her, waving her hand in readiness to slap her.

Richelieu looked on in horror. "Mother, stop that." He hurried to stop her attack. "She is a GIA agent." His mother faltered in her attack. Richelieu looked at Alex, blushing with embarrassment. "Please forgive her." He looked at Chooli. "She is an old woman, fixed in her old ways."

Camille, looked at Chooli, still fuming with rage but restrained, and then at Alex and Richelieu. "I'm not fixed in my ways and I'm not old. You should be in the war room, not chatting to these *agents*."

Alex looked on at the exchange, his emotions fluctuating between amusement and rage. "Would you like to come back to Nouveau Paris," he asked Camille, "and *chat* to us at police headquarters?"

She glared at him. "I will do no such thing. Do you know who you are talking to?"

"I assume a more mature version of the beautiful young woman in that painting."

Camille, ready with a retort, suddenly became silent and then bashful. "Well, it's so thoughtful of you to have noticed."

"I notice many things. So, whom am I talking to?"

She huffed, but answered proudly. "Dame Camille of Aquitaine. I'm of royal blood, you know. I am the elder sister of Prince Léon."

"No, I didn't know. We are just here to ask your son a few questions about the night someone murdered the Duke and Duchess of Lorraine."

Camille's eyes narrowed. "What does it have to do with him?"

"Nothing I hope. We just needed to understand what exactly preceded the murders. While I'm here, I may as well ask where you were."

"I was in the city manor all night, obviously," she said, looking distinctly affronted that Alex should have the nerve to ask such a question of her.

"So you didn't accompany your son to the dinner?"

"I'm 'too old' for such frivolous things," she said, glaring at Richelieu.

Alex thought for a moment and then asked Richelieu, "But you took someone with you to the dinner?".

"Yes, a young woman." Richelieu blushed slightly. "I am a bachelor, you see."

"Not for lack of effort from me," Camille butted in. Alex only just managed to suppress a smirk.

Richelieu glared at his mother. "I had recently met Mademoiselle Felicity Martin and had her accompany me to the dinner." He paused for a moment and then added, "We are still seeing each other."

"And when did she leave you that night?"

Richelieu reddened more but stood straight to give an impression of dignity. "She stayed at the manor all night."

"How do you know that?"

"She was with me." He looked at his mother and back to Alex.

"Oh." Alex thought for a moment more. "Well, that is all the questions I have. Do my colleagues have any?" He looked at Xavier, who shook his head, and then at Chooli.

"Does this war have anything to do with the Lorraine Duchy?" Chooli asked.

Richelieu looked at Camille to make sure she wasn't about to fly into a rage over him being asked a question by a Cetusian. She gritted her teeth but said nothing. "No," he said. "The Duchy of Champagne is just being obstinate in not accepting rule by a duke. They seem to think they can rule themselves as a democracy."

Camille huffed. "It shouldn't last long."

"But initially, I understand, you were in dispute with the Duke of Lorraine over who had the right to take control of the duchy?" Chooli continued, ignoring Camille's interjection.

"We were in discussions, yes, and yes they had hit a stalemate. But we have negotiated a suitable arrangement between us now."

"Which would have been easier with the Lorraines out of the way?"

Richelieu bristled but remained civil. "Yes, it was easier. I always had a better claim to the duchy than they did, though, through lineage. I believe Javier was just maneuvering to gain some compensation for his approval."

"I see. Thank you." Chooli looked back at Alex.

"We'll let you get back to your war then," Alex said, as he glanced at Camille before looking to Richelieu and smiling. "Thank you for your time."

Richelieu smiled in return. "You're welcome. I hope that you can complete your investigation quickly."

Alex nodded and walked out, followed by Chooli and Xavier. They went back to the AGrav and departed the estate.

"You're a bit of a smooth talker," Chooli said, grinning at Alex.

"Me? I had to say something to calm people down. You were ready to clobber her. Appealing to a woman's vanity usually does the trick."

"Appealing to a woman's vanity?" Chooli looked affronted and crossed her arms.

"Most women," Alex corrected. "It wouldn't have worked on you."

Xavier let out a hearty laugh while Chooli huffed and hit Alex on the shoulder. "You sure you two are partnered?"

"Yes, we're sure," Alex said, smiling. "We like our minor differences. Keeps us on our toes."

"Keeps him on his toes anyway," Chooli retorted, folding her arms again but smiling too.

Xavier laughed again, shaking his head.

They had just passed over the coastline of Ile-de-France, the city of Nouveau Paris in their sights, when an explosion shook their

AGrav. Chooli grabbed Alex. "What's that?" Alex asked, looking to see what had happened.

"Prepare for crash," an automated voice from the AGrav said. "Sit in position for enwrapment. Prepare for impact."

"Sit back in your seats," Xavier advised, a hint of panic in his voice.

They all sat back and cushioning bags surrounded them, preventing movement but allowing space for breathing with ease. Chooli looked wide-eyed at Alex. He felt equally nervous. Their forearms were free, so he reached over and grabbed her hand. The AGrav kept repeating the announcement. Looking out the window, Alex saw the ground speeding toward them and felt the impact moments later. The severity of the crash demolished the AGrav and threw them all in the air, Alex landing on the ground hard and passing out.

He woke semi-conscious and heard people talking.

"What should we do with them?" a male voice asked.

"Leave them. She only wants the girl. Let's get going before they wake up or someone comes."

"But she's only Cetusian."

"That's what she said. Do you want to question her orders?"

"No."

Alex lost consciousness again.

34

Alex woke up in a hospital. A medical wrap encircled his arm and several tubes connected him to machines next to his bed. He heard the usual beeps one hears in a hospital. *What on earth happened?* He remembered an explosion and then they crashed. *What happened after that?* He lay in the bed with his eyes closed trying to think, but his arm hurt where the wrap was and he couldn't remember.

Bit by bit his memory started to returned. He seemed to recall hearing voices but could not recall what they said.

No one came into the room, so he just lay in the bed trying to get his memory back.

His eyes suddenly flew open, and he sat up despite the pain. *Chooli! They took Chooli.* Holding his head with both hands, he recalled the words he had heard: "She only wants the girl." *That was it. That was what they had said.* He frantically looked around as his pulse and blood pressure skyrocketed, setting off alarms.

A nurse came rushing in. "Mr. Warner, please relax and lie down." She reached over to persuade him to lie down again.

Alex avoided her advance and swung around to get up. "Where

are my clothes? Did a woman, a Cetusian, come in with me?" He held onto the nurse's arm, a pleading desperation in his eyes.

The woman unsuccessfully tried shrugging off his hand. "There was only you and the other detective. There was no woman. They wouldn't have admitted a Cetusian to this hospital, anyway. You need to rest Mr. Warner."

"I need to get up. I need my clothes." Alex started pulling the tubes from his arms with the nurse trying to stop him. She pressed a button on her wrist and moments later a doctor came in.

"What seems to be the trouble?" the doctor asked.

"He wants to get up."

"I need to find Chooli."

"Chooli? Who's Chooli?"

"The Cetusian detective with me."

The doctor looked at the nurse.

"There was only the other male detective that I'm aware of," the nurse said.

"Mr. Warner," the doctor said to Alex, "let me go check, if you promise to stay in that bed and rest while I do it. I'll contact the paramedics who attended the crash site and see who they treated. Is that fair?"

Alex calmed down slightly. He nodded. "Yeah, OK. But don't be too long, and I don't want all those tubes in me. I'm fine."

The doctor eyed him. "Well, you've got a broken wrist and concussion, but, apart from some scratches and bruises, there's nothing else wrong with you. I'll be as quick as I can." He disappeared out the door.

The nurse eyed Alex suspiciously, but Alex turned again and lay down, waiting. The doctor was true to his word and came back ten minutes later. Alex sat up again. He had a frown as he looked at Alex. "The paramedics say there was just you and Detective Xavier Fay. They said there was another seat capsule, but it was empty. There definitely wasn't a Cetusian woman there. The attending police may have found something."

"I need to find out what happened," Alex said, a pleading look in his eyes.

"She means something to you?"

"We are partnered. Please. I need to find her."

Seeing the torment in Alex's eyes, the doctor said, "Okay, I'll release you, but you have to take it easy. You're still recovering from concussion."

Alex nodded. "Where is Xavier?"

"He's unconscious in the next room. He wasn't as lucky as you, but he will recover," the doctor replied. "Give him his clothes," he said to the nurse.

"Thank you," Alex said.

The doctor left, and the nurse went to the wardrobe and fetched his clothes. "Your belongings are in the drawer," she said, pointing to the small cabinet by the side of the bed.

"My maser pistol?"

Her eyes widened, "We don't have that. Maybe the police took it." She left the room, closing the door behind her.

Alex gingerly got out of the bed and dressed. It felt like he had broken every bone in his body, but he took the doctor's word for it that only his left wrist had a problem. Packing the things from the drawer, he left the room and went next door.

Xavier lay inert in the bed with medical wraps on many parts of his body.

"I'll find out who did this," Alex whispered to him. He was certain it had been an ambush, but he did not understand why. Deep down, he knew it involved the investigation.

Walking to the nurses' station with a slight limp, he asked for the paperwork to sign out.

The doctor came out of an office and gave him a container. "Some painkillers for you to help you sleep."

"Thanks." Alex signed out and left, only realizing that it was the next day when he got outside. He caught a taxi to police headquarters. He went up to Xavier's department and got his maser back. The people there asked about Xavier and Alex told them what he could

— he would live but would take some time to recover fully. He went into the conference room he had been using with Chooli and sat down, puffing slightly from the exertion. He did not know where first to look. Sitting back in the chair, he closed his eyes.

His comm buzzed, so he opened his eyes and grabbed it. There was no caller ID. Pressing audio, he said, "Chief Inspector Detective Warner."

"Drop the investigation if you want to see your sweet little Cetusian detective again," a chilling female voice said to him.

Alex became instantly alert. "Where is she? I'll kill you if you harm her."

"That's not very lawful, is it?"

"I'll put you away for life."

"I don't think so," the voice said in the same confident tone. "Remember, the more you dig the more harm comes to her." The comm went dead.

Alex threw the comm across the room in frustration. He swiveled the chair around and put his face in his hands, leaning on the table in front of him, tears flowing freely from his eyes. His poor Chooli. Why on earth did he come back to the GIA? Why should he care what happens on this god-forsaken planet with its warped social structure? He could do what the woman said, but how would he find Chooli? She didn't say. Was the life of one innocent man worth Chooli's? Would Chooli forgive him if he sacrificed the man's life for her? Would he forgive himself? But how could he live on without Chooli? It seemed his past was coming back to haunt him.

"Are you all right, sir?" A voice said from the door.

Alex lifted his head and wiped away his tears. A Cetusian maid stood there, concern in her eyes. He looked at her, noting the human response to seeing another human in distress and knew he had no choice but to continue with the investigation, even if it meant losing Chooli. His despair turned to anger, and he gritted his teeth. He would find Chooli and heaven help whoever had her if they harmed her. "Yes, I'm OK, thank you."

The maid seemed a little surprised by the politeness. "Would you like a drink? Tea or coffee?"

"A coffee would be good, thank you." He wiped away the rest of his tears and stood, hobbling over to retrieve his comm, hoping it still worked. The maid came back with his coffee and placed it on the table. He sat down, sipped the coffee and contemplated where to look first.

35

Chooli woke from her unconsciousness. Intense pain emanated from her left leg and a dull background of pain came from bruises all over her body. *What happened?* She lay on a hard surface but didn't want to open her eyes to see what it was. A coldness seeped into her, although she felt no breeze. She tried to remember, and slowly the events before the gap in her memory started coming back to her.

They were in an AGrav traveling back to Nouveau Paris and it crashed. *Alex!* She opened her eyes and saw she lay on a synthcrete floor inside a small room and was alone. Panic gripped her. *Where's Alex?* A sharp stab of pain shot up her leg as she tried to sit up. She inhaled quickly and held her breath so she didn't cry out. A quick look at her leg was enough to tell her she had broken it. *Where am I?*

She lay in a room five meters by five meters. A row of windows lined one wall of the room letting moonlight shine into it, which was otherwise dark. She realized it must be night time. A door stood in one of the other walls. Slowly, to cope with the pain in her leg, she slid across the floor and leaned back on the wall in a sitting position. There was nothing else in the room that she could see. *What am I going to do?* She tried to remember the time of the crash, but every-thing seemed to go blank when they hit the ground.

The door opened, and a stream of bright light entered the room. A person stood silhouetted in the doorway. "You're awake," a man's voice said. "About time." The man looked toward someone out of Chooli's view. "It's awake."

"I'll call the boss," Chooli heard another male voice say.

The degrading attitude of the first man instantly made Chooli hate him, but she could do nothing about it at present as she waited to see what would happen.

"She wants us to find the locating chip and cut it out. Says all GIA agents have one," the man Chooli couldn't see said.

"Where is it?" the man in the doorway asked.

"Dunno."

Chooli saw a gleam of teeth as a smile came to the face of the man in the doorway. "This'll be interesting," he said. Her eyes widened in fear as the man walked towards her. He grabbed her by the arm and started dragging her.

Chooli yelled out in pain as the bones in her leg grated against each other. "My leg," she yelled.

The man stopped. "What about it?"

"It's broken."

"Still have to get that chip out." He continued dragging her into the other room and across to a table. Sweat dripped from Chooli as he lifted her under the knees and shoulders onto a table. "Want to tell us where it is or shall I search?" The man had a lecherous gleam in his eyes.

"I don't know what you're talking about."

"Have it your way." He grabbed her shirt and ripped at it, sending buttons flying across the room. Chooli tried unsuccessfully to hold the shirt together to keep her dignity, but the man was too strong. "Hey, come have a look. Not too bad for a Cetusian," he said to the other one.

"Stop messing around and find that thing. We have to get out of here before they look for her. It should be just under the skin somewhere.

"Surely I can enjoy my work?" the man grumbled to himself as he started feeling Chooli's neck. Chooli squirmed and wriggled to stop him, frustrating him so much that he punched her in the face. "Stay still," he ordered, "or you'll get another one." Her eye started swelling up. She froze in terror but allowed the man to keep touching her until he started on her breasts, at which point she fought back again. He hit her again and walked off, coming back a moment later with cuffs He cuffed her wrists behind her back, greatly increasing her discomfort.

He clearly enjoyed feeling her breasts, but he didn't find what he was looking for. He stood back and rubbed his chin. "If you know where it is, you'd better tell me. I'll start searching lower otherwise."

Chooli loathed the man but wouldn't tell him where the chip was, despite the humiliation of the search. The longer it took him to find it, the better chance she had of rescue.

"I'd better search your back first." He rolled her over, eliciting a shout of agony from her. Searching again, he rubbed and pinched his way down her back. "Nope, not there." He rolled her over again and glee flooded from his eyes as he unzipped her pants, dragging them slowly down and ogling her crotch as he looked to see her reaction from time to time. "You want me to lick it for you?" Chooli shut her eyes and tears trickled down her cheeks. The man softly wiped the back of his hand along the skin of her thigh as he lowered her pants to her knees. She opened her eyes again and saw him frown as he looked at her broken tibia and pressed hard against her skin. "That doesn't look good." He continued his search, taking immense pleasure in feeling up her thighs. He finally stopped and felt a small cylinder on the inside of her left thigh, just under the skin. "Is this it?" he asked the other man.

The man came over and looked. "Suppose so." He didn't seem interested in leering at Chooli, which was fine with her.

"How do we get it out?"

"I've got a knife somewhere." The man left and came back with a flick knife. "It doesn't look deep so I should be able to dig it out with this. You keep her still."

"Easier said than done. It's a bit of a wriggler."

The man with the knife looked at Chooli. "You'll stay still. Otherwise the knife might slip and cut what it shouldn't. Hear me?"

Chooli nodded as she looked at the knife.

The man brought the knife to her thigh and nicked the skin. She flinched but tried to stay still, not wanting more injuries than necessary. Blood started weeping from the wound, but the man made another small nick to make the cut longer. Chooli whimpered from the pain, but it was much more bearable than the pain from her broken bone. He put the knife down and started massaging the chip toward the cut. She flinched as she felt his hands on her but felt relieved that they didn't stray from their task. The end of the chip became visible, and he continued massaging until enough was out for him to grab the end with his fingers and pull. A metallic cylinder a centimeter long came out. "Hope that's it. It's supposed to be virtually indestructible." He threw the chip across the room and into a corner. Chooli watched it arch through the air and noted where it landed, hoping to retrieve it. The man went away and came back with a small cloth. He placed it on the incision to help stop the bleeding. "Undo the cuffs," he told the other man. He also looked at her broken bone and frowned. "We need to get that looked at. She wants you alive in one piece for the time being."

The other man removed the cuffs from Chooli and she quickly grabbed her pants and pulled them up again despite the pain, positioning the cloth on the wound before pulling them over her hips. She tried pulling her shirt back into position, but it kept flopping open without the buttons.

The man who had cut the chip from her saw her frustration. He went away and brought back a jacket. "That should fit."

"Thank you," Chooli said, as she looked at him. He didn't seem to want to hurt her. He seemed to know he just had a job to do, and that was all that interested him. She saw a sadness in his eyes, but as she looked deeper, there was immense cruelty there too.

"We'd better get moving."

The other man grabbed Chooli again and let her flop from the table as he dragged her to an AGrav. She yelled out in agony as she fell to the floor. He dragged her into the AGrav, which was a van with no windows. Closing and locking the door, the two men jumped in the front and they programmed the vehicle for another destination. It lifted and left the building they were in, Chooli despairing of the loss of the locator and of her ever being found. She had no escape from the van, so she closed her eyes and tried to sleep during the flight, but sleep escaped her. Every time she nodded off, a bump would move her leg and send a shard of pain up it. *Please come for me, Alex*, she thought, as she cried.

The van came to a stop two hours later. *We could be anywhere.* The doors opened and Chooli shuffled as far from them as she could.

"Come over here," the lecherous man said. "Don't make me come in and get you." Chooli stayed where she was. The man sighed, jumped up and came over to her. He kicked her several times in the ribs. Chooli screamed with pain and balled herself up, sure that he had broken at least one rib.

"Stop messing around and get her out," the other man said.

The man grunted and gave her one last kick before grabbing her arm and dragging her from the van into a large covered area that looked like a warehouse. He continued moving her across the floor to the corner of the warehouse to a cage. Depositing her in it, he went back out and locked the gate behind him, imprisoning Chooli inside. She saw them both go into another room, leaving her alone in the cage. Looking around, she saw some bedding on the floor and a primitive looking toilet in one corner. A basin with a water tap stood affixed to one wall.

The man who had treated her fairly came out of the room and over to her. "Here." He dropped a food ration and a bottle of water in the cage and walked away.

Chooli suddenly realized how hungry she was. She dragged herself over to the food and leaned against the cage bars while she ate it and drank some water. *What should I do? What can I do? I don't know where I am and don't know how to contact anyone.*

She could try getting out of the cage, but then what? There didn't seem any point in trying to convince either of the men to let her go. One of them just considered her an animal. She wondered if that was how all humans on the planet thought of the Cetusian population. Why did the Cetusians put up with it?

Not knowing what else to do, she dragged herself over to the bedding and lay on it, falling into a troubled sleep as she tried to work out what to do.

She woke up with a start, as an AGrav came into the warehouse and landed next to the van. Morning had come and sunlight streamed into the room from skylights and frosted windows in the walls. The AGrav looked expensive. A man and a woman emerged from the vehicle but were too far away for Chooli to identify as she rubbed sleep from her eyes. She sat up, wincing from the throbbing pain in her side and leg. One eye was still half shut from bruising. She wished she could do something with her leg, splint it, or somehow support the two parts of the broken bone. Feeling the urge to urinate, she dragged herself over to the toilet. *This will be interesting.* Pulling herself up with the bars of the cage, she stood and somehow lowered her pants and sat on the toilet. She wanted to wash her hands afterwards and hobbled over to the basin, the effort almost making her pass out from the pain. Washing her hands, she struggled back to the bedding. She grabbed the water bottle from the night before and drank some more.

The lecherous man came out not long afterwards. Chooli groaned in dread. He unlocked the cage, grabbed her and started dragging her.

"Please," she asked, "can I try walking?"

The man looked at her and grunted. "With a broken leg?"

"Can't be any worse than being dragged."

He shrugged. "You can try, but I'll end up dragging you if you're too slow."

Chooli nodded, grateful for his compromise. She used the cage bars to stand and tried walking, nearly falling over as soon as she put weight on her broken leg. Crying out in frustration, she tried again with the same result.

"You can lean on me. I might have to put my arm around you and grab hold of something, though," the man said with another lecherous look.

She looked at him, abhorring his suggestion, but nodded. It would be better than being dragged, despite the wandering hand. With his support she managed to half walk, half hop over to the room the man took her to.

"Took your time," the other man said.

"It wanted to try walking."

"You know how impatient the bosses are. Put her over there." He pointed to a heavy metal chair with metal armrests and a high back. It had the guise of a throne. The man helped her over to the chair, and she sat and looked around. The room was relatively small. It had two entrances, the one she had come through and another on the opposite side. The door on that entrance was closed.

The first man brought over some leather-looking straps and strapped her forearms to the chair arms, her legs to the chair legs, and her chest to the back. His face was expressionless. He stood back when finished and waited against one wall by the other man.

The door opened half an hour later, and a man walked out. Chooli's eyes bulged in recognition. He was the assassin in the holovision frame from the palace. She gulped. The man stopped and looked at her before continuing to walk over to her. "Should I know you?" he asked her with a menacing smile. His words came out with precision.

"No."

"You seemed to recognize me."

"You just look very similar to someone I know."

"I see." He stared at her. She saw the darkness of hell in his eyes, his black pupils suggesting an endless, empty abyss. He took black leather gloves from his pocket and took his time sliding his hands into them. "Now. You will tell me everything that you know about the murders."

Like hell I will. "I don't know what you're talking about."

He sighed. "We've already talked to your partner. I believe he would be keen to get you back." He slid his forefinger down her cheek. "Without being damaged too much. He is more than a professional partner, is he not?"

He's alive, and they don't have him. Chooli's heart filled with hope. "We know nothing."

"Why did you go to see Richelieu then?"

"We knew he was at the dinner where the Lorraines were last seen. We wanted to ask him some questions. That's all."

"How did you find the warehouse?"

"I don't know what you're talking about."

He sighed again. "I see we will have to do this the hard way." He walked out and brought in a machine Chooli had never seen before. Bringing it over to her, he unwound two thick metallic cables with clamps. "Take her pants off."

"Pervert," Chooli said.

The man laughed. "Oh, you'll wish that was all I did once I finish this."

The lecherous man came and eagerly pulled her pants down to her shins and stepped back. The assassin picked up a leather strap, with a steel interior face, and went to put it around one of Chooli's thighs, but she held her legs together with as much strength as she could muster, stopping his attempt. He stood back. There was no expression on his face. Suddenly, he lashed out with backhanded slaps to her face, making sure his knuckles made maximum contact, sending shards of pain through her. It seemed like he broke her cheekbone. He roughly grabbed her leg again and wrapped the strap around it before she could offer any further resistance. Producing another strap, he put it around her head. It had a mouthguard in it that he positioned in her mouth. A metal strip went from cheek to cheek around the back of her head. Both straps had metal lugs protruding from them, which he attached the clamps to. He turned the machine on and it thrummed with the noise of electricity.

Chooli looked at the machine with terror and then at the man. She couldn't speak because of the mouthguard.

"You want to tell me how you found the warehouse?"

Chooli braced herself, resigned to the pain she knew was coming, and shook her head.

The man flicked a switch. Lights came on the face of the machine as a look of delight came on his face. "I know there are other methods, but I have always considered the more primitive forms much more enjoyable." He pressed a button on the machine.

A surge of electricity forced its way through her. She tried to scream as her whole body attempted to jump from the chair, spasming from the electrical stimulation. She felt the current through her and her body heating. He turned the electricity off. She collapsed limp and wet herself, perspiration dripping from her face, the smell of burning flesh, her flesh, assaulting her nostrils.

"Ready to talk?"

Chooli sat still with her head flopped forward, not acknowledging that he spoke. Another surge of electricity went through her. He must have chosen a higher voltage since it felt ten times worse than the first time. She tried screaming and screaming, but nothing came out. It was too much. She passed out.

36

Alex prepared to make a hyperlink call through to Commissioner Harris. He had sent through for identification the mugshots of the men from the hotel and also the one at the palace. Knowing who these people were might give him a clue where to find Chooli. He also wanted the locator code for her so he could use the location device he had to find out where she was. Putting through the connection request, Alex waited.

"Commissioner Harris," he said as the commissioner's image looked out from the screen at Alex.

"Oh, wasn't expecting you to call." He looked at Alex closer. "You look terrible. Is everything all right there? How's Chooli going?"

Anxiety was written on Alex's face. "I've got a problem. Someone ambushed us and kidnapped Chooli."

Harris's eyes widened. He frowned. "You sure?"

Alex nodded. "I got a comm call. Stop your investigation or you won't see her again."

"Hmm ... seems you're ruffling some feathers then. But hell, I didn't intend putting her through that when we asked her to take part in the assignment." He looked at Alex closely. "And how are you coping?"

"What do you expect? This call was almost a 'you can shove your job' call. But I want to get these bastards. I sent some mugshots through for identification. Do you know if they've done that?"

"Let me check." Harris turned to the side, and Alex saw him make another call on his comm. He had a discussion with whoever he was talking to for some time before turning back to Alex. "The dead two are known gangland mercenaries, but the other guy has no history in our hive database. They're sending through the details to you now."

"I was afraid of that." Alex frowned in frustration. "Can you give me Chooli's locator code so I can try finding her?"

"Sure. You've got the passcode for the security folder in the hive?"

"Yeah."

"I'll put it in there when we hang up."

"Thanks, that was all I wanted. There's definitely more going on here than the murders of a duke and duchess, but I don't know what at the moment. The Cetusian definitely didn't do it, that's for sure."

"Well, let me know of any progress and if you need more help," Harris said, a concerned frown on his face, "and for God's sake — and your sake — find Chooli."

"Thanks." Alex broke the connection. He pulled out his tablet and connected to the hive, extracting the locator code moments later. Activating the location finder app, a ping immediately went off when he punched in the code and he saw where it came from. *Good. It's in the city.* Grabbing his things, he rushed out and down to the parking basement to get his AGrav. He flew in the air soon afterwards, stopping off at the hotel to pick up his zaser cannon, not knowing what he would encounter when he arrived. A warehouse came into view a half hour later. His tablet showed the locator signal came from within it. He descended to the ground in front of the doors five minutes later.

Alex had no time for nonsense. If anyone inside gave him trouble, they had better be prepared to fight. He tried the doors, but they held firm and locked. He set his maser at maximum and aimed it on the door lock, pulling the trigger. The lock and half the door disappeared with wisps of smoke coming from the ends of the remaining metal. Because of the mounting of the door, it swung open enough to allow

Alex entry with no effort from him, so he looked inside. It was vacant and he couldn't see anyone.

He walked in, holding his maser ready. A table stood on the far side, close to another room. The signal came from that direction, so Alex walked over. He paused at the table. A small spattering of blood covered the top, and he made a mental note to get it tested.

Continuing onto the door of the room, he looked inside and frowned. No one was in there. Entering the room, he looked around the perimeter but found nothing of interest.

Returning to the table, he looked around near it. A small round object caught his eye, and he bent over to pick it up.

A button.

A chill went through Alex.

Chooli's button.

From her shirt.

Alex stood staring at that button, unable to move. Unable to allow himself to think about what the implications of that button being there on the ground might be. Not daring to think about it. A cold sweat moistened his skin all over.

But why was he getting the locator signal here?

He looked at the tablet again and got a better bearing on the location. He frowned again. The signal came from the corner of the warehouse. Strolling over to the corner, he wondered about the meaning of what he saw. The floor was clean with no debris except for a small metallic cylinder a millimeter in diameter and a centimeter long. Chooli's locator.

The bastards had cut it out of her.

He bent down to pick it up.

They knew she had a locator. They cut it out. A knife twisted in his stomach as he wondered how much force they had used to find it and remove it. What else might they have done to her with the locator being in her upper thigh? He held his head back, thinking. *If they went to all this trouble, they want her alive ... for now.* He put the locator in his pocket. *But where have they taken her?*

Returning to the table, he made a more thorough search around it and found three more buttons. Alex smiled but was in no mood for humor. *She must have fought back.*

Giving the warehouse one last look, he left. There was nothing else of interest inside for him. He called in a report and asked for forensics to come and collect evidence, test the blood's DNA and tell him who it belonged to, although he already knew.

The sun had started setting in the west, so Alex went back to the hotel.

THE STAFF HAD ALLOCATED him another room and several police stood in front of the door and in various positions on the floor. Alex saw one on the balcony when he went inside. He cleaned up. His broken wrist started aching, so he took one of the painkillers given to him at the hospital.

He went down to the restaurant and had dinner, washed down with two glasses of beer. It tasted horrible, but he wanted the alcohol and didn't feel like wine or anything stronger. He sat at the table looking into the amber liquid as if he was looking into a magical pool that could foresee the future, wondering what he should do, what he could do, to find Chooli.

A man walked over to him and sat down, breaking Alex's reverie. Alex raised an eyebrow.

"Detective Lamar."

"I recognize you from the office."

Lamar looked around and fidgeted. He seemed to have pent-up energy to release but nothing to expel it on. He looked at Alex. "Xavier's regained consciousness."

"Oh, good."

"This is shit!"

Alex felt a little amused by the forthright comment. "What *this* are you specifically talking about?"

"This mess with what you're investigating. I knew right from the start that that guy didn't do it. Every time we raised an objection, they shut us down. He's lucky he knows his confederation law, or he'd be dead and no one would be any the wiser. And this shit ... with your ambush, and now you agent missing ... it's getting more complicated by the minute."

Alex looked at the guy, searching his eyes to look into his soul, and he liked what he saw. "Thanks for the moral support, but that doesn't get Chooli back."

Lamar looked around again. "That's just it. I want to help. I don't care if they take my badge. This happens too often. It's not right. It's not why I joined."

"How do you think you can help?" Alex asked, intrigued by his attitude and his offer of support.

"I might help you. Get information that might be difficult for you to get. Organize things with the other guys if you need help. There's a lot who think the same as me, but they have their hands tied, families to support."

"With Xavier out of action, I can use someone in the police."

"Well?"

"What?"

"What do you want me to do?"

Alex gave a fleeting smile, followed by a heavy sigh. "I appreciate your enthusiasm. But I'm not sure what to do myself at the moment. I need to think." Alex thought some more. "You can find out where those two dead guys came from. They were gangland mercenaries, but I don't know if they came from here or from out of the system. See who they may have contacted or if they came in with anyone else."

"Great!" Lamar said. He looked like he was about to spring up from the chair in his eagerness and bounce out.

"Here're my contact details if you find out anything." Alex gave him a chip.

Lamar rose, a smile on his face. "I'll be seeing you then."

Alex watched him leave. He ordered another beer and considered his options as he drank it. Satinka came to mind for no reason he could tell. Maybe he just wanted a shoulder to cry on. He finished his beer and left, heading for The Two Moons.

~

NEGOTIATING the steps down into the club, Alex looked around. He went to the bar and ordered a drink. "Is Satinka working tonight?" he asked the barmaid.

"I think so. I'll see if I can find her."

Alex turned and looked around the place as he waited. It surprised him to find roughly equal human and Cetusian clientele in the club.

"Wasn't expecting you back here," Satinka said as she walked over to Alex. She looked around. "Where's your partner?"

A sudden flush of pain crossed Alex's face.

"Oh, sorry. What happened? Had a fight?"

"No, nothing like that. Someone's kidnapped her."

Satinka drew in her breath. "You're joking, right?"

"No." Alex felt miserable. He didn't want to download his troubles on her. "You're working, aren't you?"

"You asked for me." She sat on a stool next to him. "Anyway, I can take a break for a while. They can tell me if they don't like it."

"You want me to pay?"

"No." She looked at him. "You've got enough on your plate. You can buy me a drink, though."

Alex gestured for the barmaid to give Satinka a drink.

She picked it up and took a sip. "So ... how did she get kidnapped?"

"We were coming back from interviewing Duke Richelieu and someone ambushed us. Our AGrav crashed, and she was missing when I woke up. Had a phone call later demanding I stop our investigation, if I want to see her again."

Satinka looked at him. "But you're not."

"No." Alex looked down, pain consuming him again. "I can't. I wouldn't be able to look in the mirror if I did, and I wouldn't be able to look at Chooli again either. She would lose all respect for me."

"Despite the fact that you're saving her life?"

Alex nodded. "We value our integrity."

Satinka took another sip of her drink. Alex could see she was thinking. "Can I help?"

Alex jumped slightly. "I can't see how."

"Never underestimate the resources of our underworld."

"You're full of surprises," Alex said. *Who is this woman?* He thought for a moment. "We have an image of a suspect but have no record of him and don't know where he came from or where he is now."

"And coming up is a special guest appearance by the gorgeous Satinka," the PA announced.

Satinka winced. "Sorry. Don't move. Just have to do my routine."

Alex smiled. "I'll watch."

"Won't your partner have something to say if she finds out?" Satinka said and winked as she walked off. She went to the stage and completed her strip tease and pole-dancing act. The audience hooted and cheered her as she finished and slipped tips into her G-string. She disappeared for five minutes and returned to Alex fully dressed again, or what they considered fully dressed in this establishment.

Alex held a holo-plate of the unknown assassin. He studied it, wondering if Chooli's disappearance involved him and whether Satinka could help identify him. He looked at her as she sat back down and picked up her drink.

"Like it?"

"Couldn't really concentrate." He hesitated, but finally held out the holo to her. "This is the guy. I don't know what you can do, though."

Satinka took the holo and looked at it. "Hasn't been around here. What do you want him for?"

"We believe that he's the assassin that killed the Duke and Duchess of Lorraine."

"Wait here a minute." She got up and left, coming back five

minutes later with the manager, an enormous man, two meters tall and built like a bull.

"Satinka says you're looking for this guy," he said as he held out the holo.

"Yeah, but I don't expect you to help."

"We don't like foreigners on our turf."

"How do you know he's a foreigner?"

"I know."

"Still, he's a professional. He'll be hard to locate."

"We have resources. Let me ask around. Come back tomorrow and ask for Satinka again." He looked at her. "You'll still be here?" She nodded, so he looked back to Alex. "We'll let you know if we find out anything."

Alex relaxed slightly. *Maybe there was a way of finding this guy ... and hopefully Chooli through him.* "Thanks. Much appreciated."

"As I said, we don't like foreigners on our turf." He walked away.

"Wouldn't like to meet your manager in a dark alley."

Satinka giggled. "No, but he's harmless."

Alex looked at her, wondering what her definition of harmless was.

37

Satinka sat in the AGrav looking out at the aquamarine-blue ocean, the ripples of the waves just visible from the height they flew. The rugged basalt-colored cliffs of the Champagne coastline appeared on the holographic screen in front of her, showing the view ahead. Butterflies of excitement gripped her stomach as she thought about the enterprise they had entrusted her with. Her mother hadn't believed her when she told her the news. The memory brought a smile to her lips. She looked at the new tablet the business had bought for her, the novelty of it still holding her interest. She had never owned a tablet before. It detailed the itinerary for the trip and the appointment list of the people she would meet.

The vehicle banked as it crossed the coastline, not that she would have noticed if she hadn't looked out the window, the gravity field in the vehicle maintaining the up-down orientation of her sitting position. It could have done a loop-de-loop and she would not have noticed. The green ground below came toward her as the craft tilted. Vivid green grass extended most of the way to the horizon, interrupted from time to time by a farmhouse and surrounding buildings. She sighed as she wondered what it would be like to live such a rustic life.

The first signs of Epernay came into view half an hour later, the traditional white-walled buildings of the more prosperous Cetusian population being the first signs of civilisation. The AGrav rushed over them toward the central business district where her destination lay. More ostentatious buildings of their human inhabitants quickly replaced the Cetusian ones as her destination approached. The AGrav slowly descended to the ground on the parking pad ten minutes later, Satinka gathering her baggage and disembarking into the gentle light and temperature of the Champagne climate in spring. A large male Cetusian stood near the building entrance waiting for her. She noticed a slight raising of the eyebrows as she came into his view.

"Welcome to the Epernay branch office, miss," the man said.

"Thank you. I'm Satinka. And you are ..."

"Bidziil. I'm here to make sure you don't get into trouble."

"I see. You looked surprised when I got out."

Bidziil shuffled his feet and looked down. "Didn't think it would be a woman, that's all."

"Is that a problem?"

"I can cope with that," he said as he looked up and directly at her again.

Satinka smiled at his wording but said no more.

"Others might have another opinion," he added. "Watch they don't take advantage of you."

"Really?"

"Yeah. It's a tough place, despite the opulence everywhere."

"I'll make a note. I hope pointing this out, if it occurs, is one of your duties."

Bidziil smiled, revealing a crooked set of teeth. "Of course."

"Let's go talk to some real estate agents then."

Bidziil ushered her into the building and down to the basement parking area where he pointed to a smaller AGrav for their transportation in the city. They got in and Bidziil flew Satinka to the Prestige Realtor in the middle of the city. The façade of the establishment reeked of the opulence Bidziil had previously alluded to. Immense

Corinthian columns towered either side of the entrance. Satinka walked behind Bidziil as he escorted her into the business. Gold dazzled her as she looked over the reception area. The receptionist wore a black jacket with the collar extending up to the top of her ears and circling behind, her head surrounded by it, in line with the latest elite fashion, making Satinka self-conscious about the clothes she wore. She had bought a wardrobe in line with her increased income and her position, but she knew she couldn't even hope to afford the clothing the receptionist wore. She wondered if the job paid well or whether she allowed her boss's advances for some fringe benefits.

"May I help you?" the receptionist asked.

"I have an appointment with Mr. Moselle."

The receptionist stared at her and grimaced as she looked her over, contempt barely disguised on her face. "I shall see if he is available."

"He will be available," Bidziil added, giving the receptionist an intimidating stare.

The receptionist gulped and turned her attention to the office comm. She whispered into it and moments later turned back to Satinka. "He will be with you shortly." She gave Bidziil a nervous look before returning to her other duties.

The tall, thin form of Mr. Moselle walked through the door behind the receptionist. He wore a designer-made, black pin-striped suit, his radiant face complete with a showroom smile. "Ah, Ms. Satinka. I am so pleased to see you," he said in a very upper-class tone. "Let us go to our viewing room, where we can sit and relax while we discuss your requirements." He turned to the receptionist. "Chantelle, Champagne." Satinka saw the receptionist grit her teeth before rising to comply as she and Bidziil followed Moselle through a different doorway.

They entered a room filled with luxury. The soft red velvet lounges circled a central black pedestal. Satinka's footsteps echoed on the black-veined marble floor as she walked to the seat Moselle ushered her to. Moselle offered Bidziil a seat too, but he preferred to stand behind Satinka in a military at-ease stance. Despite the disorientation of her surroundings, Satinka reinforced her mindset to not let the unfamiliar environment intimidate her. The receptionist came in with a silver tray, three glasses and a bottle of champagne, the bottle already in a chilling bucket sitting on top of it. She placed the tray on a side desk and left. Satinka noticed Moselle's lingering lust-filled eyes follow her out the door.

Moselle opened the bottle and poured three glasses, handing one to Satinka. Bidziil refused when he attempted to offer him one. Shrugging, Moselle kept it instead. He lounged in a chair next to them. "Now, I understand that you are interested in the purchase of an establishment."

"That's correct. We wish to expand our Gentleman's Club franchise in this city but are looking at a more upmarket clientele. People who need not consider the costs of a night out enjoying such entertainment."

"I see. You have definitely come to the right person. I believe I may have the very place for you. Bear with me for a moment." Moselle rose and went to a console, bringing back a remote-control unit. He flicked through the menus until he found what he was looking for and pressed buttons. The lights dimmed and a three-dimensional holographic display lit the middle of the room above the pedestal.

Satinka's eyes sparkled as the image appeared, but she controlled her emotions so Moselle didn't notice her reaction. She stood and walked around the projection. A building stood in the middle of a lush estate, the manicured gardens displaying an elegant geometrical design. The building stood three stories tall, with brilliant white Plastocrete walls, the front façade reminiscent of a Corinthian temple with massive columns towering to the roof. An extensive patio projected out from the back of the building, complete with swimming pool, spa and other buildings that Satinka envisioned converting to rooms of pleasure. Three-meter-high security fencing surrounded the entire estate for privacy.

"Rather stunning, isn't it?" Moselle said. "I can just see the possibilities for you. Catering to men's every desire."

Satinka looked up sharply at him. "Not their *every* desire."

Moselle, realizing his misstep, looked repentance. "Yes. Still, you won't find a better establishment for your venture."

"We will see." Satinka gave him a thoughtful, questioning look as she sipped her drink. "Is that all you have available?"

Taken aback, Moselle said, "There are other properties I could show you, but none of them would come even close to what you could do with this one."

"And not with the same price tag either." She placed the side of the glass to her cheek to feel the coolness. Taking another sip, she placed it on the side table. "Let's go have a look then."

"What? Now?" Moselle looked alarmed.

"Yes now. Is that a problem?"

"No. Of course not," he said, composing himself again. "It is just unusual. Most of my clients do not wish to extend their visit to an actual inspection."

"I'm not your usual client." Satinka looked at Bidziil and quickly winked. He gave the flicker of a smile before sobering again.

"Please wait here while I make the arrangements." Moselle left, leaving Satinka to her thoughts, possibilities flashing through her mind as she stood staring at the holographic display. He returned five minutes later. "This way, please."

Satinka and Bidziil followed him through to the rear of the office and to a waiting AGrav limousine. "I see the real estate business is doing well," she said.

"We have our prosperous times," Moselle said with a sheepish smile and an attempt at humility, but Satinka noticed he soon reverted to his customary arrogance. They all got in the limousine and went to the estate, arriving thirty minutes later.

The view was everything the holographic display had shown and more. Seeing it for real made its grandeur more substantial. Satinka smelled the scent of the flowers as she ambled around the grounds. She looked up at the sky as a high-pitched sound grew louder. Two fighters suddenly zoomed overhead, one tailing the other as they both banked sharply, lasers firing from the rear craft. The smell of the flowers disappeared as alarm took over her senses. She suddenly felt Bidziil's muscular arm around her, lifting her from the ground and rushing her to the building and shelter, Moselle rushing behind him as he eyed the sky.

Disorientated, Satinka looked around. Flashes of light suddenly came from the direction of the city, followed fifteen seconds later by a roar as mushroom clouds rose into the atmosphere. "What's happening?"

"The war," Moselle said, his eyes darting around for better cover than the side of the building.

"What war?" Satinka felt annoyed that he hadn't mentioned this before now.

"Aquitaine wants to take us over."

Satinka looked to Bidziil for direction. Streaks of laser light thrust up into the atmosphere from the ground, causing other explosions somewhere high in the sky, too high for Satinka to see what hovered up there.

"Come," Moselle beckoned. "We should take better cover until this is over." He started walking to the rear of the building. Satinka and Bidziil followed, and they came to a door, which led down to a basement at least twenty meters underground.

Light streamers illuminated their path as they descended, and Satinka saw a sizeable room when they reached the bottom, its grandeur as impressive as what they had already seen. "What is this place?"

"A bomb shelter."

"With this amount of luxury? It looks more like a drawing room where people go to chat while they sip their drinks after a dinner party."

"The original builder spared nothing when he built the place. Fortunately, there is another entrance from the residence. You could use it as a private function room for whatever purpose you see fit."

Satinka saw some merit in Moselle's suggestion, but reserved her opinion until she saw the rest of the estate. Moselle walked to a screen and powered it up. The screen lit up, showing the view outside. More evidence of war came through to them. The ground shook several times, despite them being deep underground. Bidziil didn't seem bothered by the destruction above. He appeared calm and alert when Satinka looked at him. "Aren't you at least a little worried?"

He looked at her and shrugged. "Will worrying change anything?"

She smiled as she considered his flawless logic. "No." Not knowing what else to do, she pulled her tablet out and brought up the images of the men Alex wanted to find. She showed them to Bidziil. "Seen any of these around?"

He studied them intensely. "I've seen these two around recently," he said, pointing. "They've been in the club. Spending big, but not causing trouble. Haven't seen the other one, though."

"Pity. He's the one we want to locate the most."

"What for?"

"Oh, just a favor."

"If you transfer the image, I'll ask around. See if the others have seen him."

Satinka started to answer but was distracted by the sight on the screen of six large transporters descending from the sky. Her eyes widened. "What's happening now?"

"Those are troop transporters," Bidziil said. "They must be taking over the capital."

"We'll be able to get back?" Satinka asked, gripping his arm.

"Depends." He walked off to another area of the room and contacted someone on his comm. He stood talking for some time before returning to her. Eyeing her as if trying to gauge how he should phrase the next comment, he said, "We might be here for some time. Things are fairly bad in the city at present."

Moselle looked at him. Satinka thought he looked even more frightened than she felt. She also felt frustrated. She had wanted to return to Nouveau Paris that evening, but it looked like that wouldn't be happening. Looking at Bidziil and then at Moselle, she said, "Might as well look at the rest of this place while we're waiting."

38

Alex tossed and turned in bed as he tried to sleep. He kept thinking of Chooli and the worst things that could happen to her, blaming himself for her kidnapping. He knew he couldn't do anything about it. There were no leads to where she could be or who had taken her, and that frustrated him even more. He should have something to go on. There should be some clue about what happened to her, but they had gone over the warehouse with the best forensic instruments available and come up with nothing. She had just started with the GIA. He should have looked after her better. Sighing, he opened his eyes. Getting worked up over it wouldn't find her. There must be something he could do.

Latching onto an idea, he rose from the bed, even though it was only one in the morning, he went to the bathroom. He got dressed and opened up the hyperlink comm, calling Ahiga, who was first on his list of people who could help him or owed him a favor. It was four in the morning in Arbor on Caerus, but Alex didn't care.

Ahiga came on visual after a considerable time, wiping sleep from his eyes and yawning. "You know what time it is?"

"Yes, I do. I'm sorry, but I need a favor."

"What sort of favor?"

"I want you to put your considerable resources to work to identify someone for me."

"Isn't the GIA meant to do that?" Ahiga asked, raising an eyebrow. "Why? What's happened that you can't use them?"

Alex looked down to control his emotions. "Someone's kidnapped Chooli."

"What?" Came a female voice out of view.

Alex smiled grimly. "Hello, Mai."

Mai came into view. "Sorry. I didn't mean to eavesdrop. You have to find her."

"I know. That's why I called Ahiga. He amply demonstrated his resourcefulness last time when we had to find his father's killer. I still should haul you over the coals for that, now that I'm an agent again."

Ahiga grinned. "You're only there on secondment." He frowned. "So, who's this person?"

"He assassinated a duke and duchess here on Franconia, but he comes from somewhere else and the GIA hive has no record of him."

"Oh." Ahiga scratched his head. "I could ask the people my father had working for him. See if they know. They have an extensive network throughout the Confederation. You got any information on him?"

"I'll sent through a holo-image of him. He's a professional, so he won't have left many tracks, but there must be someone somewhere who knows him."

"I'll see what I can find out."

"Thanks."

"Find her," Mai said with an undertone of fear.

Alex sighed. "I know." He broke the connection and sent through the image of the assassin.

Looking through his contacts, he found the next person he wanted to talk to. He would call in a favor from him. The connection went through.

"Vapdog."

"Hello, Vapdog. Remember me?" Vapdog used to be one of Alex's informants in the underworld. Alex got a lot of useful information from him back then. He also helped Vapdog out of some serious trouble. Apart from being Alex's informant, he was also a high-powered member of the dark community he lurked in.

"Alex! Haven't heard from you for a while. What's up?"

"Nothing good, I'm afraid."

"Sorry to hear that. Is this a social call?"

"No, I want to call in a favor."

"Oh?"

"I'm trying to find out the identity of someone. Someone more in your field, if you understand what I mean. He doesn't appear in any of our hive databases."

Vapdog looked at Alex across the screen with a slight smirk. "He must be good."

"He's a professional assassin and I believe he's kidnapped one of our agents."

Vapdog's brow rose. "Assassin? Not too many of them around. They tend to die young. There's always someone better, more inventive or younger coming along and retiring him early."

"Well, this one's good, very good. We almost missed him except for some chance glitch. What about it? Can you ask around? See if there are any out there using assassin nano-bots as their tool of trade."

"Whoa. That's some serious shit."

"The list should be short then."

Vapdog looked at Alex as if considering turning down his request. He finally sighed. "Only for you. Okay. I'll see who's out there. Give me a few days."

"As quick as you can. I think I'm on a clock here."

"I'll see what I can do."

Alex broke the connection and sat back, closing his eyes. *What else can I do?* He felt at a loss until something turned up, so he went back to bed and tried sleeping through the rest of the night.

THE BELL for the unit clanged incessantly as Alex stirred from his sleep. *Just when I finally get to sleep.* He sat up and stretched, then rubbed the sleep from his eyes. Putting on pants, he went to the door and pressed the visual button on the comm. Detective Lamar stood on the other side of the door holding two takeaway coffees in his hand. Alex opened the door and Lamar walked in.

"Was starting to worry something had happened to you," Lamar said.

"Why?"

"Bit late to be sleeping."

Alex looked at the chronometer. 10:30. It surprised him. It was late, especially for him. "I made some calls during the night. Must have dozed off longer than I thought. What's up, anyway?"

"Apart from checking on you, I thought I'd come and tell you what I've got so far, which isn't much. Here, have a coffee. You need to flavor it yourself if you don't like straight black."

Alex smiled. He couldn't fault his enthusiasm. He took the coffee and invited Lamar to sit. "You got a first name?"

"Charles."

"Well, Charles. You've probably got more than me so far." Alex took a sip of coffee. "What've you got?"

"We looked at footage of the warehouse your agent went to last night."

"We?"

"I'm not the only one pissed off with all this. Anyway, we saw an AGrav van leaving it yesterday morning before dawn. It traveled north at speed, away from Nouveau Paris. Unfortunately, we lost sight of it soon after it left the city limits. It seems they know where our blind spots are."

Alex sighed. "That's something. What's north of Nouveau Paris?"

"Not much before the coast. Then there's nothing till you hit the Duchy of Champagne."

"Why would they go there?"

"Don't know. Especially since it's in the middle of a war."

"War?"

"Duke of Aquitaine is trying to take it over. Something about there being no legitimate heir to the dukedom. Makes little sense to me, but I'm just a lowlife detective."

"Oh, that war. Yes Xavier mentioned it," Alex said, and added with a grin, "You have a high opinion of yourself."

"Well, it doesn't matter what I think."

Thinking of the information Lamar had got, Alex considered what he should do. "So you think they may have gone to Champagne?"

"Doesn't make much sense, but that's what it looks like. We can trace the route they took and see whether there's anywhere they may have taken her along the way, but there doesn't seem to be anything from looking at our satellite images."

Alex took a drink of the now cooling coffee. "Let me get dressed and grab a bite and we'll have a look. I take it you have an AGrav?"

Lamar nodded. "I'll go grab something from downstairs for you to have along the way. What do you want?"

"Bacon and egg stick and some juice."

"Done." Charles rose and left.

Alex watched as he did so. Lamar's energy impressed Alex. He remembered when he was like that. Alex liked the no nonsense attitude. He finished the coffee and got dressed.

LAMAR MANUALLY STEERED the AGrav over the city as Alex munched the bacon and egg stick, looking out over their surroundings. He remembered the warehouse he had gone to the day before.

"Now," Lamar said. "The AGrav left and went this direction." He pointed north as he steered the AGrav to go the same way. "I've programmed the navigation to follow the same route. We must assume it didn't change course after we lost track of it. Not the cleanest detective work, but the best we have for now."

"I have nothing better at the moment." Alex continued looking. "It didn't stop anywhere in the city?"

"No."

They sat in silence as the scenery turned from city to countryside. Lamar slowed the AGrav and reduced its altitude to get more details of the ground and the things on it. They both looked intently until they reached the coast, neither finding anything one would consider a place for a fugitive AGrav to hide in. Lamar banked the AGrav as they went over the coast, ready to return to the city. "No point in going any further."

Alex slumped in disappointment. "We can't go to Champagne?"

"Not in this we can't. It's in lockdown, anyway. We might get shot at if we try."

"I have someone I need to catch up with at The Two Moons tonight, anyway."

"Oh?"

Alex smiled. "Not what you think. We went there to check out Yiska's alibi. I went back last night to see if they could ask around about the assassin. I got told to return tonight."

"Mind if I tag along?"

"Not at all. You in a partnership?"

"Was. Now I just bum around."

"Might suit you more than me then."

Lamar shrugged. "Not usually my taste, but I've heard things about The Two Moons. Never been there, though."

"Mind Cetusians?"

Lamar shrugged again. "We're all human."

"Satinka might interest you then," Alex said, a conspiratorial smile quickly crossing his face. Charles looked at him suspiciously and Alex grinned.

They arrived back at Alex's hotel mid-afternoon and Alex got out. "Come pick me up at eight."

"Sure. Anything you want me to chase up before then?"

Alex shook his head. "Just keep doing what you've been doing. We must find something, eventually."

Lamar lifted off and Alex watched him until he was out of sight. He started feeling nervous. Time was passing and he felt it was running out for Chooli, but he had nothing to go on to find her. He cursed as he fretted over all the scenarios of torture she might be enduring. Bad people come up with very inventive means of abusing others to get information or just for their own entertainment. He couldn't do anything about it by worrying, so he went back to his room. His comm buzzed as he went through the door. There was no recognizable name, but he recognized the code. Setting up the hyper-link, he dialed Vapdog.

Vapdog came on. "Got a name," he said, looking pleased with himself. "It wasn't easy. That area of darkness is hard to navigate and stay intact."

Alex appreciated his efforts but knew Vapdog was just bragging about his abilities. "Yeah, yeah. What you got?"

"I'll go do something more useful if you're not interested," Vapdog said, affronted by Alex's attitude.

Laughing, Alex said, "Come on. I know how you operate. I am interested and appreciate anything you might have dug up."

Appeased, Vapdog continued. "People didn't want to talk too much when I started mentioning assassin nano-bots. They clamped up real fast. I got one to talk, though. There're rumors of someone for hire whose reputation is providing the perfect crime for a price, a big price. Nano-bots are one of his specialties, supposedly."

The information sounded promising. "Did anyone recognize the face? Can he give a name?"

"As I said, I only got one to talk. He didn't recognize the image, but it's rumored the person's called 'The Reaper'. Obviously a code-name. I doubt if anyone knows his actual name."

"How do you know it's a he?"

Vapdog raised an eyebrow. "It's a he." He frowned. "The contact told me he had an accomplice. That might be a woman. Would suit the operation."

"The Reaper, then. I'll see if there's anything in our database on that."

"I doubt it."

"So do I. Thanks. I owe you one again."

Vapdog laughed. "I'll just take one off the list of the ones I owe you."

Alex disconnected. He sat back. At least he now had a name. He sent a message to Commissioner Harris to check out the information and went for a bite to eat before Lamar returned to take him to The Two Moons.

39

They arrived at the club a little after 8:30 and walked down into the place. Alex nodded to a couple who recognized him. They looked warily at Lamar, though, as if they could tell he was a cop, but Lamar looked around full of excitement, the night's entertainment in full swing. Alex walked to the bar, "Is Satinka around?" He said to the woman behind it.

"Let me get someone to check." She went away and came back moments later. "Just be a minute. Want a drink while you're waiting?"

Alex nodded and ordered one, as did Lamar. Alex looked at Lamar looking at the entertainment and smiled. "Thought you said these sorts of places weren't your taste?"

Lamar took a moment to come out of his enchantment. "Huh ... Oh, I've never been to a place like this before."

"Don't get addicted."

Alex looked around, sipping his drink while he waited. Several of the women gave them inviting glances, but Alex didn't take the bait and he held Lamar back a few times too. "You can do that in your own time." Lamar looked at him with a sulky expression but agreed to Alex's demand.

Five minutes later, the manager appeared.

"Evening, Alex."

"Evening. I was expecting Satinka."

The manager frowned. "She hasn't returned from Epernay. I'm worried about her actually, with the war going on over there."

"Epernay?" Alex looked to Lamar for enlightenment.

"The capital of the Duchy of Champagne."

"Oh. What's she doing there?"

"Just business," the manager said. "But we only meant it to be a day trip."

"So you have nothing for me then?"

"Not really. There is a whisper of someone new around, though. That's all anyone wants to say."

"Wasn't expecting too much. This guy's a pro, so he'll know how to keep out of trouble. Thanks for trying anyway."

"Got a way to contact you? I'll let you know if I find out anything else. Save you having to come in here all the time."

Alex gave him the information. "I don't think Charles minds." He gave the man an amused smile.

"So long as he behaves himself." The man winked.

Lamar looked a trifle offended but said nothing. The manager left and Alex sipped his drink in silence while Lamar continued ogling the women. Alex sighed. It felt like he was treading water.

40

C hooli regained consciousness slowly. Her leg throbbed. Past events crept back into her head to haunt her. Opening her eyes, she saw she lay on a bed in a compact room. She felt wet between the legs and realized she had urinated at some stage, probably during the last surge of electricity through her. A strange metallic taste persisted in her mouth. Spiraling into depression, she sobbed and wondered if she would ever see Alex again. A thirst suddenly possessed her that kept all but that thought at bay, and she looked around for anything to drink. A basin stood in the corner with a tap. She rose to a sitting position. The ache of over-stressed muscles engulfed her until her thirst returned and she put her physical pain out of her mind, her concentration fully on the basin and water.

Reaching the floor with her legs, she stood lopsided on her good leg and hobbled to the basin, wincing in pain whenever she placed any weight on her broken leg. She saw that someone had placed a splint on her leg while she was unconscious. Throwing her arms out to grasp the edge of the basin, she gasped for air as she leaned over. The tap turned easily and Chooli lowered her lips to gulp water until she couldn't drink any more. *Maybe not the best idea*, she thought. *I'll probably wet myself again.*

The hydration sharpened her awareness, and she looked around. Apart from the bed and basin, a toilet stood in another corner and a window let light into the room. A table stood against the wall with a chair under it. One door led to somewhere she presumed was unavailable to her. She had to escape, but how? She could hardly walk, never mind run, and she didn't know where she was or where help might be. While she stood thinking, the vibrations from explosions rattled the window and reverberated up through her legs. *Where the hell am I?*

She hobbled back to the bed and sat down, the discomfort of her wetness bringing a scowl to her face. She wished she could get out of her wet pants. Her thoughts returned to her torture. She had never seen such an unemotional person as her torturer before. He seemed to thrive on the pain of others as if it fed him. There was no doubt he was the same person as the assassin they saw in the holo-footage, but why would he care about Alex and her? Why didn't he just leave the planet? He had completed his job — or had he?

Sighing and boosting her resolve, she stood again and went to the window. It had bars on it and the bottom was just below her eye level. She looked to be in an estate. Manicured lawns and towering trees dominated the scenery outside. The sky was a brilliant blue. A large troop carrier suddenly appeared and flew across her field of view. She went over to the door, knowing already they would have locked it, but she tried the handle, anyway. It was locked. The only other orifice in the encasing walls was an air vent in the ceiling, near one corner of the room. It looked large enough for her to crawl through, but it was high above her. She had no tools to pry the cover off either. She went back to the window.

A noise came from beyond the door five minutes later. She looked as the handle turned and the door opened. The lecherous man walked in with a tray that had food on it.

"Thought we heard you walking around. Hungry?" He put the tray on the table and left.

I can't look very appealing at present, she thought. Smelling the food, she hobbled to the table and sat on the chair. A plate of stew and a slice of bread sat on the tray with a knife and fork. A knife that could pry open the vent cover, she thought as she looked up to it again. Scoffing down the food, she felt her energy level rise. *How can I get to the vent?* An idea materialized in her head, but she needed some way of concealing the knife and getting her captors to forget they had given her one. Was the lecherous one that gullible? She thought so.

She scanned the ceiling, looking for cameras. Strange they didn't have a camera in the room, she thought. She cleaned the knife on her pants and looked for a place to hide it. Going over to the basin, she looked underneath the bowl. A small returning ledge extended across the front of it to strengthen it. It was an ideal place to put the knife for safekeeping, so she put it there and hoped. Going back to the bed, she sat and then lay on it, thinking.

The door open and the lecherous one came in. He stopped and looked at her, making her skin crawl. "Assuming the position?" He asked.

Chooli ignored him. Her pulse increased as she tensed.

He laughed and continued to collect the tray. She saw him frown out of the corner of her eye as he looked at it. "Where's the knife?"

"What knife?" she asked, turning her head to look at him.

"I'm sure I gave you a knife."

"What would I need a knife for with that muck you pass off as stew?"

Looking at her, he seemed undecided about what to do. He finally shrugged. "You're probably right. I must have dreamt I gave you one." He picked up the tray and walked out, locking the door behind him.

Chooli let out a gigantic sigh and smiled. She felt her heart slow and her body relax. *That was easier than I thought.* She frowned as the stench of stale urine wafted past her nose. Feeling the need for the toilet, she went over to it and let her pants drop. She stopped mid-squat as she saw her thigh. A large burn mark and bruising blemished it where the torture strap had been. The sight sent an avalanche of fear through her as she wondered what her head looked like. Continuing with her squat, she peed and pulled her pants back up.

There was no way for her to know how much time she had before someone came back to either give her more food or collect her for more torture. She would only get one chance to escape, though. The vent enticed her to try. What was her plan? She didn't really have one except to escape the room and the torture. She didn't have any idea where she would go or what she would do when she got there, or even if there was any real escape from the clutches of those who had captured her. But she knew her torment would continue if she stayed where she was.

Steeling herself, she went to the bed, pulled the mattress off and lifted one end until the bed stood vertically against the wall by the vent. Slats across the bed base would act as ladder rungs for her. She retrieved the knife and climbed the bed up to the vent. Four screws held the vent in place, so she used the end of the knife as a screwdriver and unscrewed the screws. With the screws out, she used the knife to lever the vent, and it came away easily. Rising another rung, she poked her head into the duct. It ran in both directions but seemed to increase in size one way and decrease in size the other. It would be a squeeze, but she was sure her body would fit.

A noise outside the door froze her. *Please don't come in now.* Silence returned a few seconds later. She realized she had to act quickly and lifted herself into the duct. Since the bed would remain where it was, they would immediately know where she had gone. A shortcoming in her plan, but she couldn't do anything about that. Putting the vent back, she slowly crawled along the duct, keeping as silent as she could. The flowing cold air blew past her as she crawled and started chilling her. The duct expanded after she passed another vent. She looked down as she crawled past and saw another room. It looked like an office, but she couldn't be sure from her perspective. The movement got slightly easier after that, and she continued. It was hard to see inside the duct with the minimal amount of light finding its way into it, but there seemed to be a tee junction up ahead.

Reaching the junction, she was uncertain at first about which way to go, eventually deciding to go toward the constant drone of a fan, which was where the air was coming from. The sound of confusion and anger came from behind her as she cleared the junction. They had discovered her escape. She knew it would be near impossible for someone to follow her down the duct, but they might start pulling vent covers off until they found her, so she had a limited time to complete her escape. She increased her pace while crawling in silence.

The duct continued increasing in cross-section and before long she could crawl on her hands and knees. The duct came to a bend downwards up ahead, just after another vent. This was as far as she could go, so she crawled to the vent and realized a flaw in her plan. This vent would have screws on like the other one, She grunted and slammed the cover with her palm in frustration. To her amazement, the cover popped off and cascaded out of sight with a clanging noise. She cringed at the noise. But maybe it was her lucky day. She poked her head out through the vent and looked around.

The room was vacant and large. It seemed to be a storeroom with lines of shelving in it. A set of shelves stood directly under the vent, the cover sitting on the top. The room was gloomy with light from just a small slit of a window in one wall. Moving past the vent, she lowered herself onto the shelving, feet first, and sat on top without bending over in the space between the shelves and the ceiling. She replaced the cover to confuse her kidnappers about where she had emerged. She still sat two meters from the floor, and the shelves wobbled when she moved. Her broken leg ached, but she had to continue. Lowering herself over the side where the shelves were, she used them to descend to the floor without toppling the lot to the floor.

The room was silent. She hobbled around the shelving and came to a door. With her ear to it, she listened for any sound signaling people on the other side, but she couldn't hear anyone. She risked cracking the door open and listened again. Everything remained silent. She poked her head out and looked up and down a corridor. The noise of a fan came from the direction where the duct descended, so she assumed that the air-conditioning room was in that direction. It could have a door leading to the outside for maintenance, so she rushed to the door leading into it and tried the handle. It didn't budge. The corridor continued to a tee junction. She hobbled to the junction, but she knew that every second she was in the corridor they could discover and re-capture her. She fretted for a solution as she looked around the corner in both directions. A short corridor led to another junction in one direction and a longer one led to a set of doors at the end in the other, either to another room or outside. She hoped the latter as she went to them. To her surprise, the doors opened, and she felt the breeze of the outside air. She smiled, her first smile in some time.

She needed an AGrav to complete her escape, but there wasn't one in sight. The noise of explosions reverberated in the distance. *Where am I?* The building extended for one-hundred meters in both directions, so she randomly selected a way and went to the corner. She looked around the corner and saw nothing to help her complete her escape. It looked like the back of the building. Retracing her steps, she went the other way and looked around that corner and smiled. An AGrav sat on the ground fifty meters away. She just had to get there unnoticed and get it started. No one was in sight, so she crept around the corner and headed to the AGrav, reaching it unhindered. She got in and looked at the flight controls. A biometric lock prevented theft. Unperturbed, she recalled her training on AGravs and punched in a code. The controls came to life but still requested authority. She punched in another code, and she had access. Placing the controls in manual, she prepared to fly off when she heard shouts from outside with her two captor minions running out the building toward her. She powered the controls and lifted off, moving the AGrav in any direction that led away from the building and toward the possibility of rescue.

Everything went smoothly for thirty minutes, after which two fighter craft appeared. They flew past her. They confused Chooli.

Why would fighters be flying around the place? Was someone attacking the planet? One fighter disappeared into the distance, but the other looped around and came up behind her. The AGrav shuddered moments later from laser fire. It wobbled and lost power. Chooli could only look on in despair as the AGrav plunged to the ground.

41

A lex was beside himself, trying to work out what to do. He finally decided he would ask Richelieu to give him access to Epernay so he could go search for Chooli. At least he would be able to do something useful to move the investigation forward and rescue Chooli. She must be somewhere there if Lamar's information was correct. He called Lamar and told him to arrange for an AGrav to take them to Aquitaine.

Lamar rolled up at the hotel mid-morning in the required AGrav. Alex jumped in and they were on their way. "Hope you know what you're doing," Lamar said.

"Not really. But if I can get safe passage into Epernay, maybe I can find the trail leading to Chooli again."

"Richelieu mightn't want to see you. He would be busy at present."

"He'll see me. I just hope we don't bump into that crazy mother of his."

Lamar sniggered. "Yeah, I heard she can be weird sometimes. Never met her myself."

"She doesn't like Cetusians much. Went off her head when she saw Chooli last time."

They arrived at the estate late in the afternoon. Alex had to argue for some time, but Richelieu finally agreed to see him, once Alex wore him down with persistence. The AGrav coasted up to the entry and landed, letting Alex and Lamar out. A waiting page escorted them both into the chateau and through to a study, leaving them to wait for the duke to arrive. It was another room to the one Alex was in last time, more claustrophobic and uninviting. The decor made one want to leave, and it had no windows. Poor lighting and little decoration on the walls completed the effect. They remained standing, as there was nowhere to sit, anyway.

"One gets the impression the duke doesn't really want us here," Alex said, more to himself than to Lamar. Lamar gave Alex a glancing look without comment.

Richelieu came into the room after thirty minutes. "Sorry to keep you waiting," he said unconvincingly.

"I'm sure you have many pressing matters," Alex replied.

"What can I do for you then?"

"Someone's kidnapped my colleague. We believe they have taken her to Epernay, which is a little difficult for us to go to at present because of the war you have engaged in."

Richelieu frowned at the mention of Chooli's kidnapping. "That is not good. How did that happen?"

"We crashed on the way back from here last time and someone took her."

He gasped. "How would they have known you came here?"

"You tell me. Anyway, I was wondering if you could get us safe passage into Epernay to continue our search?"

Richelieu paced the room, glancing at Alex occasionally with a frown of disapproval. "I could issue you with a safe conduct," he finally said. "It will emit a friendly signal to my people so they don't shoot you down. Is that sufficient?"

"That should give me what I want."

"Wait here while I arrange for one." Richelieu left, leaving Alex and Lamar alone in the room again.

The door opened five minutes later, but Camille walked in

instead of Richelieu, her face suffused with anger. "What are you doing back here? Get out of here! Richelieu has enough work leading this difference of opinion in Champagne."

"Good afternoon to you too, Dame Camille," Alex said with a dutiful smile. "Do you always resolve a difference of opinion with warfare?"

"That is none of your concern." Camille shuffled across the room toward Alex.

Alex was much taller than Camille, but she still managed to emit a menacing presence. Her attitude came across as haughty and arrogant, and whoever she addressed had better acknowledge it. It was the same confrontational stance as the first time they met. Unfortunately, her portrait couldn't deflect the icy façade she presented this time. Alex decided stoking the fire might be interesting. "Someone ambushed us the last time I saw you. You had nothing to do with that, did you?"

Camille's eyes burned him like lasers. "Why would I want to do something like that?"

"Good question, would you want to do something like that?"

Warming to the verbal duel Alex had started, Camille replied, "Where is that Cetusian tart who was here last time?"

Alex gritted his teeth and glared at her. He knew she was more than a worthy opponent, and he had asked for such a reply. "You still haven't answered my question."

"And I will not answer it either. The likes of you have no right asking such a ridiculous question. You haven't answered mine."

"I don't know where she is. They kidnapped her right after we left you. Is that a coincidence?"

Glancing at Alex, Camille looked away again, not answering for a fraction longer than was necessary. "Must be. What does it matter, anyway? She's just a Cetusian. You can do better than that for yourself."

"I didn't say there was anything between us."

"Ha, a blind Franconian batwing can see there is."

"That's beside the point," Alex said, blushing slightly.

"You're here looking for her when we have more important things to think about, like wrapping up your investigation. Stop making a nuisance of yourself and let my son get back to his work. And you," Camille said as she pointed to Lamar, "you should have more sense than to bring him here."

Lamar smiled but said nothing.

"I resent you saying Chooli is unimportant. She's a detective in the GIA."

"She's your tart. Your bit of exotic excitement. Get a proper woman."

Alex opened his mouth, but nothing came out. He wanted to shout the riot act at her, but he knew that was exactly what she wanted so she could throw him out. Instead, he said with all the calmness he could muster, "That was uncalled for."

"It's the truth. You can't face the truth. That's your problem."

"Listen," Alex shouted, heaving with anger. "You will refrain from talking to a GIA agent like that or I will arrest you."

Lamar looked at him in alarm.

"Like to see you try," Camille said calmly, a satisfied smile crossing her face.

Richelieu came rushing into the room, "What is going on?"

Camille looked smug. "Just telling this *GIA agent* the facts of life."

"Oh Mother, I wish you wouldn't meddle in things." He looked at Alex, who was calming down.

Alex knew he had overstepped by losing his temper, but he couldn't let her talk about Chooli like she didn't matter and meant nothing. "I am sorry. I shouldn't have gotten angry."

Richelieu gritted his teeth and glared at Camille. "My mother has a flare for upsetting people, sometimes just for sport, but I am wondering if there is something more to it than that in this case. Mother?"

"Don't be ridiculous. I just don't like the way he's taking up so much of your time when you have other things to worry about."

"Yes, well, I am rather busy." Richelieu looked at Alex. "Here is your chip. I hope you find her."

"Thank you. I think we'll be off. That should make your mother happy." Alex glared at Camille before he left the room with Lamar in his wake.

42

C hooli woke coughing and spluttering from the wreckage of the AGrav. Recalling what had happened, it amazed her she had survived. She lay still, wondering if the crash had injured her. Her broken leg hurt, but she couldn't feel any other pain. Considering she could feel all her extremities, she felt lucky, again. *It must be my lucky day.* She rose to a sitting position inside the smoldering craft. Smoke started filling the enclosure, so she opened the hatch.

Her eyes met a city in turmoil, with smoking buildings and wrecked AGravs like hers littering the pedestrian corridors. She coughed and realized the pungent smoke inside was increasing. Her eyes watered from it. A fire started behind her. She needed to get out before the vehicle blew up. Checking herself, she saw some cuts but nothing that suggested any serious injuries, so she got to her feet and hobbled out, moving over to the nearest building. She had just rounded the corner when the AGrav exploded, shaking the ground under her. Debris flew past the edge of the building. She leaned against the wall and cried, as much in relief as despair. She didn't know where she was or why she seemed to be in the middle of a war, but she was alive, and while she was alive, there was hope of her returning to Alex's arms again.

Chooli couldn't tell how long she stood there, but she finally realized she had to work out what to do. She heard shouting nearby but wasn't sure whether to go toward it or away. It seemed to come from around the corner a hundred meters away, so she went to investigate what it was before deciding. Starting off in that direction, the sound of maser shots came to her above the shouting, followed by yells of pain. Chooli froze. Did she really want to find out what was happening around the corner? She could do with no further excitement for one day. Heaving a sigh, she had to find out, so she continued to the corner. She looked around and saw people exchanging gunfire in the distance.

"Who are you?" Chooli heard from behind her.

She froze, but then slowly turned to face her surprise visitor. A tall brawny Cetusian man stood behind her with a maser pointed at her. She gulped. "Detective Chooli Richards from the GIA."

"What's someone from the GIA doing around here? Don't you know there's a war going on? Or are you a spy?"

She shook her head. "I'm not a spy. Someone kidnapped me and took me to someplace nearby. I escaped, but a fighter shot me down."

The man looked at her, skeptical of her story. He then looked her up and down and frowned, looking at her leg. "You're injured."

Chooli leaned against the wall and sighed, then smiled a wry smile. "It's the second time they have shot me down. I don't know when the first time was. It was when they kidnapped me. I broke my leg in the crash."

"Maybe you should stay away from AGravs," the man said as he lowered the maser.

She sniggered. "Yeah, maybe."

He walked to the corner and looked around it and then back at Chooli. "Anyway, we can't stay here. The fighting's getting closer. I would tell you you're on your own, but you're from the GIA. I respect them. I take it you can walk?"

Chooli nodded. "Slowly."

"Well, follow me then. I'll take you someplace safe." The man started walking away from the corner but kept close to the building wall, looking behind him, past Chooli, once in a while.

They passed two blocks of buildings and the man slowed to give Chooli a rest from the quicker pace he had been forcing on her. She leaned against the wall, sweating from exertion and pain.

"Sorry about that," he said. "I had to get us away from the fighting before we got caught up in it. I'm Gaagii."

"I'm pleased to meet you, Gaagii. Wasn't sure what I would do otherwise. Where are we?"

"You don't know? Where are you from?"

"Caerus."

Gaagii looked at Chooli like she was a god. "You're from Caerus? Our birthplace?"

Chooli looked at him. "Yeah. So, where are we now?"

"You don't know? We're in Epernay, the capital of Champagne." He looked around. "We should keep walking. I won't walk as fast."

Chooli nodded. "Where are we going?"

"Somewhere safe."

They continued walking through the walkways of Epernay, ducking under cover when the occasional AGrav passed overhead. Chooli winced in pain several times but she continued on, despite Gaagii wanting to stop to let her rest. They continued for another thirty minutes until they came to a building damaged by cannon fire.

Chooli raised her brow. "We're going in there?"

"Yeah. It's not as damaged as it looks, and we're going down."

Chooli shrugged. "Lead the way."

Gaagii opened the door and ushered Chooli through. They continued down a corridor until they came to a door. Gaagii knocked, and a scanner appeared and checked his retinas before Chooli heard a click and the door opened. A set of steps projected down into darkness.

"You OK to go down the steps?"

"I'll manage."

They went down two flights, Chooli taking her time, until they came to a basement level. Gaagii then led her through a maze of corridors until they came to another door. He went through the same procedure as the first and they entered a vast room with a multitude of people in it, everyone busy doing something, but Chooli couldn't tell what. Gaagii led her around the bustle and to an area set aside as a hospital. He talked to a nurse, and she went off.

Minutes later, a medico came over to them. "What are you doing bringing an outsider in here?" he asked Gaagii.

"She's injured and needs help."

"She could be a spy."

"She's not a spy. She's GIA."

The medico looked at her suspiciously. "What are you doing here?"

Knowing she needed to explain herself, Chooli said, "The assassin who murdered the Duke and Duchess of Lorraine kidnapped me. They brought me here, and I escaped. A fighter shot down the AGrav I escaped in and Gaagii found me." Chooli could tell she hadn't convinced him yet.

The medico examined her. "What's that mark on your temple?"

"I didn't know there was a mark. I haven't seen myself in a mirror recently. My guess is an electrode made it when they tortured me with electroshock treatment."

The man's eyes widened. "Why would they do that?"

"They wanted to know why we went to see the Duke of Aquitaine when we questioned him about the murders."

"Who's we?"

"The chief detective and me. We work for the GIA. We are here to confirm the guilt of the alleged murderer."

"That trumped-up charge. Are you here to pacify the dissidents then?"

Chooli got angry at the implication. "No! The person is innocent. I'm here because people don't like what we are finding out."

The man looked away, chastised by her reaction. He looked back and pondered for a moment. "Come with me. Let's look at your leg." He led her to an examination bed. "Sit on there."

Chooli hobbled over and sat on the bed.

"Lie down." She turned and lay on the bed. The medico examined the burn on her temple, then looked at her leg. He took the splint off and cut the material of her pants leg to see her leg properly. She felt uncomfortable, but knew he had to do it. He looked at her broken bone and shook his head. "When did this happen?"

"Don't know exactly. Three, four days ago."

He stood back. "Where's the matching mark to that?" He pointed to her burn mark.

"On my other thigh."

"Gunna have to remove your trousers then. Sorry, but we'll give you some fresh ones." He cut her pants away and flinched as he saw the burn on her leg. "How much current did they put through you?" Placing his fingers on the burn to probe at it, he looked at the injury from a few angles. The pain made Chooli gasp, but she gritted her teeth. He looked at her again. "You're stronger than you look. The burns will heal with a bit of treatment. I'm worried about that bone, though. It's been through a lot without being looked at, and we're not set up to treat it properly here."

"Just patch it up and I'll get it looked at properly when I get back to Nouveau Paris."

The man shook his head. "You're not going anywhere at the moment, not with all those fighters around. You're lucky you made it out alive this time."

"But I have to get back to Alex. Can I at least let him know I'm alive?"

He shook his head. "They'll know where the transmission came from."

Chooli grunted in frustration. "Patch me up then. I'm not lying here all day."

The medico put some cream and bandages on her burns and a

medi-boot around her leg. He went away and came back a few minutes later with another pair of pants. "These should fit. You might need to cut them to fit over the boot."

Chooli pulled the pants on but needed him to cut the bottom part for the broken leg to fit. She rose and gingerly stood. Seeing Gaagii standing a little way off, she attempted to walk to him. Pressure on her leg with the boot on felt strange, but it was better than what she had and she quickly got used to it, walking almost normally by the time she got to him. "I need to contact my boss."

Gaagii looked at her. "You can't do that from here. We've got enough problems without drawing the attackers here like wasps."

She pouted in frustration and looked for somewhere to rest. Seeing a seat nearby, she hobbled over to it and sat. Gaagii followed her and pulled another seat over, sitting too. "So all this fighting ... is this because of Champagne not having an heir and the Duke of Aquitaine wanting to take it over?" she asked him.

"Yes, our duke died without leaving an heir, so the Constitution for the planet says one of the related duchies needs to rule it in proxy. But we want to rule ourselves. The duke was arranging it before he died but didn't finish the process. So the Duke of Aquitaine thinks he can rightfully take us over. We don't want that. The matter is made worse by the fact that the population here is mainly Cetusian, and they think we don't have any rights."

Just then an explosion resounded through the basement, inter-rupting Gaagii. Maser fire, smoke and shouting billowed through in its wake. They both looked in that direction and alarm rose inside of her.

"Stay here," Gaagii said as he rushed off, pulling his maser from its holster.

Chooli stood and found a corner to hide in while the fighting continued, which lasted half an hour before silence filled the room again. A combat soldier suddenly appeared around the corner with a laser cannon strung around his shoulder, waving back and forth for something to shoot at. It slowed and leveled at her when the soldier saw her. "Move!" he barked. Having no choice, she hobbled in the direction he pointed and found herself in a corner of the basement with other rounded-up people, including Gaagii, a trickle of blood still creeping down his face, and showing a look of defeat. Others came after her and joined the prisoner group. The troops led them to a transport, and they flew away.

43

Richelieu came back to the chateau tired and worried. The takeover of Champagne was taking far too long. No sooner had his forces gained control of one area than another flared up, tying down his troops until they struggled forward and regained control again. There were too many damned Cetusians running around. They were desperate fighters, and that made them excellent fighters, throwing themselves into battle without fear of death. They seemed well armed too. He wondered where they were getting all the equipment from. The solution would be easy if he didn't want to minimize casualties. The political fallout would be hard to manage with a large death rate, especially civilian casualties. He wondered what else he could try. His generals had run out of sensible ideas, and he dared not ask his mother for advice. Her ideas would be worse than those of the generals.

Trudging into his study, he poured himself a whisky with ice and stood by the window looking out over the estate. The serenity of the grounds calmed him, but his troubled thoughts lingered as he sipped the fiery liquid. The door opened behind him and he froze. Only one person would come in without knocking, and he didn't particularly want to see that person now.

"I thought I heard you come in."

"Hello, Mother." Richelieu turned and walked over to her, giving her a dutiful peck on the cheek as usual.

"Have you wrapped things up with this takeover yet? What's taking so long?"

"No, we aren't much further than we were two days ago. They're putting up too much resistance. I'm wondering if it's all worth it."

"What do you mean, worth it? You can't pull out now. Think of the embarrassment. We'd be the laughingstock of the planet."

"We?"

"What, do you think the vultures will stop at laughing at you? Not on your life, I know plenty who would grab any chance to belittle me in front of the nobility. No, you can't pull out. You need to intensify your attack."

Richelieu sighed. "I'm already stretched to the limits. We're chewing away at our capital reserves so fast we'll be begging on the streets soon."

"I'm wondering about you now. You've been showing promise lately, but you're turning out just like your father. Weak, indecisive."

"That's enough, Mother. I am using every tactic in our strategic arsenal, but they always seem to have a counter-attack. Those damned Cetusians are bloody skillful fighters."

"Stop swearing. You know not to swear."

"Stop mothering me." Richelieu glared at his mother before turning back to the window.

"Well, finish it, just finish it. I'll not have people laughing at us like they did your father. I saw them. Sniggering behind our backs."

"You're being paranoid. No one's sniggering at you."

"I expect to see some progress, and soon." Camille walked out.

Richelieu smiled half-heartedly. "Yes, Mother, whatever you say." There were days he wanted to strangle her and her obsessions about status. Shaking himself, Richelieu brought himself back to the harsh reality of the present. He finished his drink and weighed his options for increasing his firepower as he left to prepare for dinner.

44

The transport landed in another part of Epernay and Chooli and the other prisoners obeyed the orders of their guards and walked off. She found herself in a makeshift prison cell with several other Cetusian women ten minutes later. Darkness fell, and she found a quiet place to lie down and sleep, waking the next morning still tired, grumpy and aching. Sitting on a bench, she moped about her misfortune in silence.

During the day, several of the women were led off without explanation, returning half an hour later bruised and whimpering. Chooli gritted her teeth and glared at the guards in disgust, challenging them.

Evening fell across the city and a guard came to her cell. "You," he said, pointing to her. "Come with me."

The bravado Chooli had shown before quickly evaporated as she stood and obeyed. She followed him through the complex and saw cell after cell filled with Cetusians, some groaning in pain from their injuries. She saw several that didn't move at all, eyes unblinking in death. She gritted her teeth in silent rage. *What were these barbarians doing?* Her fear left her and she knew she had to do something for these people. The guard finally pulled her up outside a door. He opened it and pushed her through. She found herself in an interrogation room with a table and a chair on either side of the table. The door closed with a thud and she sat on a chair, waiting.

The door opened again ten minutes later, a high-ranking officer walked through and sat in the other chair. He stared at her for a long time, Chooli remaining silent, choosing to let him speak first. "Who is your commander?" he finally asked.

"My name is Detective Chooli Richards and I work for the GIA. I would appreciate it if you released me immediately."

The man laughed. "What business does the GIA have with rebel troops? No, you are one of them. Who is your commanding officer?"

"I'm telling you the truth. I came here with my Senior Detective to review a murder conviction."

"Where is this Senior Detective of yours then?"

"I don't know. Our AGrav crashed, and someone kidnapped me and brought me to Epernay." Chooli saw immediately that he didn't believe her unlikely story, but she couldn't help that.

"What's his name?"

"Chief Inspector Detective Alex Warner."

"Chief Inspector?" The man raised an eyebrow, feigning it impressed him.

"Yes. I suggest you release me and return me to Nouveau Paris if you don't want the Confederation coming for you."

"You're in no position to make threats."

But, despite his stance, Chooli could tell that the news about her position had unnerved him. "Wait here." He rose and left.

Chooli saw guards at the door as it closed. She thought about her situation while she waited. Unlike the other women, it seemed she was not going to be physically tortured or molested. *Why was that? Did the others come to this room, or have these people got a different treatment in store for me?* Her questions troubled her. She wished she could get a communication to Alex somehow, even if it was only to let him know she was alive. That would not happen while they held her captive. Her leg ached again, but not as badly as before. *The boot must be doing some good*, she thought.

The door opened, and the officer walked back in. He studied her as he paced the room. He finally stopped behind the chair he had used and placed both hands on top of the backrest. "You are very fortunate," he said with a sneer. "I've been told to keep you unharmed for the time being, instead of giving you the treatment the others received, filthy scum that you lot are. I haven't finished with you, though."

"I want to make a call to Detective Warner."

"There will be no calls." He stared at her, sending a shiver through her. "Guard." A guard came into the room. "Take her to a high-security cell."

The guard grabbed Chooli roughly and started leading her off. She turned her head just before she left the room. "I'm that dangerous, am I?" She saw the officer grit his teeth as he disappeared from her sight. The guard led her through to another area of the complex. It too had large cells full of Cetusians. She wondered why they had just rounded up Cetusians. People stared out at her as she passed, looking despondent with no hope — men, women and children, all crowded in the same compact space. Their treatment angered her. She wondered what they had done to deserve such savagery, other than being born Cetusian.

A face peered out at her as she passed one cell, a face that looked familiar. She couldn't place it for a second and then memory came back, the woman from the strip club. *What was her name? Sarina? Sabrina? No, Satinka. What is she doing here?* Chooli started saying something, but the guard pushed her past the cell before she could. A large brute of a man stood behind Satinka.

Chooli's march ended soon after. She reached a cell large enough for maybe three or four prisoners, but it sat empty. The guard shut down the force-field and shoved her in. The steady hum of the active force-field started again before she turned around to give the guard a resentful look. He didn't even give her a second glance.

The room was clean and had the basics for hygiene, which Chooli appreciated. Definitely an improvement on where she had been. She wondered what had improved her fortune. The officer didn't really seem scared that she worked for the GIA. They could easily cover up her death, she realized. Going over to the one chair in the room, she sat and thought about what she could do. The place wouldn't be as easy to escape from as the last one, even if she got the opportunity, which she doubted she would get. She felt more defeated now than ever. Time wore on and she suddenly felt tired, her head nodding as she dozed in the chair. A bed stood next to the wall, but she didn't have the energy to go over to it yet.

A person who looked like a Cetusian orderly came, accompanied by a guard, and gave her some food. He looked at her with fear as he put the tray on the table in the cell. There seemed to be a silent communication between them, though, as if they found strength in each other despite the circumstances they were in. He left. The food looked and tasted edible, and she wondered as she ate her meal if the others got the same. She went to the bed after that and lay down, sleep finding her quickly.

Some noise woke her in the middle of the night, and she lay on the bed listening. Cetusians were being pushed and shoved past her cell, their body language showing defeat and a look of despair in their eyes in the dim light. They quickly passed and silence came again until one guard started talking. "What are we going to do with all of them?" he asked.

"I heard we're gonna get rid of them," another replied.

"What do ya mean?"

"Get rid of them. Exterminate them like bugs."

"You're making that up. I know they're just Cetusians, but execute them all? Even the children?"

"Just telling you what I heard."

"From whom?"

"The boss himself. I was in with him earlier delivering a message and he was on the comm with someone. He was talking about how to get rid of so many. He seemed scared. Didn't want others overhearing him. He shooed me away when he saw me linger, but I stopped outside the door and listened in. He was talking about constructing furnaces or something."

"Not sure I like that. It doesn't sound right. Wonder who he was talking to?"

"Don't know. I had to walk off before someone saw me. Anyway, that's what I heard." The guards went silent again.

Chooli's heart thumped in horror. What monster would do that? She didn't know how, but she had to get out and warn someone.

45

Dawn broke as Chooli stirred from her sleep. She rose and washed the sleep from her eyes, drinking some water as she did. With the sun not fully risen, the cell and surrounding area still had the glare of artificial lighting. The conversation she had heard the night before came back to her, and she knew she had to escape and tell someone of the evil plans being devised. She wondered how she could overpower the guards and how she could get out of the complex if she did. Going back to her bed, a sprout of a plan came to her as she sat on it with her legs drawn up and her arms embracing her knees. Would she get an opportunity? She needed to be ready if she did.

The light level increased, and activity started for the day. The orderly came along with a meal. Chooli watched closely as the guards opened the force-field to let the orderly in. The two that guarded her seemed lax in their tentativeness, not even bothering to train a weapon on her while the field was down and casually talking and laughing with each other. The orderly placed the food on the table and left, and the force-field came on moments later. Chooli sprang from the bed and rushed to the edge of the field, looking where the guards stood and who else occupied the corridor. The two guards were the only people in sight. She went to the table and ate the food, thinking. They gave her a metal knife and fork, which she thought unwise. Her idea for escape bloomed into an actual possibility as she washed the utensils and hid them.

The orderly came back an hour later and looked at her when he noticed the missing utensils. She placed a finger to her lips, and he smiled as he picked up the tray and left. She now knew she could trust him not to interfere with what she intended to do. Getting the knife out, she looked at the edge and end. The end was blunt, so she wedged it between the metal framing of her bed and bent it from side to side until the end broke off, giving her a sharpened point for a weapon. She hid it until the opportunity presented itself.

Sitting in the chair, she used the time to think about her life and the sudden twist it had taken with her first case. No one would have believed her if she told them about the predicament she found herself in. Frowning, she wondered if she would get the chance to tell anyone. Deciding to think positively, she waited.

The hours wore on and she heard the orderly come down the corridor again. This was it. She retrieved the knife from its hiding spot, rushed to the edge of the force-field ready for it to go off, the knife ready in her hand. She breathed in and let the air out slowly to calm her nerves. She was obviously a prize captive, given the cell she found herself in, but would the guards accidentally shoot her?

The field came down and Chooli spun through the entry, surprising the guards. The knife flashed and dug into the closest guard's throat, making him drop his laser rifle and grab his throat before collapsing, She had aimed well and pierced one of the carotid arteries; blood gushed over the floor. The other guard jumped, as did the orderly. Chooli grabbed the rifle of the first man as she saw the guard bringing his rifle up to aim at her. He was too slow, and she pulled her trigger, putting a hole in his chest. She did the same to the other guard to put him out of his misery. The orderly stood agape in shock, frozen to the ground.

"I won't harm you," Chooli said.

He nodded.

Chooli rummaged through the pockets of the guards; one had an ID chip in his, the other still held his from using it to open the cell field. She grabbed both and both rifles. Looking up and down the corridor, she felt sure security would notice quickly and others would be on their way. Her plan required quick action, so she dashed down the way she had come, finding the cells with the Cetusians trapped in them quickly. Mentally crossing her fingers, she swiped the lock for the force-field and it switched off, to the surprise of all the Cetusians inside.

"Quick, come out now. You must fight," Chooli said as she waved the people through.

Satinka and Bidziil approached her, and Chooli smiled.

"What's happening?" Satinka asked, recognizing Chooli.

"You must get out of here now and fight. They intend exterminating all of us. Maybe not me, but the rest of you Cetusians."

"What?" Satinka said in shock, gaping open-mouthed and frozen.

Chooli looked at Bidziil. "We don't have time. You need to organize these people to overpower the guards and break free of this place, otherwise you all die." Bidziil nodded.

"Here, take this." She gave one of the ID cards to Satinka. "Open as many cells as you can."

"Where are you going?"

"I have a different destiny. I have to get word to Alex."

"He's worried sick about you."

Chooli smiled. "Good to know I'm appreciated."

Bidziil laughed in relief as he turned back to shepherd the people out of the cells.

Chooli suddenly remembered her two rifles. "Here take this." She gave one to Bidziil. They heard shouts and rifle fire getting closer. "Let's go," she said as she led them further down the corridor, opening cells with Cetusians in as she went.

People streamed out. Satinka and Bidziil shouted to follow them. They heard gunfire and people shouting up ahead. Dead guards lay on the floor as they passed before long. Chooli's plan for the Cetusians was working, but she still needed to get to a communications room and she couldn't find any. She picked up a laser pistol lying on the floor. Sheer numbers overwhelmed the guards before long and the crowd came to the perimeter of the camp, killing and disarming guards as they went. Before long they had control of the camp and the heavy weaponry protecting it. She looked around for Satinka and saw her up ahead, but too many people separated them. Satinka turned and their eyes met. She nodded in appreciation, and Chooli knew it was time for her to chase her own destiny. She wove her way back to the buildings but didn't know where she should go.

Looking back, she wondered if she should follow the crowd instead and find a working comm. It wouldn't happen, she thought, as she suspected that they would have jammed all communications in the duchy except for those from the military. She needed to get to their communications room. Thinking about where she had gone when they interrogated her, she retraced the way and found the room. She kept walking and came to a corridor. She heard people shouting orders up ahead from a room she couldn't see into. Her hopes rose, feeling she had found what she was looking for.

Three soldiers came running out and down her way. She hid, but they were on her. They stopped in shock, not knowing what to do. Using the delay, Chooli raised the pistol and shot all three of them. She smiled bitterly. She was getting good at killing. Other heads looked out of the room as they realized something was wrong and Chooli shot at them too but missed. She stood looking at the door in a quandary what to do. It hid the activity in the room behind it from her position, and she couldn't get much closer without placing herself in a vulnerable position. There were at least two others in the room and she heard someone from within talking as if on a comm.

Feeling her only option involved a full-on sudden assault, Chooli braced herself and breathed in deep, focusing her eyes on the door. She started running and dropped to her knees just as she passed the door, shooting inside as she slid along the floor of the corridor. The scene went into slow motion. Three people stood in the room. One shot their laser rifle out the door, aiming at where he thought Chooli would be, realizing too late that he shot too high. Chooli shot back, dropping him to the floor. She got off two other shots before the door frame slid past, blocking her view again. Turning as she slid to a stop, she replayed the scene. Definitely one had a fatal hole in him, but she wasn't sure about the other one. Silence came from the room, which seemed promising. Standing, she crept back and glanced past the frame. She didn't see any movement, so she had a better look. Two soldiers lay on the floor and a third sat slumped in the chair behind a desk console, his back facing her. Keeping her pistol trained on his back, Chooli crept into the room, looking both ways to check for anyone else. She lowered her pistol. A laser hole penetrated the person's head. It would have killed him instantly.

Chooli relaxed and looked around. A comm stood on the console desk. Screens littered the front of the desk, providing views of the prison. Cetusians swelled throughout as they looked for a means of escape to freedom. Satinka stood waving at people on one screen, directing activities and, to Chooli's surprise, the others seemed to obey her. They had several soldiers tied up being led to a prison cell they had occupied previously. She felt glad that the Cetusians had not executed the soldiers out of hand.

Returning to her reason for being in the room, Chooli pushed the person off the chair. He thumped to the floor, leaving the chair for her to sit on. Chooli sighed a deep breath as she relaxed in the chair. She closed her eyes as she leaned back on the backrest, exhausted, ... and her head filled with pain before she lost consciousness.

46

Satinka and Bidziil shouted at the others as they streamed out of the prison. Satinka told them all to fight for freedom. Some congregated around her, wanting to know what to do. She suddenly realized they saw her as a leader and froze. What could she do to lead them? She was just a stripper. Looking at Bidziil and seeing the same expectation from him, she looked around. Fighters flew across the sky. Fortunately, they weren't flying toward them yet, but she knew it wouldn't take long before they were directed to the prison. Four ground-mounted attack canons stood nearby, apparently deserted during the chaos of the escape. "The canons," she shouted. "I need people to take control of the canons." People still stared at her. "You, you, you and you," she said as she pointed at the closest people to her. "Can you shoot canons?" They nodded. "Go then, shoot down any fighters that come our way or any troops headed toward us." The four rushed off and she heard cannon fire mixed in with all the other noises soon afterwards.

Many of the people had rushed away, looking for safety, but a sizeable group remained. She recognized some from the underground bunker Gaagii had taken her to and many others who wore similar attire. They must be the resistance. *Where are their leaders?*

They seemed frozen, as if they were part of a hive with a destroyed hive mind. "I need a group to find their armory and hand out weapons to everyone." Several hands shot up. "Go." They came back half an hour later, well-armed and ready to lead the others back to get theirs.

Satinka looked up and saw an AGrav take off and move away from them. One gunner took a shot at it but missed, and then it was out of range. "We need to find the communications room," she told the others. "Is there anyone here able to comm the others and tell them what's happening?" Two people put their hands up. "Good. You others come with me. I want some in front and others protecting our backs." Twenty broke into two groups, five for the vanguard and the rest bringing up the rear as Satinka walked back into the prison looking for the communications room, Bidziil by her side, armed and apparently protecting her, and the other two right behind her.

The prison compound seemed eerie as Satinka entered its menacing corridors again, the corridors that had led to the cells trapping her and the others only an hour ago, until Chooli had rescued them. She was a brave woman and deserved recognition for her bravery, but where was she? Satinka shook her head to help her concentrate on the path ahead as they crept slowly through the compound. The vanguard finally stopped and motioned for them to stop at a corner. She didn't know why until one came back.

"We think we have the room in sight but there seems to have been a fight. Three soldiers are dead in the corridor. We will check the room. You stay here until we know it's clear."

Satinka nodded and watched the person go back. The five disappeared around the corner and Satinka waited, the tension building as time ticked by. The same person finally came back.

"It's safe."

Not realizing that she had been holding her breath, Satinka exhaled and moved around the corner and into the room. It looked like the communications room to her. Two other soldiers lay dead on the floor. Chooli had headed that way, but there was no sign of her. She motioned for the two comm operators to get to work. They grabbed the two chairs and started working the comm, adjusting the transmission frequency and signal direction. One was talking to someone before long. He looked around. "It's ready."

Satinka looked at him and then at the others. They all looked at her. "Why would they believe me? They've never heard of me," she muttered to Bidziil.

"From where I stand, you have more balls than the rest of us combined," Bidziil said.

Satinka let out a loud laugh. "Not sure if the analogy quite fits." She sobered and thought about what she should say to these people. She finally had a speech, she hoped. "Who's online?" she asked the operator.

"All the major resistance cells."

She gulped. "Nothing like a bit of pressure." Taking a large breath, she calmed herself and came to the comm. "Hello. This is Satinka. You don't know me, but Aquitaine forces captured me and took me to a prison camp together with many of your friends in Champagne. While we were there, we learned about a plan the Aquitaine military had devised to exterminate all Cetusians in Champagne. The brave person who uncovered the plot broke free from her cell and let the rest of us out. We do not know where she is, but we owe her our lives. Anyway, this fight has changed its aim. I believe that it started because you wanted to keep your freedom. Freedom is no longer an option for Cetusians. This is a battle for your lives. You must take up arms and fight, every one of you to the last, if you love your family. We must fight or die." Satinka took a calming breath and waited.

The comm came alive. "Fight, fight, fight ..." it seemed like a million chanted. Tears trickled down Satinka's cheeks. This wasn't what she came to Champagne for. Bidziil came over and hugged her. The others in the room were also chanting. The rallying call eventually faded.

"How do we coordinate this?" someone at the other end said.

Satinka didn't know what to say. "You have leaders in your groups, don't you?"

"Yes, but we need someone to coordinate our efforts so we don't interfere with each other. Someone who can see the overall picture."

Confused, Satinka looked around. She didn't understand why they didn't already have such a person. The purpose of the room suddenly hit her. Screens and monitors had information on all the Aquitaine troop and fighter movements. They had no time to remove or destroy the systems in the rush to escape. "We can do that from here. We have live information on what they are doing. Let's get to work." She looked at the others. "I need people analyzing these screens. I want to know who is going where and how many so we can tell our people where to defend and where they can attack."

Three moved forward and went to work.

"We need desks and chairs," Bidziil said to someone outside. "Go find some and bring them here. You others stand guard."

People went into motion. Satinka smiled.

47

Chooli woke with a splitting headache and the sensation of movement. She realized she was in an AGrav and when she opened her eyes saw her wrists and legs restrained.

"We finally caught up with you," a dreaded but familiar voice said behind her.

"Where are we going?"

"Away from the war."

Rolling over onto her other side, she saw the emotionless face of the assassin, with its undercurrent of menace and ruthlessness. He sat on a seat close by and was the only other person in the AGrav cabin. One leg was slung over the armrest of his chair.

"Can I sit in a seat?"

"If you want."

Chooli silently chastised herself as she struggled up into a nearby seat. She should have heard him come in but hadn't and she hadn't got any message to Alex. *It isn't fair. When will I get a break?* Glancing over at the assassin, she saw him still looking at her, making her nervous. "What are you going to do with me?" she asked as she steeled herself to look back at him.

"That's up to the person instructing me, but in the meantime I might have some fun with you when we get to where we're going." He let a sinister smile linger.

"Why?"

"Why?"

"Why do you do this?"

"It pays well and I get fringe benefits during my playtime." A shiver went down Chooli's back. "You're taking your predicament rather calmly. I'm impressed. Most of my captives either descend into a sniveling mess or spend most of their time fainting."

"I've had time to get used to you."

"You will beg me to kill you by the time I'm finished with you."

The AGrav had windows. Sick of the conversation, Chooli turned her head and looked out. The ocean lay below and it was still daylight, so she couldn't have been unconscious for long. Islands blemished the surface of the water in the distance. "Where are we?" she asked, turning her head back to the assassin.

He looked out the window. "I'm told we're over the Strait of Rousseau."

The name sounded familiar. She closed her eyes to think as she tried recalling a map of Franconia she had studied during her research of the planet. An image of the map came to her mind, and she recalled the Strait of Rousseau being between Champagne and Aquitaine. "We're going to Aquitaine then?" she asked as she opened her eyes again.

The assassin laughed. "Very good, I am impressed again."

"Why are we going to Aquitaine?"

"I don't know. I do what I'm told and ask no questions unless it affects me."

"Is your client there?"

The assassin smiled but didn't reply. The conversation died, as Chooli assumed she would if she couldn't figure out another way of escape. She wondered what Alex was doing. *Is he even looking for me?* Yes, he would be. He wouldn't give up searching until he found her. She hoped he wasn't feeling guilty over her situation, as she knew how protective he was of the people under his command, how he felt them to be his responsibility. *Will I ever see him again?* Remembering when they first met, she smiled. Their mutual attraction to each other was uncanny. The quickening of her heart whenever she saw him made it ache now. Returning to her predicament, she stared at the assassin, wondering where his weaknesses lay. He wouldn't have many, not in his profession. If he did, he would have been dead by now. "Did you use assassin nano-bots?"

Raising his brow, Chooli saw him calculating how to answer her. "You continue to impress me. Maybe I should convince you to become my partner."

"I don't think so."

"No, nor do I, but you have a sharp mind. No wonder you're in the GIA at your age."

"Yeah well, it's looking like a brief career."

The assassin laughed. "What? Giving up already?"

Chooli didn't answer. She wouldn't give up hope until her last breath. It was the way her father had taught her. Never give up. She clenched her teeth as she looked out the window. Land approached fast, and they crossed the Aquitaine coastline a few minutes later as the sun dipped below the horizon, bringing the first signs of evening to the west. Getting as comfortable as she could with her hands behind her back, she closed her eyes to sleep if she could. Her head still throbbed from the concussion she received when the assassin knocked her out.

Pain spiked through her as she woke with a start. Her hip hurt and she felt herself being dragged by her wrists as the assassin maneuvered her out of the AGrav. She felt every bump. "Ow!"

"Get used to it."

Chooli bumped down the ramp and across the ground. She saw the stars overhead before entering a building that seemed to be a workshop. There were many small cubicles to hide behind for cover, but that didn't help her. Taking her to an alcove, the assassin tied her wrists to a post and looked at her. His eyes were black again as he stared at her in the semi-darkness. It was as if he had transformed into a monster. He kicked her hard in the ribs. She yelled in agony as she gasped for breath.

He laughed. "Welcome to pain," he said as he kicked her again.

Chooli realized he was a complete psychopath. She sensed that he felt no pain, neither his own nor in sympathy with others. He roughly lifted her by the wrists and hung her from a hook just off the ground, although she could just touch it with her toes.

He punched her, first in the ribs and then her cheeks and eyes. The punches were fast and sharp, hard enough to cause injury but not enough to make her pass out. She smelled her blood as a ring on his finger opened a gash over her brow. He stood back. "This is fun."

"Why are you doing this?" Chooli croaked, her cheeks bruising already.

"Does that aureola hurt if I punch it?" The assassin did just that.

Chooli screamed in pain as an ingrained agony she had never experienced before rocketed to her brain like an exploding asteroid.

"Guess that's a yes," he said as he delivered another punch.

Hanging limp, Chooli's head fell to her chest. She didn't know how to bear such pain. Her eyes, now closed from bruising, could see little out of the slits she still had. More stabs of pain registered as he hit her again on the cheeks and jaw. She just wanted it to end. Why couldn't she lose consciousness and die? Moments later, he granted her one of her wishes.

CHOOLI WOKE STIRRING SLOWLY as pain welcomed her from every part of her body.

She heard the assassin talking.

"She's here, safe and sound. I'm just having some fun with her to pass the time."

A talking noise came to her that was too soft to decipher.

"Don't worry. She'll still be good enough to bargain with. What's the difference with someone of your standing anyway? You'll soon have what you want," he said sarcastically. "I'm the one taking all the risks."

Some more mumbling.

"Yeah, well, just transfer the credits and don't make me wait too long. I might get bored and get carried away."

Everything went silent until Chooli heard the assassin walking. She tried to pretend she was still unconscious.

He prodded her. "You're awake then." He hit her on the aureola and she screamed. "Let's see. What else can I do?"

Chooli heard him walk away and come back a few minutes later. She looked up and tried to focus on him and what he had in his hand. She drew breath between her teeth. "No, don't. Please don't." Her arms were on fire from hanging on the post as she struggled to get away from him. Her wrists bled from the restraints.

A swish came to her ears and the front of her shirt came away, a trickle of blood welling from the slightest hint of a cut running down the center of her chest. "I need to tattoo you with my marks before we part."

Chooli looked at him — and saw a maniacal smile reflected back at her. Her assailant was insane. He rotated her so she faced the post and tied her to it at the hips and around the legs so she couldn't move. He ripped her shirt away soon after. The feel of flesh being cut lanced through her and she screamed again. She felt his breath on her as he came close. "Got to have something to remember me by," he whispered in her ear.

"Please stop."

"Stop? But I'm having fun. Aren't you having fun?" He continued cutting into her back and she felt blood flowing down. The cutting stopped fifteen minutes later. "Now that's a work of art. Want to see?" She heard him take a holograph. He brought his comm around and showed her the image.

She gasped and whimpered. He had put ink or soot in the cuts and a black-outlined image displayed on her back. It had two eyes, one on each shoulder blade, and the outline of the face of a monster she had never seen before. It looked satanic and oozed evil, like the blood still seeping from the wounds. The monstrosity went all the way down her back to her sacrum. She sobbed at the mutilation.

"Everyone will know who you bumped into. Hey, what's your boyfriend going to think? He'll wonder if your back is all I poked." The assassin broke out into a demonic laugh. "Now what else could I do to complete this side? Ah, I know."

Chooli dreaded what he had thought of as she waited, her nerves stretched to shreds. A lance of agony shot from her aureola, just above her left ear. She screamed as she arched her back, drool and spit flying from her mouth. Seconds later another came from the area of the right ear. Her back arched again. She couldn't understand how she wasn't passing out, as she gasped in air, trying to breathe.

"That gets a reaction. Never realized how sensitive that area was. I will definitely have to do that again. Just one more area to finish my masterpiece." He untied the restraints from her hips and legs and turned her again, returning the restraints as they were. She saw him step back to examine her. "Those breasts will make an impressive feature for my pièce de résistance."

Chooli struggled as she opened her eyes as wide as the bruising would let her. "Please don't, please don't."

He steadied his knife as he brought it closer to her chest but frowned and a flash of anger crossed his face. "Stop wriggling," he said as he slapped her across the face with the back of his hand.

She stopped, not to comply, but because the last of her strength had left her. The knife started its cutting. She whimpered but bore the pain as he carved his art into her chest. Sometime later, she couldn't tell how long, she heard him stand back.

"Perfect. Now it won't make any difference which way he looks at you, he will always see me in you. Want a look?"

She didn't answer. All her strength and will had left her. He took an image of her chest and showed her, anyway. Dragon scales covered her front from her breasts to her navel, again highlighted with the black substance he had rubbed into the cuts. She had no strength to respond or even sob.

A noise came from the front of the workshop.

48

Alex took off from Richelieu's estate and sped to Epernay. "What do we do when we get there?" he asked Lamar.

"We can go to the local police, if they still operate, and check the local security footage. See if we can spot the AGrav coming in from Nouveau Paris."

That seemed like an excellent plan. Alex nodded and the hope of finding Chooli returned to him. The frustration of losing her trail and the inability to enter Champagne safely had taken its toll on him, his despair of ever seeing her again mounting every moment. Having worked many kidnapping cases, he knew the likelihood of finding the victim alive diminished as time went by and too much time had gone by for his liking. Still, Chooli was smart and resourceful. He had to maintain hope that she still survived whatever ordeal her kidnappers were putting her through.

They crossed the coast of Champagne two hours later and received clearance to proceed in safety from the Aquitaine military command.

The streets of Epernay displayed the destruction of war. Collapsed buildings and burning shells of accommodation littered the suburbs as they progressed to the city center and the police head-quarters. Alex felt distressed that people were being killed because of ideals, but people would go to impressive lengths for their freedom and Richelieu was pushing them into no other alternative but to fight.

They arrived at the police station and went inside. A sergeant met them and led them to the archive room where they kept surveillance files. Retrieving the files for the day Chooli left Nouveau Paris, they started the painstaking process of reviewing them. They finally had success three hours later.

"There," Lamar said as he pointed to a vehicle crossing the coast of Champagne. "That's the same one that left Nouveau Paris."

A spark of hope came to Alex as he followed the craft into Eper-nay, landing on the outskirts of an industrial estate on the edge of the city.

"You want to keep looking at this or do you want to look at the estate?"

"Let's go look," Alex said. "We can always come back and continue if we need to."

"Let's go then."

They got back into the AGrav and headed for the warehouse, arriving an hour later just after midnight. The place looked deserted as the AGrav landed near the front entry doors. Collecting their arms, they crept to the access door. Lamar tried opening it, but it remained locked. Alex looked at the locking mechanism and it seemed simple enough. This time he had his trusty box with him. He pulled it out of his pocket and placed it over the lock, letting it analyze the mecha-nism. A slight click sounded and Alex tried the door again, opening it with ease. The interior was pitch black. Using a portable light to see, they both went inside. Alex searched for a power board so he could turn the lights on, finding it five minutes later. The place lit up with glaring light when he flicked the switch. "Hope the neighbors don't ring up to report a break-in," Alex said.

The place looked deserted and disused, but they saw signs of recent activity when they searched rooms further in. The remains of food wrappers and other waste lay on tables and the floor. One room caught Alex's attention. Its only furnishing was a sturdy metal chair. The room reeked of urine, and a sense of dread rose in Alex's gut. It had the hallmarks of a torture chamber. They moved on and looked in other rooms, coming to one where a bed stood on end near an air vent that had its cover ripped off. He scrutinized the room for any detail of who or what had been in it. He found nothing. He hoisted himself up using the bed as a ladder and looked inside the air duct. There was nothing there, and he started lowering himself again, but something caught his eye. A small patch of fabric clung to a sharp protrusion. Picking it up and inspecting it in a better light, his heart skipped a beat. "This is Chooli's. Chooli was in here."

"Really? Where did she go?"

"Through the air vent to escape, I'd say. Let's look around some more." They looked through the rest of the complex but found nothing else of interest. Alex wondered if Chooli had escaped successfully and where she would have gone if she had. How long ago had she left the place? "Looks like it's back to the station to look at some more footage."

Lamar sighed. "Looks that way."

Switching the lights off, they left the warehouse and headed back to the station and archive viewing room. Lamar went out and returned with some fast food and steaming hot coffee. The aroma instantly filled the room, distracting Alex from looking at the holo file. His stomach grumbled and his mouth salivated.

"Any luck?" Lamar asked.

Alex shook his head. "And there won't be before I get some food in me either." He gulped down the food and sipped the coffee afterwards as he returned to the viewing. After looking through a day and a half's footage, Alex finally saw something of interest. Someone came out of a back door of the building. He stopped the spooler and magnified the image. The image ended up being too grainy to see who it was, so Alex let the file run in slow motion. The person looked injured and limped toward the front of the warehouse. Alex magnified the image again, but not as much as before, and stopped. He continued frame by frame until the person looked directly at the camera. His heart stopped. It was Chooli. The image blurred too much to see any real details, but it was definitely her. Bruised and battered, but her. Zooming back out, he continued the file and saw her get in an AGrav and take off. He felt proud of her resourcefulness.

They found files showing the progress of the AGrav and followed it. Alex's hope left him ten minutes later when he saw her AGrav shot down by a fighter. He smashed his fist hard on the table. "Damn." The AGrav crashed but looked like it remained intact. Chooli crawled out several minutes later and hobbled away. She seemed to disappear after that. They couldn't find any file showing where she went. Alex shot up off the chair in frustration and walked to the wall, placing his forehead against it. He should have been there for her. Not only had he failed her, he had failed his own creed. He turned, still leaning on the wall. "Now what?"

"I suggest we get some sleep," Lamar said. "We'll have clearer heads tomorrow."

Alex sighed. "Where?"

"We might have to stay here. I doubt any hotels are open for business with what's going on."

Alex nodded. They left the room and found a quiet spot where Alex made himself as comfortable as he could, falling asleep soon after from total exhaustion. He woke with a start. Lamar was shaking him. The aroma of fresh coffee wafted into his nostrils. Looking around, Alex sat up and wiped the sleep from his eyes. "What time is it?"

"After eight. I didn't have the heart to wake you straightaway, so I got us some breakfast."

The food was welcome, and Alex devoured it. The coffee woke him completely, and he stood, stretching to get the kinks from his bones. "Any idea what we do now?"

Lamar shook his head. "I asked around but found nothing helpful. We could go check out where we saw her last. See if she left any clues."

"Let's do that."

They went to the AGrav crash site but found no further sign of where Chooli might have gone. Alex felt the stab of defeat. He had come to another dead end. *Where is she? Is she even still alive?* Maybe she had been injured in the crash and had died from her wounds; maybe she had been taken away and buried. He kicked through some rubble aimlessly as he heard Lamar's comm sound.

Lamar walked away to talk. He came back a few moments later with a frown. "That was Nouveau Paris HQ. The Aquitaine military contacted them yesterday to find out if Chooli really was a GIA agent."

All his attention refocused on Lamar, Alex asked, "Where is she? Is she all right? Can we go get her?" He knew he sounded hysterical but he didn't care.

"She's in a military compound just outside of the city. I've been told to go there."

"What are we waiting for then?"

"An alert just came through saying there's some kind of disturbance there."

"Well, let's go find out." Alex made to go to the AGrav but Lamar stood his ground. "Is there a problem?"

"It might be dangerous."

Alex scoffed. "You're a cop, aren't you? We have the passes to be here, anyway."

"You're assuming that the Aquitaine forces are still in control there."

"We won't know if we just stay here."

Lamar rubbed his neck. "I suppose you're right." He followed Alex, and they were airborne moments later.

Alex looked out as they approached the camp. A multitude of people milled around a large fenced complex and streamed outside of it. He frowned as he wondered what was happening. Lamar frowned, too. "What do you think?" Alex asked him.

"We had better be cautious." Lamar directed the AGrav to descend and slow down as they approached the camp.

People manned the large canons, and they fired them at passing fighters occasionally. He was grateful they seemed to leave them alone. One shot from a canon and there wouldn't be much left of their AGrav or them.

The AGrav landed just outside the gates and people instantly surrounded it. Some shouted and their voices penetrated the hull of the craft, making Alex nervous about opening the hatch. He braced himself with Lamar behind him and pressed the button. The volume increased as the door opened with angry faces confronting him. A pang of fear lanced through him, but he kept his resolve and held up his GIA identity chip, hoping someone in the crowd would recognize it and calm the others. Luck was on his side and a man looked closer, waving the others to desist once he realized who Alex was. The people in the immediate area calmed down, and the shouting changed to questions about why they were there. Since the person who recognized the chip seemed to have some authority, Alex asked him, "Are you in charge here?"

The man shook his head and pointed inside the compound.

"Can you take us to him?"

"Her."

"Her."

He nodded.

Alex and Lamar climbed out of the AGrav and followed the man as he led them into the camp, the milling people parting to let them through. People acting as guards stopped them several times, enquiring about their business and who they worked for. After many stops and much frustration in answering the same questions, Alex finally arrived at the communications center, apparently the office of whoever was in change. He rounded the door post and froze.

"What are you doing here?" Satinka asked when she turned and recognized him.

Finding his voice, Alex replied, "I could ask you the same thing."

"Sorry, I was just surprised to see you. You're looking for Chooli."

"Yes," Alex said, hope increasing as he expected Satinka to tell him she was nearby, but he saw Satinka frown. "What's happened to her?"

"I don't know," she said, walking closer to him. Someone said something to her, but she ignored him. "I really wish I could tell you. She's responsible for us being free. She said she had another destiny and ran off. That's the last I saw of her, although I think she was in here before we took over. Several dead soldiers lay on the floor when we arrived. She was in no mood for messing around."

Alex's shoulders slumped, and he leaned on the doorframe. He seemed to be in the habit of just missing her. The agony in his heart increased, and he shook his head.

Satinka walked over and rubbed his shoulder. "I'm sure she's all right, wherever she is." She gave him a half-believing smile.

"What're you doing here, anyway?"

"Apparently, I've become a resistance leader here," she said with a wry smile. "I'm trying to coordinate their counter attack on Aquitaine. That's another thing she did. Somehow she found out that Aquitaine doesn't want to just take over Champagne. It wants to get rid of all the Cetusians here too."

"What? That's a war crime. The Confederation would remove the system from the alliance for that."

"Only if they found out. Anyway, that's our problem. I can't help you with yours." The person talked behind her with more persistence and Satinka turned, annoyed. She turned back, "Looks like I have to get back to the problems here."

"Yeah, thanks for letting me know."

Satinka returned to the pestering person and her own activities.

Turning to Lamar, Alex asked, "Now what?"

He shrugged his shoulders. "Since they haven't found her, maybe someone who escaped took her with them. We could see whether any AGravs left here during the uprising."

"That's good." Alex turned to Satinka. "See you round." She waved her hand behind her as she concentrated on her own activity.

ALEX AND LAMAR hurried to the AGrav and took off, heading for the surveillance section of the police headquarters in Epernay, arriving a half hour later. They rushed inside and pulled out the archive footage for the Aquitaine compound, watching it from the beginning of the day. Most of the footage gave them nothing till activity increased when the prisoners started escaping. The number of people rounded up astounded Alex. He started giving up hope when they saw an AGrav take off, heading toward Aquitaine. They watched the rest of the footage anyway, but nothing else of interest came up. Going back to the AGrav, they followed it until it crossed the coast of Champagne and disappeared off the Champagne surveillance system.

"What do you think?" Alex asked.

"It seems headed for Aquitaine. We had better go there and see if we can pick it up coming in."

"Right. Let's go." Hope returned to Alex as they left. He tempered it after his many previous disappointments. All he wanted was to see Chooli again, see that she was safe and alive. As he sat back in his seat, he wondered why they had wanted to pick her up from the compound, if they were just going to remove her again. Stranger yet, she had escaped and let the others out, according to Satinka. How had they recaptured her? He looked across to Lamar, wondering whether to broach his concern with him, but decided against it. Something in his gut didn't sit right, something he couldn't put his finger on. The AGrav raced across the ocean and then the land as he went through the events of the preceding few days.

After a while, the AGrav descended. Alex looked out and saw a group of buildings with nothing but countryside around them. "Why are we stopping here?" Alex asked as he frowned, confused.

"I had a tip-off before. They said to check this out." Lamar avoided Alex's eyes.

"What sort of tip-off? Is Chooli here?"

"Don't know. They just said to check it out."

The AGrav settled on the ground in front of a building next to another AGrav. Alex felt nervous as he glanced at Lamar and felt for both his weapons. The door opened, and they got out. They walked toward the nearest building, Lamar pointing the way but staying slightly behind, making Alex wonder what was going on even more. It just didn't seem right. *How did Lamar know to go here? Who called him?* Alex opened the door and stepped inside.

49

"I thank you Lamar for being so efficient," a disembodied voice said from the back of the building and behind a partition.

Alex spun around to look at Lamar, but when he did, he saw a maser trained on him. His eyes widened in surprise and then it all fell into place. "What are you doing? Who is that? What is he talking about?"

"No hard feelings," Lamar said. "Just doing my job."

"What do you mean? You're a police officer. Where does this fit into your job description?"

"As I said when we first met. This shit happens all the time. I decided I can get more money doing jobs on the side."

Alex's mind struggled to comprehend what was going on.

"It was you, wasn't it? It was you who planted the knife in Yiska's apartment. You caused the AGrav's crash, making it possible to kidnap Chooli. It's you who's been spying on me and undermining Xavier."

"Well, you were getting too close to the truth," Lamar responded in a reasonable tone. "Something had to be done to deflect you."

"Why wasn't I kidnapped then? Why Chooli?"

"Look, I don't make the decisions. I guess because she's just a

Cetusian, fewer people to care what happens to her. Might have been more fuss if you disappeared. Trouble is, you wouldn't give up, would you? I tried to warn you. You've only got yourself to blame that it's come to this."

"I'm leaving," Alex said in disgust, forgetting for a moment about the disembodied voice.

"I don't think so." Lamar jabbed him with the maser. "There's someone who wants to meet you."

Alex stumbled forward. "Who?" He was shoved toward the back of the building. It looked like some kind of workshop. He rounded the partition and stopped. "You."

The assassin stood in front of Alex with a cheesy grin on his face. "We finally meet. I compliment you on your tenacity and acumen. You've got it all figured out, haven't you?"

Alex drew in a sharp breath. "The Reaper, I presume?"

"I'm impressed — you GIA agents really are quite intelligent," he mocked.

"Why am I here? What do you mean *agents*? Where's Chooli?"

"Oh, I forgot to put it on the invitation. I have something to show you." With the same cheesy smile still beaming, the assassin stepped aside to reveal Chooli. She dangled from a hook, slowly rotating on the rope tied around her wrists. "Like my artwork?"

The world stood still. Everything went black as the image of Chooli burned into Alex's retinas, his eyes bulging in disbelief. What sort of monster could do this to another human being? Alex had seen some inhuman sights with the police cases he had worked on, but nothing compared to what he saw before him. This was ... monstrous ... personal. A knife slashed through his gut as the image became real, and then an anger he had never felt before set in. A hatred burned from his eyes as instinct caught Lamar off guard. Alex rotated, smashing him to the ground.

Dazed by the jolt and surprise, Lamar shook his head before turning his maser back onto Alex. It never reached its destination. He stiffened and collapsed to the floor as Alex shot him with his maser on stun at full strength. Alex turned back to the assassin, but he had disappeared. "I will kill you!" Alex shouted.

"Now, now. That's not what a good policeman should do. Don't you take an oath or something?"

"I'm not a policeman now." Alex waved his maser from side to side as he tried to locate the source of the voice. He crept forward as he looked around. There were too many places for the assassin to hide and too many ways for him to get behind Alex.

"I really enjoyed my time with Chooli. She made a magnificent canvas for my artwork."

Alex gritted his teeth. He knew exactly what the assassin was doing, making him blind with rage so he would make a mistake and lower his guard.

"It remains a mystery to me how you found out about me. Chooli is a magnificent agent. She kept her mouth shut the whole time. And believe me, I have some delicious methods of finding out information."

Maser ready, Alex inched past benches and partitions with implements on them. Perspiration dripped from his brow as the tension mounted. He knew he only had one chance of disposing of the monster.

"Oh, by the way ..." Alex heard the assassin's voice slowly circle around the other end of the line of benches. The lighting was poor on the sides of the workshop, so Alex couldn't see where he was. "... I kept her pure. I'm not a monster." The assassin gave a coarse laugh.

Firing where he thought the voice came from, Alex tensed.

"Now, now, you really must control that temper."

Cursing, Alex continued scanning the darkness. He neared Chooli and his heart bled for her. He saw her eyes flicker, but she looked dead otherwise. Considering whether to cut her down, something hard crashed into him, smashing him to the ground and forcing the wind from him. The assassin had swung a hoist hook into him. Alex saw the assassin lunge for him with a knife as he struggled to regain his breath. He just rolled away as the knife passed, plunging into the dirt floor. Alex rolled back to get a shot at his assailant, but he knocked the gun from Alex's hand. It went flying across the floor.

The knife lifted and started its plunge again, but Alex grabbed the wrist and stopped it just short of his neck, forcing it back. Increasing the pressure on the assassin's wrist, he felt the grip loosen and pushed the assassin away with his other hand and legs. The assassin fell backwards and Alex instantly leapt for him, grabbing the wrist of the hand holding the knife again. He straddled the assassin and punched him in the face as he forced the knife from his hand. The grip loosened, and the knife dropped to the ground. Alex flicked it away before his opponent could grab it again.

Alex's lungs ached from exhaustion, but he wouldn't relent. He punched the assassin again before the assassin pushed him off and lunged for him, offering his own blows to him. Blood and saliva splashed from both their faces as wounds opened and mouths bled. They traded blow for blow, energy draining from both of them as Chooli dangled and watched. Giving one last massive blow with the little energy he had left, Alex reached for the maser they had rolled close to and grabbed it. He grabbed the assassin by the throat, seeing mockery in the assassin's eyes as he pressed the muzzle to his head ...

"Don't," Chooli croaked.

His chest heaving to get every bit of air he could, Alex glanced at her for a moment, then refocused on the assassin, his rage threatening to pour out with the energy of the maser as he put pressure on the trigger. "Why shouldn't I remove this scum from existence?"

"Don't." Chooli labored to get the words out. "He knows who's behind all this."

Hesitating, he reduced the pressure from the trigger. He wanted to pull it. Oh, he wanted to pull it more than anything in the world, but Chooli was right.

Alex removed the muzzle from the assassin's head and landed a heavy blow to his temple with the butt instead, rendering him unconscious with the mocking smile still on his face. He struggled to his feet, still catching his breath, and staggered over to the unconscious Lamar to get the handcuffs from him. He came back, rolled the assassin over and cuffed him. Finding some rope, he tied his legs together and then tied him to a nearby post. He did the same with Lamar.

His gaze returned to Chooli, and the agony of seeing her returned. He got the knife and cut the rope holding her up as he wrapped his arms around her and gently lowered her to the ground. Her face was barely recognizable from the beating she had received, and the cuts still bled. Alex sat on the ground behind her and wrapped his arms around her as tears welled in his eyes and streamed down his face, falling on Chooli's hair. "Chooli, what have I done to you?"

50

Chooli's eyes opened as far as they could and she turned to study him, pain showing on her face. "I know what you're thinking," she said with an effort. "This isn't your fault. You couldn't have prevented it."

They stayed in each other's arms for minutes in silence, Chooli snuggling closer as Alex tried soaking the pain from her, even though he knew he couldn't. He eventually wiped his tears away. "I'd better get you to a hospital."

"No, we have to go to the Aquitaine estate and see Richelieu quickly."

"Why? You need medical care."

"I heard him talking to someone from the Aquitaine household. Someone there is behind this."

"Do you know who?"

"No, but it's part of a bigger plan. We have to stop something even more monstrous happening."

"What do you mean?"

"It all involves a grab for the Champagne Duchy and the increase in power and influence that would bring them. The worst bit is that they want to exterminate all the Cetusians there."

"That's what Satinka was talking about."

"Did you see her?" Chooli gave a weak smile.

Alex grunted as he smiled too. "She's leading the resistance there. The part that you released, anyway."

"You're joking."

"Really. It seemed she was doing an impressive job too, from what I saw."

"From stripper to soldier," Chooli said and she started laughing, but quickly winced.

"We'd better get going."

Alex gently released her and stood up, groaning as the effort and pain of the fight made its presence known. He took his jacket off and wrapped it around her. She flinched from having it touch her wounds but grabbed each side with her hands to keep it there.

"Can you walk?"

"I think so."

Helping her to her feet, Alex let her rest against him as she hobbled to the door of the workshop. He saw the determination on her face as he looked at her. They reached the AGrav moments later, and he settled her in a seat. He left again and came back a few minutes later, dragging the assassin behind him. He thought about throwing him from the moving AGrav when they took off, but the thought evaporated quickly, as he wanted a more enduring punishment for the monster — but he wondered if it would make any difference to his demented and psychopathic mind. Roughly getting him inside, he secured the assassin to a seat, making sure he couldn't get loose and escape. Lamar still lay in the workshop, but Alex left him there. He would get someone to pick him up later.

He set the destination for the AGrav and settled back in his own seat next to Chooli, cradling her hand as the AGrav rose from the ground, headed for the Aquitaine estate. He wanted to go straight to a spaceport and leave the warped world of Franconia with its distorted society, but he knew he had to see the case through to the end and it seemed Chooli had put the last pieces of the puzzle together.

51

The AGrav settled on the grounds of the Aquitaine estate; the chateau gleaming in the midday sun. Alex initially thought Chooli sat asleep beside him, but she stirred as soon as they landed. Pain and bruising distorted her face. He wished he had more than his jacket to cover her torso. He wanted to protect her so badly, and the guilt of not doing so still accused him.

The assassin lay unconscious and restrained in another seat. Alex wondered if he had done enough to prevent him from escaping or whether he should take him with them. But it was too much effort to carry him and support Chooli. An idea came to him. He should have thought of it before. The AGrav had a secure and ventilated cargo hold, large enough for a human, so Alex undid the restraints fixing the assassin to the seat and dragged him into that, locking the hold with his personal seal. Alex had commed the Aquitaine police to collect Lamar, getting them to stay on standby to come to the Richelieu estate for further arrests.

"Let's go then," Alex said as he returned to Chooli, wiping perspiration off his face. Chooli rose from her seat, stooped over with pain. She shuffled her feet as Alex held her. "You sure you want to do this?"

"Yes, I must."

Progress was slow, and Richelieu's staff stared at them as they entered the chateau. The Cetusian staff, in particular, looked horrified. They had to stop several times before they arrived at Richelieu's ground floor study for Chooli to take a rest. It seemed like they intended going to another room, maybe the one used to entertain them on a previous occasion on the first floor, but they changed their mind. They went into the room and Chooli sat on a seat by the window, exhausted from the effort.

They were only there for a brief time before Richelieu walked into the room. He looked preoccupied and worried, his brow creased in thought, but stopped in his tracks when he saw Chooli. "What on Franconia happened to her?"

"Maybe you can tell us?" Alex replied.

"What are you inferring?" Richelieu's tone changed instantly from one of concern to indignation.

"We believe you are behind the murders of the Duke and Duchess of Lorraine. You hired an assassin. And then when your plan started unraveling because the GIA got involved, you kidnapped Chooli to distract us and prevent us from finding out the truth."

"That's preposterous. I highly resent and deny your accusations. Why would I do that? Javier was my friend."

"A friend who impeded your expansionist goals."

Alex noticed Chooli had been watching the exchange. She waved at him and he came over to her. "Water, please."

"Do you have water?" Alex asked.

Richelieu waved to a servant standing at attention by the door. He bounced into action immediately, as if it was his duty to help Chooli. He brought a glass and Chooli took several sips. She put the glass on a table next to her and looked at Richelieu. "Please come closer so I don't have to talk so loud."

Initially looking at her as if she had no right requesting him to do anything, Richelieu relented and went over to her.

"We will understand that matter soon, but there is a more urgent matter to sort out. Your troops in Champagne are rounding up the Cetusians there to exterminate them. You must stop them."

His body jerking up, Richelieu looked at her in disbelief. "Have you gone mad? Why would they do that? I gave no such order."

"I am happy to hear you say that. But someone did. I overheard your senior generals discuss it where they imprisoned me in one of your compounds near Epernay. The compound was full of Cetusian prisoners — men, women, and children. They were preparing to execute them."

The news physically jolted Richelieu. He went pale and rushed over to another seat, sitting before he collapsed. "Are you sure?"

"That is what I heard. If you are not behind this, please call them to stop it before people die."

Frozen to his seat, Richelieu sat motionless while he thought through the revelation. He came out of his reverie and stood up. "Yes, immediately," he said as he left the room. The servant still stood to attention, but Alex saw shock on his face too. Richelieu walked back in half an hour later, pale and tormented looking. Alex thought he had forgotten about them. "This makes no sense," Richelieu said.

"Did you stop it?" Chooli asked.

"Yes, it took some hard questioning, but my ground staff finally confessed their orders. They insist the order came from higher up, though. There are only a few people between them and me, and I thought I could trust them with my life." He sat down near Chooli again. "Did you get any idea who might have given the order?"

Chooli, relaxing when she heard he had stopped the action, sighed and shook her head. "I only heard one say that the order came from higher up."

Richelieu stood and paced the floor. "This is disastrous. This will destroy my reputation if word gets out. Thank God I could stop it in time." He looked at Chooli. "We owe you a great debt." Pacing again, he said, more to himself than to anyone else, "I stopped the war. I knew it was a mistake. All that money and resources down the drain just to get a minor portion of land. What was I thinking? It is pointless now."

Clearing his throat, Alex butted into Richelieu's monolog, "We still have the matter of my accusation."

"What? Oh, that's absurd, preposterous. You're lucky I don't have you thrown off the planet for making such an accusation."

"I heard the assassin talk to someone from here over his comm," Chooli said.

"But that just can't be. I know it wasn't me. There is no one else."

They all looked at each other in silence.

The door opened.

"Oh, I'm sure we can come to an arrangement," Felicity said to Camille as they walked in.

Alex instantly raised his head. "You!"

52

Standing up to stretch her aching back, Satinka rubbed her eyes. She couldn't remember when she had slept last. Every time things seemed to settle down, and she went to get a few winks of sleep, someone would come to tell her of another flareup for her to attend to. The fighting was endless, but she was proud of her fellow Cetusians. They fought on regardless and they were slowly pushing the Aquitaine soldiers back, even with the extra firepower of the fighters and the occasional energy blast from the enemy's destroyer-class ships in orbit. If only they had fighters of their own to put up an aerial front and even cause some damage to the destroyers, they would stand half a chance. Despite the brave face she displayed and the dedication of the people fighting, she knew they couldn't continue forever and there would be only one outcome unless something changed. Bitterly smiling, she remembered she had come over to Champagne with enthusiasm and hope of doing something good, hoping to get enough money to pay for her mother's operation. Now she would probably die here, and her mother might never know what happened to her.

It staggered her to realize that she was such a good strategic thinker. She could almost see the tactics the enemy would adopt before they did. They started becoming predictable and a few of her counterattacks completely routed them. She moved to stretch her legs as she walked out of the communications room. Bidziil followed her. If nothing else, he was loyal. He never left her side, maser rifle at the ready. She looked at him as they walked. "Bet you never thought when you met me that this was what you would be doing."

"No. It wasn't what I thought I would be doing."

She patted him on the back. "You're an outstanding man. Let's go grab something to eat."

They had set a simple canteen up close to the comms room, and Satinka entered it with Bidziil. The people there instantly stood, but Satinka waved them down. She didn't understand why they did that. Grabbing a tray, she put a plate of pre-dished food on it and a glass of juice, taking it to a table to eat. Bidziil sat opposite her moments later. Shoveling food into her mouth, she looked at Bidziil and chewed and swallowed. "Do you think we'll get out of this alive?"

Bidziil looked at her. "No."

"A pessimist."

"Realist."

"I agree with you, but we can inflict as much damage as we can while we're still alive." She took a drink of juice and more food. A vibration shook the room. Another fighter had gotten through and masered the compound. "I'm amazed this compound's survived for this long. Would have thought their destroyer would have blasted it. Maybe they can't afford to destroy one of their assets." A stronger vibration hit the room, making Satinka look up. Maybe this was the end for her.

One of her runners came dashing into the room and over to her. "You must come quickly."

"What's up?"

"They are starting a fresh attack."

"So I hear." Another vibration rang through the complex.

"Not here. In the city."

"Oh." Satinka shoved as much food in her mouth as she could and took the drink with her as she rose and followed the runner back to the comms room, finishing the drink as she got there and wiping her mouth on the sleeve of her shirt. "What have you got?"

"Major groups of soldiers are congregating here, here and here," the person manning the screens pointed out.

Satinka studied the screen. They were coming at one of the largest Cetusian group of fighters, seemingly to isolate and overpower them. It would be a major blow if she lost the entire group. She should pull them out while she could. Better to retreat to fight another day. The troop movements suddenly reversed and the Aquitaine soldiers withdrew. "What's happening?"

Her screen operators busied themselves to update their information, puzzled faces reflecting off the screen surfaces. A comm sounded in the corner.

"They're withdrawing, Satinka," the supervisor said.

"Why would they do that, unless they're planning something massive and destructive?" The constant vibration of the fighters over her seemed to have stopped too.

"Satinka, you have a call," the person who answered the comm said.

Looking over to him, she looked back to the screens, frowning. She didn't like what was happening, but walked to the comm. "Yes?"

"Is this Satinka?"

"Yes."

"I have been told you are in charge. Duke Richelieu here." The comm was on audio only.

Satinka staggered back. Her gut started twisting with dread at what he would say next. "Oh, yes, what is it?"

"I am calling off the offensive. You can stand down."

"What?"

"I'm—"

"I heard you. It wasn't what I was expecting. Why?"

"This was a mistake from the very beginning. Let's just say I don't have the stomach for it anymore. You will understand why in the next few days. In the meantime, I am resuming negotiations with Champagne's Lord Chancellor."

Satinka's face burst into a smile. "You can't believe how happy I am right now."

"I probably can't, but I think I can imagine a little. Enjoy the rest. I was told that you are leading the fighters, and I wanted to tell you personally."

"Thanks, I appreciate that." The comm went dead and Satinka turned to a sea of expectant and unsure faces looking at her. "It's over," she whispered, and then shouted, "It's over!" She jumped up and down and rushed over to hug Bidziil, giving him an unexpected kiss.

The room went crazy with excitement and joy. The news spread fast and the whole compound danced and sang in celebration soon after. Satinka got the operators to spread the news to all the cells in the city. Someone found a cache of alcohol somewhere in the complex and handed it out. A person brought two bottles of champagne to the comms room. Bidziil grabbed one and opened it, spraying Satinka with the contents with screams and laughter coming from her. She eventually got a glass of the bubbly liquid that covered her as she wiped her face so she could see properly.

"Maybe you can go home now," Bidziil said to her.

"Yeah, maybe I can go home."

53

F elicity looked over to Alex and froze as their eyes locked on each other. Malice slowly oozed into hers.

"Arrest her immediately," Alex ordered.

"What for?" Both Richelieu and Camille said.

"Complicity in the kidnapping and detention of a GIA agent. I recognize that voice anywhere."

"You're mad." Felicity stared back at him in defiance.

"But I've been dating her. We are discussing the possibility of a steady relationship," Richelieu said plaintively.

"She is the one," Alex insisted, Felicity's smug defiance annoying him. "Maybe we'll get The Reaper to help us identify her."

"Ha, good luck with that. I've been told he's the best there is."

Alex smiled as he saw a crack in her façade. "And how would you know that? How would you know who he or she is if you had no involvement?" He eyed her with a hunter's stare. "As for getting him to identify *you*, it shouldn't be too difficult since we have him in custody."

Felicity's smug look wavered — as did Camille's, Alex noticed — and then pure hatred emanated from Felicity as she stared at him.

"What is the meaning of this?" Richelieu asked no one in particular, but his eyes settled on Felicity.

"Richelieu, don't believe them," she appealed. "They're insane. You know I would never do such a thing."

"Did you know the extent of your accomplice's handiwork?" Chooli's soft, calm voice asked from the chair she still sat in.

Felicity and Camille both looked at Chooli for the first time.

"What is she doing here?" Camille spat out venomously. "See how filthy she is. Typical. They're all the same. If it wasn't for us humans ramming some civility into them, they'd still be in the jungle."

Chooli struggled to her feet and hobbled over to them, looking at Felicity and then Camille, both of them glaring back at her. "Do you want to see some of his handiwork?" She let Alex's jacket fall to the floor and turned full circle to give them all the complete picture. Camille gasped. Felicity stood stony-faced. The servant bent over and retched. Richelieu staggered to a chair. Chooli leaned over with effort and retrieved the jacket, putting it back on. "He called it his masterpiece. Maybe he can give you a matching work of art?" She looked directly at Felicity.

Before Alex could respond, Felicity lunged forward and grabbed Chooli, wrapping her arm around Chooli's neck. After drawing a small laser pistol from a pocket, she pointed it at Chooli's head, and moved, making sure Chooli was between Alex and herself.

With pure reflex, Alex whipped out his maser and pointed it at Felicity, but he couldn't get a clear shot with Chooli in front of her. His heart thumped and perspiration burst from the pores on his forehead, his palms damp.

"Let me pass," Felicity said to Alex before glancing at Camille. "This would be a straightforward job, you said. Earn easy money so your precious son can get control of Champagne with the Lorraine duke out of the way."

"Shut up," Camille hissed.

Felicity turned her attention back to Alex. "Let me pass, or she dies."

Time stood still. The entire room disappeared and all he saw was

Chooli in front of Felicity. He hadn't experienced such focused concentration before. But he just didn't have a clear shot. He couldn't kill Chooli, he just couldn't, but he didn't want her to die in the hands of that monster either, as he knew she would as soon as she was of no further use to Felicity. His finger remained frozen, just touching the trigger. Licking his lips, he pleaded, "Let her go."

"She's my bargaining chip out of here."

Chooli stood frozen in agony as the mutilation from the Reaper's artwork tormented her, her eyes on Alex. Those eyes that Alex loved. How could he get her to move for a better shot?

Richelieu stared at Felicity, aghast. His mouth opened and closed, but no words came out at first. "But, Felicity—."

"Oh, you blind fool," Felicity spat, losing all patience with him now that she knew the game was up but keeping her eyes fixed on Alex, "it was so easy to manipulate you."

Silence filled the room as the impasse dragged on.

"Take the shot," Chooli finally gasped, her eyes staring at Alex in resignation.

"I can't." Tears falling from his cheeks.

"You can't let her go either."

Indecision and torment of losing Chooli froze Alex into a statue. This woman had healed him, and now the only way for justice was to shoot her? There must be another way.

"This is your last chance," Felicity stated, jabbing the muzzle of the pistol into Chooli's head.

The hatred and malice in Felicity's eyes drilled nails of torment into Alex's soul. His eyes flicked to Chooli again. After a split second, something other than resignation and sorrow projected from them. Determination? Yes, determination.

"Take the shot," Chooli said again, just before her hands shot up, grabbing the hand and pistol and shoving them away from her head.

A shot blasted from the pistol and hit a portrait of Camille hanging on the wall, blasting a hole in its forehead.

With the same motion, Chooli twisted out from in front of Felicity.

Seeing his opportunity, he quickly change the maser setting to stun and fired, hitting her in the chest. Felicity dropped to the ground, almost bringing Chooli down with her. He so much wanted to blast her out of existence, but he needed her evidence.

Alex wiped the tears from his eyes and rushed over to Chooli, holding her in his arms, not wanting to let go of her. Time started its normal speed again.

Alex stared at Camille, "You're under arrest for conspiracy in the murders of the Duke and Duchess of Lorraine."

"Don't be ridiculous," Camille yelled. "Lies. Don't think you'll get anything by coming up with a story like that."

"It shouldn't be too difficult to corroborate Felicity's version. I have The Reaper to ask, and I have ways of asking that will get the truth." His face turned stone cold. "Ways that are not pleasant. Even he may flinch."

"No one will believe them over me, the sister of the prince. There is not one shred of evidence that will stand up in court."

"And did you order my army to round up the Cetusians in Champagne to execute them?" Richelieu roared at his mother as he stood, his face red with rage.

Fear settled on Camille's face for the first time in the interchange when she turned to look at her son. The emotion vanished, and she stood straight. "It was the only way to get this stupid war out of the way. You weren't doing anything. You're as spineless as your father. I can't understand how I produced such weak offspring."

"You're a monster. I knew you were manipulative and ambitious, but I never imagined you scheming such cruelty, such savagery. What were you thinking you would get out of it?"

"You still don't get it, do you? A simpleton like your father, too. With Champagne in your possession you will have more land and power than any of the other dukes, and you could even take over Lorraine now that they don't have any real duke to take over from Javier. Your power would take preeminence of all the others, and I would at last have the recognition and honor I deserve. And now you've ruined everything."

Richelieu stood stony-faced in front of his mother. "I do not have a mother. I disown you. I never want to see you ever again." He strode over to the intercom and called security.

"You can't run this duchy on your own. You need me."

"I would rather it fall apart than stand another second with you in my sight."

Camille flinched.

Four security staff walked in. "Take these two and place them in a secure location. Take directions from Detective Warner here, when we finish our current discussions. Now get them out of my sight." The security people looked at Camille and back at Richelieu, confused. "Yes, her." They complied and escorted Camille from the room. Two of them carried Felicity with them. Richelieu sat down again. Shaking his head from side to side as he held it in his hands, pulling back his hair as he looked back up at Alex. "How did this mess happen?"

"I don't know, but some people are master manipulators. They are so good you don't even know you are being manipulated. As for the rest of it? I don't think she really cared how all this would affect you. All she cared about was the status it would bring her. I think she brought in Felicity to keep you busy while she put her machinations in place."

Richelieu stood up. "I really thought she might be the one to settle down with. Mother even liked her. Now I know why Mother liked her."

"Maybe you need to look more with your mind than your pants." Richelieu's eyes flared in anger. "Sorry for the bluntness. There are plenty out there I'm sure you would have a long and happy life with."

As he took in Alex's words, Richelieu stared at him for a moment. He then looked at Chooli. "I am deeply sorry for what you have been through. I will pay for any treatment you need to restore your health and remove that monstrosity from you." He walked over to the door and turned. "If you will excuse me, my servant will escort you out. I have a war to wrap up."

54

The prince's palace stood resplendent in decorations, inside and out. Prince Léon had organized a special assembly of the dukes and prominent people in society who sat expectantly in the palace's ballroom. He had kept the purpose for the event secret, so the room was abuzz with chatter and conversation about what it could be. They all knew that such assemblies where only organized for major announcements and presentations.

It was just over a week since Alex and Chooli had arrested Camille and her associates. That news spread throughout the entire world like wildfire with comments of disbelief or knowing refection. The bruises on Chooli's face had mainly disappeared, but her broken leg, mutilated skin and tortured body and mind remained to heal in the weeks and months ahead. She hobbled up the central aisle of the assembly with Alex helping her, conscious of the looks from those there, having refused a hover chair to help her. She self-consciously made it to the front row and sat with Alex next to her. "Why are we here?"

"I don't know," Alex said. "I was just told that we were to come, both of us."

She sat patiently, pleased to have Alex's warmth next to her. The room hushed five minutes later, and a fanfare started. Everyone stood but Alex and her. Finding it difficult to turn just her head by the neck, she moved her entire body and saw Prince Léon walk up the aisle in his royal regalia of office, followed by other dignitaries she didn't know. She looked at Alex and raised an eyebrow. He shrugged and stood, helping her to stand too. The dignitaries stopped at the foot of the dais at the front and Léon climbed the three steps to the dais itself, his throne center stage and toward the back, which he sat on. The audience sat again, as did Alex and Chooli.

An official made several introductions, and they sang the planetary anthem before Prince Léon stood and came toward the front of the dais. He looked at those assembled and his eyes rested on Alex and then Chooli. There seemed to be special kindness in them as they rested on Chooli.

"I have assembled you all here today for two reasons. It is a special day of celebration for us, and I intend to make it as memorable as possible.

"First, I wish to thank personally the two fine and dedicated officers from the GIA, Chief Inspector Detective Alex Warner and Detective Chooli Richards, for their outstanding work. I doubt we would have ever found out the true culprits behind the despicable murders of the Duke and Duchess of Lorraine without them. In fact, we would have likely executed an innocent man. I am sure that, in the humility that the GIA usually exhibit, they will say that they were only doing their job." A wave of soft laughter encircled the room. "But I think you will all agree that what they did went well beyond the call of duty and I intend writing a formal letter of gratitude and commendation to the relevant authorities within the GIA. Please stand and show your appreciation."

The entire audience stood, and a deafening roar of clapping echoed round the room. Chooli looked at Alex and he motioned for her to stand, which she did with Alex's help. They turned and the volume of noise increased. It eventually subsided and everyone sat down again.

The prince looked to the side and nodded. A page boy came out holding a box with both hands and walked over to the prince, standing at his side and facing him with the box's lid open.

"Second, it is my wish and great privilege to perform this next duty. This will be unprecedented, but the reason is also unprecedented. This person went through extraordinary pain and suffering to prevent what would have been a great humiliation to this planet, making us the pariah of the Confederation. People hatched a plot to rid Champagne of its Cetusian population during the recent war between Aquitaine and Champagne. I must add that this was behind Duke Richelieu's back; he did not know of this. Through the hardship of capture, torture and escape did this person uncover the plot and stop it before it started. We cannot show this person enough gratitude for doing this. Chooli Richards ..." Léon looked at Chooli and she froze. "Please come forward and accept our Medal of Honor as a symbol of our appreciation for the sacrifice you have made."

The room instantly fell into hushed conversation. A Cetusian had never received such an honor. Chooli sat frozen, unable to think through what was happening. Alex gently nudged her and gestured at the dais with his eyes.

"Do you want me to help you?" Alex asked.

Chooli took a breath and shook her head. She would do this on her own. She stood and hobbled forward. Stumbling on the first step, Léon took a step to help her, as did Alex, but a duke, of all people, immediately rushed forward and grabbed her arm. She turned and thanked him and continued up the three steps. Tears started trickling down her face as she neared the prince, stopping in front of him. Léon took the medal from the box and pinned it to the GIA jacket she wore. He held her on the shoulders with both hands and smiled at her.

The prince wiped her tears away. "Thank you, Chooli," he whispered to her.

She turned and the entire room thundered in applause as everyone stood in her honor. She stood straighter as she looked at Alex, tears replacing the ones the prince had removed. Alex stood and applauded her too. She could see how proud he was of her, and that made her cry all the more. The noise crescendoed and receded. She looked at the prince, who signaled she could leave. She went down the steps and Alex went to her as she made the last step, helping her back to her seat and hugging her. Silence returned to the room.

"Well, that was quite emotional," the prince said to the laughter of the audience. "In all seriousness, it was an emotional experience. You can see it was for Chooli, but for me too. I first met her recently, and even then I knew she was an exceptional person. It has been an honor to know you, Chooli." More applause sounded. "And you are welcome to visit me any time you are on Franconia — or contact me if you wish to come. I'll make sure you and Alex will have a *pleasurably* memorable visit if you do. Now, this brings us to the end of our formalities. There will be a formal dinner tonight in Chooli's honor, but before then you are free to mingle or come and go as you please."

The audience stood and started talking to each other.

Prince Léon came down from the dais and over to Alex and Chooli. "How are you feeling?"

"Embarrassed," Chooli said, but smiled.

"I didn't want to embarrass you."

"She knows," Alex butted in. "It's unexpected."

"Hey, I can talk for myself."

Léon raised an eyebrow.

Alex and Chooli laughed.

"And how are you healing?" Léon asked.

"It will take time."

"Let me know if you need any specialist treatment we have on Franconia. I will make sure you get it."

"Duke Richelieu has already offered to pay for my treatment."

"Good. He is suffering too. I know how the daggers can come out when something like this happens. Anyway, I must leave you and prepare for other things. I will see you at the dinner tonight. Feel free to ask my staff for anything you may need." He left them alone.

Several others came up to thank them and congratulate Chooli, including Xavier who had almost recovered from his own ordeal.

She felt strange. Given the social inequality the planet still had, it was surreal that the nobility seemed to be ignoring her Cetusian origin. Maybe it was strategic of them since it gave them favor with the prince.

After what seemed like an endless stream of nobles and dignitaries coming over to meet them, someone shy and unsure approached them.

Alex saw her first. "Come over, Satinka."

She did. "This is so great for you."

"You should have gotten this," Chooli said, plucking at her medal.

"No, I am getting my reward for my effort, but nothing would have happened if you hadn't done what you did. You deserve this."

"Will you be at the dinner tonight?" Alex asked.

"Yes, I don't know where I'll be sitting, though. An invitation for a Cetusian to such an occasion, as a guest, is unheard of."

"I heard you had quite a celebration when the Aquitaine troops withdrew."

Satinka laughed. "They drenched me in so much champagne I had to stand under the shower for a week the get it off me. I can still smell it." She sobered and looked directly at Alex. "I remember when I first saw you, I envied any woman who could catch such a man. I think you have a more remarkable partner."

"Thank you. I think so too." He hugged Chooli. "Although I have to say she had a tinge of jealousy after we left you."

"Did not," Chooli butted in, but laughed. "What will you do now?" she said to Satinka.

"Well, I have the money I need to pay for my mother's operation. I don't know what will happen with the club. They have offered me an executive position, but I'm getting offers from other organizations too, especially in Champagne. I'll take some time off to help my mother and think about things."

"Hope it all goes well."

"I need to go. Have to get ready for tonight and all that."

"Women," Alex joked as he rolled his eyes.

Satinka left, leaving Alex and Chooli alone for a moment. Chooli didn't know what to say to him. There really wasn't anything to say. She looked at him as he did her. "I love you."

"I love you too," Alex said as he hugged her. "Probably inappropriate to kiss just now."

Chooli giggled. "Probably. Let's go wander around in the gardens for a while."

They left the ballroom and went outside strolling in amongst the flower beds and shrubbery, Alex with his arm around Chooli's waist. Despite her ordeal, she felt more at peace now than she had ever felt before. Coming to a small alcove manicured into the greenery, she led Alex into it and reached up to kiss him. He obliged. "You know what we need to do now?" She asked afterwards, her aureola shining bright golden yellow.

"What?" Alex said as he stared into her eyes.

"Go home."

Alex nodded in agreement.

~

The End

You can read the first book in the Halwende's Legacy Series - Halwende's Redemption.

Type https://books2read.com/Halwendes-Redemption into your browser.

Thanks for reading this book. If you loved the book and have a moment to spare, I would appreciate a quick review on the site that you purchased the book from, as this helps new readers find my books.

Subscribe to my Newsletters and receive three free episodes of The Chronicles of Gatacus Todd.

Type http://subscribepage.io/g4r4f8 in your browser.

ALSO BY JOHN WEGENER

ABOUT THE AUTHOR

John Wegener grew up in the Adelaide Hills of South Australia. He now expresses his imaginative dreams by engaging in writing after a 34-year career as a Chemical Engineer in the steel industry, which has taken him to many countries and allowed him to experience many cultures. John currently lives in Wollongong, Australia with his wife and children.

Click on johnwegener.com to find more of my books or read his blogs. Type subscribepage.io/g4r4f8 to subscribe to my emails for more stories and information.

f

www.ingramcontent.com/pod-product-compliance
Lightning Source LLC
Chambersburg PA
CBHW071232250626
47163CB00001B/154